EAVES OF DESTRUCTION

A Fixer-Upper Mystery

Kate Carlisle

BERKLEY PRIME CRIME
New York

BERKLEY PRIME CRIME
Published by Berkley
An imprint of Penguin Random House LLC
375 Hudson Street, New York, New York 10014

Copyright © 2017 by Kathleen Beaver
Penguin Random House supports copyright. Copyright fuels creativity, encourages
diverse voices, promotes free speech, and creates a vibrant culture. Thank you for buying
an authorized edition of this book and for complying with copyright laws by not
reproducing, scanning, or distributing any part of it in any form without permission.
You are supporting writers and allowing Penguin Random House to continue to
publish books for every reader.

BERKLEY is a registered trademark and BERKLEY PRIME CRIME and the B colophon
are trademarks of Penguin Random House LLC.

Hallmark Movies and Mysteries is a trademark of Crown Media.

ISBN: 9780399586460

First Edition: November 2017

Printed in the United States of America
1   3   5   7   9   10   8   6   4   2

Cover art © Robert Crawford
Cover design by Steve Meditz

PRAISE FOR KATE CARLISLE'S FIXER-UPPER MYSTERIES

"Carlisle uses her trademark clever wit and complex plotting to pen a mystery that can only be solved by a smart, funny, and courageous heroine such as Shannon Hammer . . . an immensely satisfying page-turner."
—Jenn McKinlay, *New York Times* bestselling author of the Library Lover's Mysteries

"Sleuth Shannon Hammer knows her way around a building site and a murder—I fell for this feisty, take-charge heroine, and readers will too."
—Leslie Meier, *New York Times* bestselling author of the Lucy Stone Mysteries

"Another winner from one of the leaders in the genre!"
—*RT Book Reviews*

"Carlisle's second contractor cozy continues to please with its smart, humorous heroine and plot. Fans of Sarah Graves's Home Repair Is Homicide series will appreciate this title as a solid read-alike."
—*Library Journal*

"Highly entertaining . . . quick, clever, and somewhat edgy. . . . Shannon's not a stereotype—she's a person, and an interesting, intelligent, likable one at that, which makes it easy to become invested in her tale."
—Smitten by Books

"Kate Carlisle can always be relied upon for a lead character whose wit is as finely honed as her intelligence. . . . Full of clever humor and more than one plot twist, this novel serves up equal amounts of generous holiday goodwill and delightfully entertaining characters."
—Kings River Life Magazine

OTHER BOOKS BY KATE CARLISLE

BIBLIOPHILE MYSTERIES

Homicide in Hardcover
If Books Could Kill
The Lies That Bind
Murder Under Cover
Pages of Sin
(Novella: E-book Only)
One Book in the Grave
Peril in Paperback
A Cookbook Conspiracy
The Book Stops Here
Ripped from the Pages
Books of a Feather
Once upon a Spine

FIXER-UPPER MYSTERIES

A High-End Finish
This Old Homicide
Crowned and Moldering
Deck the Hallways

This book is dedicated to my dear friend and fellow writer Jenn McKinlay, who, despite her bad breakfast choices and incorrigible tomfoolery, makes me happy to be alive and working in this crazy business. I love ya, kiddo.

Chapter One

I really love my job. But I've got to admit, some days are better than others.

I've been working on construction sites since I was eight years old and my father started taking my sister, Chloe, and me to work with him. Our mom had died a month earlier and it just made sense for Chloe and me to hang out with Dad after school instead of going home to a big, sad, empty house.

Chloe and I had thrived around the construction workers, who took us under their wings. They bought us little pink tool belts and hard hats and showed us all kinds of cool stuff to make. The first time I used a stud finder, it was a revelation. And when one of Dad's brawny carpenters demonstrated the joys of the common socket wrench to me, I was seriously hooked. I soaked up everything the guys taught me, from laying tile to hanging drywall. And I knew what I wanted to do with my life.

Then, six years ago, Dad suffered a heart attack.

Chloe had finally gotten her big break in Los Angeles and was working on a home-makeover TV show, so Dad asked me if I would be willing to take over Hammer Construction. I didn't have to think twice; I said yes. And ever since then, I'd been living the dream. Each day presented a new and exciting challenge.

But every once in a while, I would find a fly in my personal ointment, so to speak, and get a client who was, frankly, horrible. Petsy Jorgensen was one of those clients. She was the quintessential "client from hell." Having to work with Petsy was almost enough to make me wish I had become a barista. Or a brain surgeon. Or a hobo.

It was a glorious spring morning following weeks of rain. We had desperately needed the rain, of course, so nobody had complained too much. Still enough was enough, and all of this lovely sunshine was like a miracle. I had driven over to Cranberry Circle with my foreman, Wade Chambers, to talk to the homeowner about some work she wanted done to her beautiful Victorian home.

In a town where one Victorian mansion was more sumptuous and ornate than the next, the Jorgensen house was the pinnacle of elaborate, gracious excess. It stood at the end of the cul-de-sac on a large plot of land surrounded by several homes around the same age, and six newer Victorian-style homes that had been built with love by my father's company to blend in with the originals.

I took a lot of pride in those homes, and now that I was working on the most beautiful old Victorian in the circle, I wondered, could I get any luckier?

The Jorgensen house was a classic Queen Anne design, with a three-story tower to the left of the wide wraparound veranda, three chimneys, and multiple gables and dormer windows, all topped off by a lovely widow's walk that spread out from the top-floor tower across the pitched rooftop.

I couldn't wait to see the inside of this house.

"Hello. I'm Shannon Hammer," I said when a well-dressed woman opened the front door. "This is my foreman, Wade Chambers."

"It's about time you got here," the woman said, swinging the door open wider. I'd never met her before and now I knew why. We clearly didn't move in the same social circles—if her initial attitude toward us was any clue. She actually managed to look down her nose at us, which was a real feat, seeing as both Wade and I were taller than she was.

She was thin and beautiful in a Jackie Kennedy sort of way, with dark hair worn in a stylish bob and great taste in clothes. But she had hard blue eyes and frown lines that were starting to dig deeply enough into the sides of her mouth that you could someday plant corn there. "I'm Petsy Jorgensen."

I brushed aside her previous comment implying that we were late—in reality we were five minutes early for our appointment. Stepping into the surprisingly large two-storied foyer, I gazed around, taking in the artistry of the heavily carved newel post, the dark wood paneling, the polished handrail, and the unique spiral balusters that graced the wide staircase straight ahead. I blinked up at the dramatic crystal chandelier hanging from the center of an elaborately gilded ceiling rose and had to smile. This house was a gem.

"What a beautiful foyer," I said, admiring the scrollwork on the corbels that extended out from either side of the archway leading into the formal dining room to our left.

"Yes, yes, of course, but I'd prefer to cut the chitchat. I don't have time for it." She spoke in a clipped way that sounded very much like Queen to Peasant. "Follow me." She walked into the dining room and we trailed behind her.

If I hadn't already fallen in love with the house, I might have turned around and walked out. Life was too short to deal with deliberately rude people. I was good at first impressions, and while Petsy Jorgensen was "ice princess" beautiful, she was a socially incompetent, angry, impatient woman. I wondered whether it would be worth our time and energy to continue with the interview, but I decided to keep going for now. Maybe she was just having a bad morning.

Petsy strode toward the opposite wall and gestured down at the dark wood wainscoting that circled the large, elegant space. "Will you just look at this?"

I did as she asked and knelt down to get a closer look at the wainscoting. It was actually made up of individual wood panels fitted together, each about three feet tall by two feet wide. A lovely sculpted grapevine pattern, accentuated by birds and the occasional flower, wove itself across each panel. The carvings were wonderful. Some nineteenth-century craftsman had worked his butt off to create these beauties.

"It's a gorgeous room," Wade said.

"Very funny." Petsy scowled at him. "If you can't see that it's a disgusting mess, then I'm not sure you know what you're doing." She looked at me. "All I want to know is, can you fix it?"

Before I could answer, she jabbed her finger in my direction. "And don't lie to me. If you can't do it, I want to hear you say it, because I'll have to hire someone more capable immediately."

I took in a slow breath, let it out, and managed to smile at her. "I can guarantee you won't find anyone more capable than me and my team. But if you would prefer to make a change, now is the time to let us know."

She pressed her lips together in a tight frown. She didn't like being pushed. Funny, because I didn't, either. After a few long seconds, she nodded briefly and waved at the damaged walls. "Fine. Go ahead. Let me know what you think."

I nodded, satisfied that she knew where we stood. Deliberately taking my time, I walked to another panel section and hunched down to study the grapevine pattern more closely. My stomach dropped as I noticed all the tiny holes that had been drilled into the wood.

"Wormholes?" I whispered, and shivered involuntarily. I hated seeing the damage that woodworms could do to a beautiful piece of wood. But besides the wormholes, there were also large chunks of wood missing in the bas-relief images of the birds and grapevines. In some spots the grapes were cracked, and some leaves were completely gone. Several of the frolicking cherubs had fractured noses and a few birds were missing parts. Woodworms hadn't done that damage. It looked more like the work of some destructive humans. Had someone been playing bumper cars in here?

I could fix the carvings, but it would take time. The

wormholes were more problematic. While plenty of people liked that worn, rustic look, there was always the possibility that the little buggers were still living in the wood. They would keep drilling, and eventually the entire wall of wainscoting would collapse.

I moved on to examine the next panel. It was just as bad. I checked a few more. Same problem. How had that happened?

"Well?" she asked in a demanding tone, as though I'd taken too much time inspecting the wood. I hadn't taken more than a minute or two, but I supposed Mrs. Jorgensen was a busy gal.

"Yes, of course I can fix it," I said. *I can fix anything,* I thought. *Even your stupid wormholes.* But I again pasted a smile on my face, and added, "I'll be happy to do it."

"Good," she said. "Because I'm sick of looking at it."

"How did all this damage occur?" Wade asked.

She rolled her eyes. "My husband let his bratty little nephews loose in here a few years ago and they destroyed everything. I'm absolutely certain it's the reason we didn't win the grand prize last year."

First of all, unless the kids really had been playing bumper cars, I couldn't believe a couple of them could've caused this kind of wholesale damage. Maybe a nick or two here and there, but not all of this destruction. And those wormholes weren't caused by kids. So was Petsy just kidding us? Or was she lying about the source of the damage? I shook my head. Why would she lie about something like this?

Second, not that it mattered in the current scheme of things, but Petsy's husband, Matthew, was a good friend of my father and a really nice guy. Would he have allowed his nephews to tear this room apart? And while we were on the subject of Matthew, how in the world did he put up with his wife's crabby moods?

And third, the grand prize she was talking about was the large cash award given each year by the judges of the Lighthouse Cove Victorian Home and Garden Tour. There were dozens of lesser prizes given out as well. It was exciting to see how prestigious the annual tour had become, but now it seemed as if half the town was willing to sell their souls for one of those impressive awards.

Apparently Mrs. Jorgensen fell into that category.

I hunched down to take one last look at the woodwork. I wasn't about to call Mrs. Jorgensen a liar, but there was no way a couple of kids had wreaked all that damage.

I stood up and met Wade's gaze. I could tell he wasn't happy. In fact, he looked more than ready to blow off this job and I was pretty close to following him. But I rarely turned my back on a challenge, and there was Matthew Jorgensen and my father's friendship to consider. So in that moment, I doubled down on my decision and turned and faced Mrs. Jorgensen.

"I assume you also want to get rid of the wormholes," I said, pulling my tablet from my bag to take notes.

"What a ridiculous thing to say. Of course I do."

I thought of Dad and took a few deep breaths. "Fine. The wormholes will be easy enough to fix. But the missing pieces of the carvings will be more difficult and time-consuming."

Her eyes narrowed. "What do you mean, time-consuming? Can you do it or not?"

"I told you I can do the work, but it could take a while."

"You have four weeks."

I breathed in and out, hoping I could maintain my calm outer shell. "I understand you want it done before the Home and Garden Tour, but my team and I have other jobs we're working on this week. We'll have to start here next week."

"What? But that only gives me three weeks." She sighed. "All right, fine. But I insist you work for me exclusively."

"That's not going to happen," I said genially. "But as far as the time frame goes, I would suggest that rather than repairing each panel individually, which could take a month or longer, there's an alternative that I—"

"But I was promised—"

"Let me finish, please," I continued softly, trying to remain serene in the face of her impatience. "If you'd care to consider it, we can replace the panels with beautiful wood onlays in a similar style to your grapevine pattern. We would stain them the same rich color and you would never know the difference."

"Onlays? I don't like the sound of that."

"I can show you some beautiful pieces that would be perfect in this room. I've got a website you can look at to see if—"

"What do you mean, a website? What are wood onlays?"

"Let me show you." Turning my tablet around for her to see, I clicked onto Victorian Home Works, a website that displayed beautifully sculpted onlays in different sizes and patterns and designs in every type of wood imaginable. You could find almost anything and it was all very high quality. I skipped to a page showing hundreds of different pilasters, pediments, ceiling roses, cornices, corbels, and crown moldings.

I explained that this company specialized in both *inlays*—which were designs carved straight into wood—and *onlays*, which were pieces designed and carved separately and then applied to smooth wood or walls. There were scrolls and shell patterns with fancy flourishes; all sorts of fleur-de-lis patterns; roses with leafy froufrous; fan shapes and stylized pinecones. There were even carved bows with ribbons dangling off to the sides. And there were grapevines of every size and style. And all of these were offered in maple, cherry, and other hardwoods.

"As you can see, your choices are quite varied."

She shook her head in disbelief. "But these things are . . . why, they're . . . they're fake! I want someone who will actually come into my home and do the work. Someone who knows how to carve the designs into the wood. Why would I use this company and cheat myself?"

I was about to laugh—until I got a better look at her horrified expression. "Let me assure you that this is a perfectly acceptable way of creating the look you want. The pieces are manufactured in England."

I covertly rolled my eyes as I said the words. As if something coming from England made it more legitimate? But for some people, that fact made all the difference.

"Everyone in my industry uses these products," I added.

"Not in my house," she said, sniffing with contempt. "I was told you did custom woodwork. Is that true or not?"

"It's true," I said mildly, although I was getting fed up with her attitude. I could tell that Wade was fuming.

"Then that's what I want. I won't accept anything less. No cheating." I wouldn't have thought it possible, but her frown lines deepened.

"It's not cheating, Mrs. Jorgensen," I said through clenched teeth. "But never mind. I'm happy to do the sculpting work for you. But as I said, it's expensive and time-consuming. I just wanted to offer you an efficient alternative in case you didn't want to pay for the extra—"

"I thought I made myself clear," she said. "I want to win this contest at all costs. Money is not part of the equation. I want quality work."

"And you'll get it, I promise you." I gave her another big smile—fake!—and made a mental note to ask Dad just how close his friendship with Matthew Jorgensen was. Because if they were just casual acquaintances, putting up with this woman was not worth my aggravation.

She glared back. "I certainly hope so." She huffed impatiently as though she were dealing with recalcitrant children. "And don't forget, I want my orangery built in plenty of time for the tour."

"I haven't forgotten." How could I? Our original purpose in taking the Jorgensen job had been to construct a charming Victorian orangery on the side of her house where French doors led to a small, flower-filled yard.

I had thought an orangery—or greenhouse, or solarium, or conservatory, or whatever you wanted to call it—would be a fun challenge for me and my crew guys to tackle. Petsy had already ordered the massive kit from England and it was now sitting in her backyard, waiting to be put together.

"I've already pulled the permits for the orangery construction," I continued, "so that won't hold us up. But as I explained earlier, my team has a full schedule this week, so the earliest we can get started on your orangery is next Tuesday morning at eight o'clock. And I can begin the wainscoting repair at the same time, if that works for you."

"I'm not happy with the idea of waiting, but I suppose I'll have to. Please be on time."

"Of course. I'll drop off the contract tomorrow afternoon."

"My husband will sign it and write you a check." With that, she turned abruptly, walked out to the foyer, and disappeared through a door, her high heels tapping furiously against the polished wood floors as she moved.

Apparently we were dismissed.

"I guess we'll show ourselves out," I muttered.

Wade turned and looked at me. "Shannon, she's awful."

"Maybe we shouldn't have shown her the website."

"We always show clients that website. It's beautiful and most people love it." He blew out a frustrated breath. "Of course, *most* people are smarter and nicer than this one."

It wasn't often that Wade said something harsh about a client, but I couldn't blame him for feeling that way.

"Funny how she'll buy a mail-order orangery kit," I mused, "but when it comes to wood paneling, she insists on having the so-called real thing."

"Good point."

I took one more glance around the dining room. In Petsy's defense, the wainscoting panels were exquisite.

Or they would've been if they hadn't been allowed to disintegrate over the years.

Under ordinary circumstances, I would've loved to immerse myself in the Jorgensens' woodworking job. But my guys and I were swamped with work. It didn't make sense to spend my time doing this when I could spread out and do six different jobs and accomplish a lot more.

Especially when this particular client had such a lousy attitude!

As we walked to the front door, I shook my head. "Fake onlays. Give me a break."

"She's a piece of work, for sure."

"Maybe I should've explained that the original Victorian decorators cheated all the time."

"Not sure it would've helped," Wade groused, then broke into a grin. "Wait'll she finds out about the polyurethane corbels we're using in her orangery."

Horrified, I looked up at him. "Oh God, don't tell her."

"Believe me, I won't say a word. All I need is for her to come at me with a frying pan, yelling, *Fake! Fake!*"

I shouldn't have laughed, but I couldn't help it. It was so unreasonable. Nobody could tell the difference, and the polyurethane pieces were so much lighter and easier to work with than the old plaster forms.

What she didn't know wouldn't hurt her, I decided, as I walked over to my truck and unlocked the door.

After climbing up to the passenger seat, Wade pulled out his tablet. "Since you're going to be stuck on this woodworking job, we'd better work out a new schedule."

Grumbling, I shut the door and started the engine. "What we really need to do is hire another carpenter."

* _ *   *

I spent the rest of the week with Wade and two of my crew guys across town at the Spauldings' house, renovating their old kitchen and laundry room. The rest of the crew was working with Carla at my friend Emily's house. She wanted us to refurbish the front veranda railing and lay down a new concrete walkway in preparation for the Home and Garden Tour.

Because we were also rebuilding the short wall in front of Emily's home where some erosion had occurred during the rains, I had gone to the building-inspection office to apply for a permit to do the concrete work. The last thing I wanted was a job slowdown due to inspection issues, especially with the tour coming up so quickly.

While I was at the inspection office, I had also applied for a permit to renovate my friend Jane's garage starting next month. She wanted to turn the old structure into three new suites for the Hennessey Inn and I couldn't have been more thrilled. I had helped her refurbish her grandmother's Victorian mansion a few years ago and it was now considered one of the most elegant places to stay when traveling along the Northern California coast.

My company had several other jobs around town that Wade, Carla, and I were taking turns supervising. We were super busy and that made me very happy. Well, except for the unpleasant prospect of having to work with cranky-pants Petsy Jorgensen next week. But I could handle it. And once we got through that job, we would all be able to rest easier.

*   *   *

It was the following Monday afternoon and I had just called it a day at the Spaulding house. I had started to pack up my tool chest, ready to head for home, but had run into a snag while rearranging my screwdrivers.

That was the moment when Wade approached.

"Look at this," I said, holding up my claw hammer. "Why can't I get this to fit? It squeezed in here just fine earlier today, but now I've got to move all these screwdrivers around to make room."

"It's a question for the ages," he said, leaning one shoulder against the wall. "Listen, I've got news. I think I might've found us a carpenter."

I stared up at him. "Are you serious?"

"Yeah."

I stood and rested my fists on my hips. "A good one? Not just a hammer-and-nails guy, but someone with actual artistic ability?"

He smiled. "Yes."

It was almost too much to hope for. "Do you know him?"

He grinned. "It's a woman."

"Really?" I blinked in surprise. Sadly, there just weren't that many women working in construction.

"Yeah, really. Rumor has it, she's at least as good as you."

I laughed at his teasing tone. "No way. Who is it?"

"Do you know Bob Clemons?"

"The brick guy? Sure." *But he's a* brick guy, *not a* carpenter, I thought as I unbuckled my tool belt.

"I ran into him up at the hardware store and mentioned that we're looking for a highly skilled carpenter.

He recommended a gal he's been working with over in Flanders. She's supposed to be fantastic. A real artist, he says."

I lifted my tool chest and walked with him out to the street. "Could we get that lucky?"

"Why not?" He shrugged. "Bob swears she's amazing. What do you think?"

"I think I'd like to see some of her work. What's her name?"

"I wrote it down." Wade glanced at a piece of scrap paper. "Amanda Walsh."

I thought for a moment. "I don't think I know her."

"According to Bob, she just moved to the area a few months ago. He gave me her number. Do you want me to call her?"

With all the jobs we were picking up in preparation for the town's annual Victorian Home and Garden Tour, I had already hired some extra crew. I wanted experienced workers, though, so I was being picky. It was one of those good problems to have.

"Do you trust Bob?" I asked.

"He wouldn't lie to me about this."

I nodded slowly. "In that case, I wonder if Amanda can start tomorrow."

Wade grinned. "I'll give her a call and see if she's available. Unless you want to make the call."

I checked my watch. "I've got to meet my dad in fifteen minutes." I hefted my tool chest into the back of my truck. "Why don't you call and ask if she's interested in the job? And if she says yes, then find out when she's available to start. We'll give her a try on one job, and if she works out . . ." I held up my crossed fingers.

"If she works out, this Amanda Walsh could really make all of our lives easier." He started to walk away, but then turned back. "Will we see you at the pub later?"

"Definitely." My crew and I had a standing reservation once a week at the pub on Main Street for dinner and shooting the breeze. They were a good group of guys, but after going through some scary moments recently, I'd made it my goal to check up on them and make sure things were going well in their lives. The casual pub atmosphere made for easy talking—and it didn't hurt that I picked up the tab.

And that gave me an idea.

"Hey, Wade, why don't you ask Amanda if she'd like to meet us at the pub tonight? We can make sure we all get along before bringing her onto the jobsite."

He chuckled as he shook his head. "Talk about a trial by fire."

I smiled. "We'll see if she can stand the heat."

"You're tough, boss."

I blinked at him, slapped my palm dramatically to the center of my chest, and said innocently, "What? I'm a pussycat."

"Yeah, right." He laughed. "See you later."

"What do you think? Isn't she a honey?"

"She's a beauty, Dad. But are you sure you want to buy a boat? It's a lot of work, isn't it?"

"I'm not afraid of a little work."

No, but I am, I thought. Ever since his heart attack, I lived in fear that my father would overextend himself and end up in the hospital again. I knew the doctors had said he was fine. And Dad was continually reminding me that *he* was the parent here and perfectly healthy to boot. But no way did I want to relive rushing to his bedside in that cold, sterile hospital setting.

Still, did it matter that he was alive if my hovering kept him from *living*?

We stood on the dock of the marina, admiring the shiny blue hull and the clean white trim. The boat really was a beauty. It slept three people comfortably, plus a few more out on the deck on a warm night. It had a fully equipped galley and a remarkably large bathroom—or head, as Dad called it. I could picture my father and Uncle Pete and the rest of their pals having a grand old time on this floating man cave.

"And working on a boat isn't like work at all," Dad insisted. "It's a labor of love."

I knew that wasn't exactly true, but there was no way I was going to rain on his parade. "Is Uncle Pete going in on it with you?"

He shot me a sly smile. "He's got a little invested in the project."

"I hope so. You guys are lifelong fishing buddies. He would want in on a deal like this."

"You know it. But Pete's not going to live on the boat like I am so he's only going in for thirty percent."

"Sounds reasonable." But then I played back what he'd said. "Wait. I didn't realize you were going to live on the boat. Are you giving up the RV?"

"No way," he said with a wink. "That'll always be my original man cave."

"Pretty deluxe for a man cave." Dad had originally bought the luxury RV with the idea of traveling the back roads across America. Once on the road, he quickly realized that while he loved spending time in the RV, he didn't enjoy traveling all by himself. So he came back, turned the family home over to me, and moved into the RV instead. When Dad wasn't using it to go fishing with Uncle Pete, the RV was parked in my driveway, which was fine with me.

"Yeah." He turned and gazed longingly at the sleek thirty-seven-foot cabin cruiser. "But this baby opens up a whole new world. Heck, I could catch my own dinner every day."

I gave him a hug. "As long as you're happy, I'm happy."

He wrapped his arms around me. "I love you, sweetheart."

I drove home to change clothes and feed my critters. Pushing open the back gate, I glanced up at the apartment over my garage and worried for a few seconds that there were no lights on—until I remembered nobody lived there anymore.

MacKintyre Sullivan, the well-known mystery author, had lived upstairs for over six months while my crew and I refurbished the old lighthouse mansion. He had just moved a week ago, and even though his new home was only three miles up the coast, I missed him.

Sighing, I climbed the steps and opened the kitchen door—and was instantly greeted by an adorable barking Westie and a fluffy, striped orange cat who wrapped herself around my ankles. "Hello, my darlings."

I set my tote bag and purse down on the kitchen table and picked up Tiger for a quick cuddle. The cat purred loudly and I relished the warmth of her soft fur against my cheek.

"Woof!" Robbie protested, as if to say, *What am I, chopped liver?*

With a laugh, I set Tiger down and lifted Robbie up to give him a hug. "I love you guys."

A minute later I was cleaning and refilling their water bowls. Then I filled their food bowls and placed them on their individual mats.

My cell phone rang and I checked to see who was calling. It was Mac Sullivan so I quickly answered. "Hi, Mac."

"Hey, Irish. I'm going stir-crazy. Do you want to save my life and grab a bite to eat with me?"

I smiled. Mac wrote the Jake Slater thrillers and was in the throes of finishing his latest adventure.

"I would love to," I said. "But since today is Monday, would you mind if we went to the pub?"

"Oh, right, you've got dinner with the guys tonight. Guess I lost track of the days."

"That's understandable." I'd seen for myself that when the man was on a tight deadline, he often forgot to eat. Or shave. Or sleep. It wasn't pretty.

"But yeah," he said, "I'd love to join you. How about if I pick you up at six thirty?"

"Sounds perfect. I'll be ready."

"Can't wait to see you."

"Me, too," I said, then ventured to ask, "Is the book going well?"

"I've got two more chapters."

"Wow, you're writing this one fast."

"I'm motivated. I want to have it finished before the Home and Garden Tour starts."

"Then why are you still on the phone talking to me?" I teased.

He chuckled. "I'll see you in an hour."

We hung up and I ran upstairs to take a quick shower and do something with my hair.

This year the town council had voted to make Mac the official celebrity judge of the fifteenth annual Home and Garden Tour. I was pretty sure Mac considered it a greater honor than any writing award he'd ever won. Personally, I thought it was because writers were inherently nosy, and as a judge, he would be invited to poke his nose into everyone's house and wander around their gardens without anyone questioning why he was there. Mac would love that. As far as "judging" duties went, basically he would be helping to count the ballots and announcing the winner. The actual voting was done by all of the people taking the tour.

While I was getting dressed, my cell phone rang. I didn't recognize the number but answered anyway. "Hello?"

"Is this Shannon?" a woman asked.

"Yes, it is."

"This is Joan Derry. I live over on Cranberry Circle."

I was pleasantly surprised. She lived in the house with the beautiful and authentic orangery.

"Oh, hello, Mrs. Derry. Your house is beautiful."

"Thank you, and please call me Joan," she said. "I spoke with my neighbor Petsy Jorgensen a few minutes ago and found out that your company is installing her orangery."

"Yes. I understand she was so enthralled with yours that she wanted one for her very own."

"*Enthralled* is one way to put it," she said wryly, and chuckled. "Anyway, I was wondering, since you'll be in the neighborhood tomorrow, if I could beg you to run over and take a look at our basement. I'm scared to death we might be dealing with dry rot down there."

"I'm so sorry to hear that." I did a mental check of my schedule. "I'll be happy to stop by in the morning. Is seven o'clock too early for you? If that doesn't work I can make it around ten a.m."

"I'm an early riser, so seven is perfect. Thank you so much. You're a lifesaver."

I smiled into the phone. After dealing with Petsy Jorgensen, it was nice to talk to an appreciative client. "No problem. See you then."

A half hour later the doorbell rang. I opened the door and Mac stepped inside and pulled me into his arms. "Hi."

"Hi." I held on to him a few seconds longer than usual since I hadn't seen him in almost a week. "Do you think you'll get the book finished in time?"

He leaned back to look at me. "That's the plan, but don't jinx it."

"Oops. Sorry."

"You're forgiven," he said, rubbing my shoulders. "Seriously, though, I would hate to have to turn down my first chance to be a celebrity judge of such a prestigious event."

"That would be horrible." I rested my head against his chest. "But don't worry. You're going to be the best celebrity judge our town's ever had."

"Pretty sure I'm the *first* celebrity judge the town's ever had."

I thought for a moment. "You're probably right."

Since the pub was only two blocks away, we decided

to walk. It was staying light later in the day and kids were still outside playing basketball, the rhythmic thump of the ball sounding like the heartbeat of the block. With summer coming, the tourists would start streaming into town soon. There would be more noise, more traffic, more people, and just when it was all starting to make me a little grumpy, fall would arrive and sanity would return to the Cove.

As we walked, I told Mac about the run-in with Petsy Jorgensen.

"She sounds like a character. I can kill her in a book for you if you'd like."

I laughed, but it wasn't such a terrible idea.

"What sort of work are you doing for her?" he asked.

"We're redoing the wainscoting in her dining room because it's rotting. And we're building an orangery for her."

"An orangery? You mean, like a sunroom?"

"Oh, never say that word," I said, laughing. "She insists that we call it an *orangery*. Or I suppose you could get away with calling it a conservatory."

"Sounds Victorian."

"Doesn't it? Her neighbors the Derrys have a real one, built back in the eighteen hundreds. And it's gorgeous."

"So she's trying to keep up with the Joneses."

"Exactly. But you see, last year the Derry house won the grand prize. So Mrs. Jorgensen has decided that if she only had new wainscoting and a beautiful orangery, she could be the big winner this year."

Mac laughed and tucked my arm through his. "Do people honestly plot and plan that way? Why not just plant a pretty garden and maybe paint a room or two?"

I frowned as I thought about how some of my friends and neighbors had turned into cutthroat competitors over the last few years. "It's because of the prizes."

"I guess having your house featured on the cover of *Northern Home* magazine would be pretty awesome."

"And don't forget the ten thousand dollars that goes along with it."

"Oh yeah," he said, nodding sagely. "People would kill for a lot less than that."

Chapter Two

Half a block from the pub, my phone rang. "It's Wade," I explained to Mac, and answered the call. "Hi."

"Good news," Wade said. "Amanda can start tomorrow, and she's meeting us at the pub tonight."

"Really? That's great."

"I got a look at her portfolio, Shannon. She's exactly what we're looking for. Her work is fantastic."

"Wow." High praise coming from my very particular foreman. "Can't wait to see it."

"I think you'll be impressed."

I felt silly for asking, but I forged ahead anyway. "Is she nice?"

"She's a peach," he said cheerfully. "You'll like her. And she seemed really excited to be working on the Jorgensen house. I guess she's heard of Cranberry Circle."

"Cool." Anyone who liked Cranberry Circle was okay in my book, since my father had built some of the newer houses on the cul-de-sac.

"Hey, how did you see her portfolio?" I asked. "Have you already met her?"

"Yes. We're both at the pub, waiting for you." He laughed. "I came outside to call you and I can see you walking this way."

"Oh, how funny." I waved at him, then quickly told him about Mrs. Derry's dry rot problem, and he agreed to join me at her house tomorrow morning at seven o'clock. I ended the call and gazed up at Mac. "Looks like we're about to meet my new carpenter."

"Fantastic. So, having her around will free you up to do other things, right?"

"Exactly. I just hope she gets along with the guys."

Mac gave me a shoulder bump and a wink. "Your guys are easy to work with. And so are you."

"Thanks."

He grinned. "Are you going to warn her about the scary new client?"

I sucked in a breath. "I'm not sure that's a good idea. I don't want her to run away screaming before she even starts."

"Maybe she can find a way to get along with her."

"Maybe," I murmured, although I doubted anyone could really get along with Petsy. "At least her husband is nice. Maybe he'll intercede once in a while."

He took my hand as we strolled up to the pub. "It'll all work out."

"From your lips," I said, pushing on the door of the pub.

Mac pointed out Wade and the rest of the guys at the big round table in the corner and we weaved our way through the restaurant to join them. Everyone, including Amanda Walsh, was there.

My first thought was that she was really pretty. She had long brown hair—the word *chestnut* came to mind—and beautiful brown eyes. Even though she was sitting, I was pretty sure she was about my height, and I liked her immediately. Not because she was tall, but because she had a ready smile and was laughing at something one of the guys said, which told me she had a good sense of humor. But I warned myself to be cautious because, while I usually had good instincts about people, I had been wrong a time or two and the results had been disastrous. And frankly, I tended to be a real people person, which meant that I was inclined to like almost anyone I met—until they turned mean or betrayed me. For some reason, Petsy Jorgensen's image flashed through my mind. I shook it off.

Since Wade had already seen Amanda's portfolio and offered her the Jorgensen job, though, we would just have to see how things played out between me and her.

I was glad to see that Carla Harrison had made it, and I went over to give her a big hug before sitting down. She was my second foreman and one of my oldest friends. I trusted her implicitly. Wade would've already filled her in on who Amanda was, so I felt confident that Carla and Wade would jump in with questions of their own.

"I brought my portfolio with me," Amanda said after Mac and I had ordered beers. "You can take it with you later if you'd rather not look at it here."

"I'd like that. Thanks," I said. "So, how did you learn carpentry?"

"From my dad. He was a master at woodwork and I just loved hanging around with him."

It sounded so much like my own story that I had to smile. I could tell that my crew guys liked her already. But of course they would, because, duh, she was pretty.

"Where are you from?" Carla asked.

"Baltimore. Born and raised." Amanda frowned as soon as she said it, and I wondered why. But not everyone had had the idyllic childhood that I had.

"Did you like growing up there?" I asked.

The frown was deliberately forced into a smile. "Oh, yeah. I love Baltimore. But after my parents died, I thought I would venture out to see the rest of the world."

"I'm sorry about your parents," Wade said.

"Thanks. It's still a little painful to think about it. My dad just passed away a few years ago."

So, that's why she frowned, I thought. I could sort of relate to that, too.

"How in the world did you end up in Lighthouse Cove?" I asked.

"Well, to tell the truth, I actually planned to end up in San Francisco. I had fallen in love with all the Victorian homes I saw in photographs of the city. You know the ones they call the Painted Ladies?"

"I love those," Carla said.

"Me, too." Amanda smiled. "And they've got plenty of work there. But I guess I was whining about all the traffic one day, and one of my fellow workers suggested that I check out Lighthouse Cove because it's a small town, which appealed to me, plus you've got Victorians everywhere. My friend thought I might be able to pick up some custom carpentry jobs, so here I am."

"Are you happy here?"

She took a deep breath. "I know it sounds corny, but I feel like I'm finally home. I loved it the first time I drove down Main Street. It's like I've found a little piece of heaven whenever I walk around the town square."

"That's so nice," Carla said softly.

Sean flashed her a warm smile. "Your move here was lucky for us, too."

Todd took a quick slug of beer. "And we've pretty much got Victorian houses and buildings coming out of our ears around here."

"They're fun to work on," Billy said.

Sean grinned. "Especially when you're up on one of those slanted roofs, trying to maintain your footing."

"That's why I insist that you all wear safety belts," I said, well aware of some of the guys' willingness to take chances.

"Aw, Mom," Billy said, causing everyone to laugh and hoot. I didn't care. I had once seen a worker fall off one of those treacherous slanted roofs and it haunted me to this day. I would rather have my guys be safe than have to visit them in the hospital. Or worse.

Our waitress came over with our beers and we all ordered dinner, mostly burgers and fries and a few orders of fish and chips. Amanda ordered the cheeseburger with extra onions and French fries. I silently approved of the order—then instantly wondered why it mattered to me. Would I take off points for a chef's salad? I smiled and shook my head at my own silliness.

"What's up?" Mac asked quietly.

"Just thinking about dumb stuff," I confessed.

"You'll tell me later."

I rolled my eyes, still feeling goofy. "Probably."

We chatted and laughed all through dinner about regular stuff. It was easy, with Amanda sliding right into the give-and-take as if she'd always been there. Everyone talked over one another trying to fill Amanda in on the insanity of the annual Home and Garden Tour. When she found out that Mac was a famous writer, she was both shocked and thrilled to know him, but didn't go overboard with her fawning admiration, which he clearly appreciated.

All in all, she was kind of perfect. She fit right in with the group. And with me. Maybe this would work out.

I called for the check, then said, "Wade tells me you're available to start tomorrow. Is that still true?"

She grinned. "You mean, am I still willing to work with all you crazy people?"

Everyone laughed, including me. "Yeah, that's what I mean."

"I would love it."

"Good."

To my surprise, everyone applauded. Amanda looked a little stunned and I laughed. "Now you're stuck."

"It's a good kind of stuck," she said, giving a quick glance around the table. "I'm happy."

Wade leaned forward. "Uh, Shannon? Maybe we should warn her about Petsy."

"Oh God, you're right." I sighed. I hadn't wanted to give her a warning, but she was just so darn nice, I couldn't throw her into the lion's den without at least a little preparation. "The client you'll be working with is really difficult."

She glanced around the table again, checking everyone's expression before looking back to me. "What do you mean?"

"She's rude," Wade said.

"And demanding," Sean said.

"And snooty," I added, then winced. "And since you'll be working inside the house, you might get some sharp comments from her. I hope not, but it could happen. If she bothers you, just say the word and I'll deal with her."

Amanda smiled. "I'm sure I can handle it."

"I just don't want you to quit."

She held up her hand in a pledge. "I promise you I won't quit."

"Good," Wade said with a firm nod.

"It's weird," I said after a moment. "I don't think Petsy cares about making improvements for the well-being of the house itself."

"No," Wade grumbled. "She only cares about winning first prize in the Home and Garden Tour."

Sean crumpled up his napkin and set it on the table. "You're right. She doesn't care, because it's her husband's house. His family has lived there for over a hundred and fifty years. Mrs. Jorgensen has always resented it."

I gaped at Sean. "How do you know that?"

"I know their daughter, Lindsey." He looked at me. "Don't you remember her?"

I had a vague memory of a shy, gangly girl. "She didn't go to school with us, did she?"

"She was a year younger and only got through second grade before they sent her off to boarding school. My sister Amy is still friends with her, so I see her every so often."

Mac nodded slowly and I could imagine him creating a mental character chart on the woman for one of his dark thrillers. "Mrs. Jorgensen's crabby attitude makes sense if she's always hated living there."

"It's still weird," Wade said, unwilling to give Petsy the benefit of the doubt. "Just because you're miserable doesn't mean you have to take it out on everybody else."

Amanda shook her head, perplexed. "That's so sad. I've seen the house you're talking about. Who wouldn't want to live in a beautiful old house like that?"

The awe I heard in her voice gave me a warm and fuzzy feeling. It told me she revered old houses. I knew it took a certain type of personality to enjoy the sort of work we did. Among other qualities, it took someone who was willing to put in a lot of hard work to make an old house shine again.

I really hoped my instincts were right this time. I handed my credit card to the waitress and then turned to Amanda. "So, we'll see you tomorrow."

"Absolutely. Thank you so much for this opportunity."

"You're welcome, but I've got to warn you. Based on Bob's glowing recommendation, I'm expecting great things."

She laughed. "I won't let you down."

I tore a piece of paper from the notepad in my purse and scribbled some information. "Here's my phone number." And I wrote down the address, too. "But it sounds like you know where you're going. Can you be there at eight o'clock?"

"I can be earlier if you need me."

Wade made a face. "Mrs. Jorgensen insists that we

start at eight. But Shannon and I will be in the neighborhood around seven. We've got an inspection down the street from her."

"If you need me, I can show up at seven," she said amiably.

Wade and I exchanged glances. She was almost too good to be real. "If you're willing to inspect dry rot, then by all means, come early. The Derry house is across the street, two doors down. It's a big yellow house."

"Oh, dry rot can be awful," she said. "But I'll be there." Standing, she pulled a mini tablet out of her bag and handed it to me. "I'm going to take off now, but I didn't want to forget to give you this. It's my portfolio."

I frowned. "I don't want to keep your tablet if you need it."

"I only use it for taking photos, so it's no problem. I'd like to get it back in a day or two, though."

"Of course. Thanks." I was anxious to see samples of her work. She'd impressed Wade, so now I was even more curious.

"Thank you for dinner. I really enjoyed myself." She waved to everyone at the table. "I'll see you all tomorrow morning."

The rest of us stayed at the table for another half hour to chat and finish drinks. Then as Mac and I headed for the door after dinner, Carla sidled up next to me. Glancing around, she leaned closer. "So, what'd you think of the new girl?"

I smiled. "I like her. I took a quick look at her portfolio and I'm impressed, so that's a big relief. Also, she didn't come across as a mean girl, so I'm hoping we'll all get along. What did you think?"

"Nice. Smart. Funny. Her work looks really good. And she came highly recommended by Bob, so . . ." Carla shrugged. "Guess we'll see how it goes."

"Guess we will." I gave her a hug good night. "Have a safe drive home."

"Hey, guys," Sean said, jogging to catch up with us as we started to cross the street outside. "Talk about a coincidence, huh?"

"What do you mean?"

"I mean how I met Amanda last week and now here you are hiring her."

"You met her last week?"

"Yeah. Didn't Wade tell you?" He laughed. "Guess not. I was going to recommend her to you myself, but the next morning I left for a few days to visit my sister."

"For your niece's graduation?"

"Yeah. Talk about silly." He shook his head. "I mean, the kid graduated from *kindergarten*."

I chuckled. "Hey, that's an important rite of passage."

"Yeah, sure," he said, shaking his head. "But I've got to admit, the little kids were pretty cute."

"So, where did you meet Amanda?" I asked.

"Right here at the pub. It was after we all met for our Monday night dinner last week. Remember, I stuck around because Todd and Billy owed me a beer? So we went up to the bar after everyone left, and a few minutes later, Amanda came and sat down next to me. We struck up a conversation and she told me how she worked in construction and asked if I knew of any jobs around town."

"And you said yes?"

"Yeah." He scratched his head sheepishly. "But then, like I said, I left the next morning and totally forgot to tell you. Sorry about that."

"It's okay. You had vacation on your mind."

"I sure did." He grinned. "So, I'm on my way here tonight and Wade calls to tell me you've hired this woman named Amanda and invited her to dinner. And it turns out it's the same gal. So, anyway, it's cool that it all worked out."

"Very cool."

"Well, here's my truck," he said. "I'll see you tomorrow."

"Be careful driving home," I said.

"You got it."

Amanda was waiting for me when I parked my truck on Cranberry Circle the next morning. She had her hair pulled back in a ponytail and wore a baseball cap. Her clothes looked like the same basic uniform that I was wearing—blue jeans, long-sleeved shirt, vest, tool belt, and boots. I was missing the ball cap, but I did have my long, tangled curly hair pulled back from my face. All that hair could constitute a workplace hazard.

Wade jogged up the steps to the Derrys' front porch to join us. Frowning, he stopped and stared back and forth at Amanda and me. Then he grinned. "Wow. This should be interesting."

I knew what he was thinking, that Amanda and I were dressed way too much alike, all the way down to our boots. Maybe he was right, but I ignored him and rang the doorbell.

Joan Derry greeted us as if we were long-lost friends and whisked us into her house, where she offered coffee and bagels. She was dressed in a white tennis outfit and it suited her athletic build and outgoing personality perfectly. She was a completely different species from her dour neighbor and I liked her immediately.

All three of us shook our heads. "But thank you," I said. "That's very kind of you to offer."

She smiled. "I appreciate your wanting to get right to work. So follow me."

She led us into the spacious laundry room, where a door opened to reveal steps going down to the basement. The subterranean space had been refurbished in the last ten years, so it wasn't as dank as some old Victorian basements I'd worked in. She snapped a switch and the room filled with light. There was little furniture except along one wall where a large state-of-the-art wine-storage unit stood. Two comfy chairs and a small table faced the unit. *The perfect spot for some serious wine tasting,* I thought.

"Wow, that's a beauty," Wade said. "Looks like it holds about two hundred bottles."

"Yes, that's about right," she said, and added fondly, "My husband loves his wine."

On a hunch, I headed to the west side of the room and quickly found the dry rot.

"Found it," I muttered.

Wade rushed over. "Oh yeah. Figures it's the western wall."

"Is that significant?" Joan asked.

"Only because it's closest to the ocean," I explained. "But it really doesn't matter. It can happen anywhere when the air is damp like ours."

"But then why is it called *dry* rot?" she asked.

I smiled. "That's a good question and I honestly don't know for sure. It may be because it occurs after the wood has dried out following some water-related event. A flood or, in our case, constant moisture from the ocean. And also, you can see that the affected wood looks like it's turning to powder."

She sighed heavily. "What do we have to do?"

I glanced around. "First we've got to remove and replace all the affected wood. Then we'll clean all the nearby surfaces thoroughly and apply a fungicide and a sealant."

"Is the fungicide safe? My husband loves spending time down here."

"It's toxic," Amanda said flatly.

"That's right," I said with a quick look at her. "You'll want to keep him out of here for several days. We'll have a portable ventilator going while we work and we'll all be wearing respirator masks. Once we're finished, we'll wash down all the surfaces, including the wine safe and the chairs and table."

"And after that," Wade continued, "you'd be smart to install a dehumidifier. That'll prevent a new outbreak of dry rot and also guard against mold and termites."

"Wow. Okay," she said, sounding a little shell-shocked. "You guys sure seem to know what you're doing. How soon can you start?"

I glanced at Wade, then said, "We'll have to juggle some schedules around, but we'll make this a priority because it's dangerous to let it go. I can have two of my guys start this afternoon."

"I really appreciate that." She walked over to the stairs.

"Joan," I said, "would you be willing to show me your orangery? I would love to take a few photographs, if you don't mind."

She grinned for the first time since we'd entered the basement. "I don't mind at all. That way, you can see what a *real* orangery looks like."

I forced myself to bite my tongue, but Wade laughed out loud. Joan seemed delighted with his reaction. It was pretty obvious—and thoroughly gratifying—that the two neighbors were not exactly the best of friends.

After dragging my tool chest out of the back of my truck, I stood on the sidewalk and gazed around at the homes that lined Cranberry Circle. Several of the houses on this street were near and dear to my heart since my own father had built many of them years ago. In among the newer homes were the original Victorians that had been here for well over a hundred years. Some, like the Jorgensen and Derry homes, had been in the same families for all that time. The lots were big, at least a quarter acre, and all of them were well maintained with lovely trees and green lawns.

I doubted Petsy Jorgensen would've tolerated an unkempt property in her neighborhood.

I turned to Amanda. "Ready?"

She nodded. "And excited."

I checked my watch. Five minutes after eight. I hoped Petsy hadn't noticed us coming from the Derrys' house.

Would she make a stink because looking at Joan's orangery had caused us to be five minutes late?

"Guess we'll find out," I muttered, hating this feeling of dread at the thought of dealing with my client. That was no way to run a business. The fact was, I had accepted the job knowing full well that Petsy was a difficult person, so now it was up to me to make it as pleasant as I could for my entire crew.

I walked up the long walkway to the stairs leading to the front porch. When I turned to say something to Amanda, she wasn't there. I whipped around and saw her standing back on the sidewalk, staring up at the imposing home as if she was mesmerized. It was a marvelous house, but still.

"Amanda?" I called. "You okay?"

She shook off whatever had captured her attention, straightened her baseball cap, and came striding up the walk. "Sorry about that."

"No worries. These houses are pretty amazing, aren't they?"

"Beautiful," she murmured.

"By the way," I said when Amanda reached the porch, "your portfolio pictures were really fantastic. I'm still looking at them, so if you don't mind, I'll return your tablet tomorrow."

"Not at all."

"You're really good."

Her cheeks were turning pink. "Thanks. That means a lot, coming from you. I hear you're, like, the best carpenter in the world."

I laughed. "Yeah. Not quite."

I knocked on the door, and when nobody answered I circled over to the porch rail and took another moment to appreciate the cloudless blue sky and mild spring weather. From here I could see the surrounding hills and trees and even the very tip-top of our famous lighthouse three miles up the coast. Because of last month's rains, the new leaves on the trees were bright green and spring flowers bloomed in vibrant shades of pink and yellow and red and purple.

It couldn't have been better timing. In three weeks, the array of colors for the Home and Garden Tour would be glorious.

Wade was crossing the street toward us, carrying his tool chest and a stepladder. He waved and continued along the side of the house, where the orangery kit was waiting to be put together.

Just then the front door opened and Petsy stood there, making a point of checking her watch.

"It's about time," she said, but made no further comment as she swung the door wide enough for us to enter.

"I'd like you to meet Amanda Walsh," I said. "She'll be working with me on the wood panels. There's nobody better at woodworking in all of California."

"We'll see about that," Petsy said, staring at Amanda.

I turned to Amanda. "This is Petsy Jorgensen."

Amanda looked way too solemn as she nodded at the older woman. "Hello."

Petsy shook her head, basically ignoring Amanda's greeting, and I had the strongest urge to slap her. But I didn't. Instead, Amanda and I followed her through the archway leading into the dining room.

"I have an important meeting this morning," Petsy said, "so I won't be able to stay and supervise."

"We know what to do." I glanced toward the dining room. "My foreman is already here to start building the orangery. Three of my other crew members will join him shortly while Amanda and I work in here."

"Fine. My husband and daughter are both home in case you have any questions while I'm out."

"Thank you."

But she didn't walk away, just continued to stare at Amanda, who was starting to look uncomfortable. "Do I know you?"

"I don't think so," she said. "I've only recently moved to town."

Petsy squinted to study her for another few seconds. Did she think Amanda was lying? I was about to intercede, but then without another word Petsy turned and left us alone.

I leaned closer to Amanda and whispered, "I'm sorry about her attitude. I plan to be here as much as possible over the next few days, so I'll make sure she doesn't bug you too much."

"Oh, she's not so bad," Amanda said, waving off the odd moment. "I'll be fine."

"You're a better woman than I," I muttered.

An hour later, Amanda had finished assessing the damage to the wainscoting panels and estimated that she could complete the project in about two weeks.

"That would be fantastic," I said. "Petsy was adamant that we wrap it up before the Home and Garden Tour."

"No worries." Amanda wrote out a list of supplies she would need and the two of us drove to the big hardware store out by the highway. In the car, I explained how Mrs. Jorgensen had refused to use any wood onlays, insisting that the work be done by hand.

"I'll be doing it by hand," Amanda assured me. "But does she realize I've got to make molds of the patterns? Those may or may not be made of wood, but I promise they'll look exactly the same as what's on her walls now. They'll be beautiful."

I'd seen her portfolio and I believed her. "I know they will be. But at this point I'd rather not share that information with her. She'll just get cranky."

She smiled. "Thank you for trusting me. I know she'll be happy with the results."

"I'm not sure Petsy will ever be happy," I muttered. "But your word is good enough for me."

"Is Petsy a nickname? Do you know?"

"I do, because I looked it up in the town newspaper archives."

When she grinned at that, I shrugged. "I was curious— what can I say? Petsy is short for Petronella."

"Wow. That's rough."

"I know, right?" I chuckled. "That name was more popular in the forties and fifties, although I wouldn't say it was ever really *popular*."

"But *Petsy* is kind of cute."

"Really?"

She laughed. "Well, it would be if it belonged to someone a little nicer."

Driving back, we were chatting like old friends. When we reached the Jorgensen house, I helped her set up a worktable at one end of the room, using two sawhorses and a thick piece of plywood. We draped drop cloths over the dining room table, the chairs, and the fancy dish cabinet along the side wall.

To avoid filling the room with sawdust, we agreed that any filing or sawing she needed to do would be done in the side yard where the guys were building the orangery.

And speaking of the orangery, I was anxious to check up on Wade and the guys. But first, Amanda and I pried off several of the wood panels that were still in good shape and placed them on the plywood. She would carefully remove the cleanest sections of the appliqué scrollwork designs and trace the patterns onto heavy butcher paper. This would create a template that she would use to carve out a new piece, using either wood or plaster, depending on what worked best in any particular spot.

For some trouble spots, she would actually create plaster molds that would replace the broken panels.

"Shannon Hammer, is that you?"

I turned and beamed at the handsome older man who'd just walked into the room. "Hi, Mr. Jorgensen."

He gave me a hug, then glanced around. "I'm glad we're finally getting these old pieces replaced."

"This is Amanda Walsh," I said. "She'll be doing most of the sculpting and creative stuff for you."

"Brilliant. Nice to meet you, Amanda." He jogged around me to shake her hand.

"Nice to meet you, too, Mr. Jorgensen," Amanda said.

"Please call me Matthew, both of you. You're making me feel like an old man with that 'Mr. Jorgensen' nonsense."

I had to smile. His temperament seemed the complete opposite of his wife's and I couldn't figure out how they could live in the same house together. But then, love and marriage baffled me on a regular basis.

"Can you tell me how these panels got so damaged?" I asked.

He winced. "Yeah. It's probably my fault. I've got three siblings and they each have two boys. Petsy hated to have them racing up and down the stairs whenever they visited, so we started turning the dining room over to them. We have a big family table in the kitchen and rarely use this room, so it made sense at the time. Needless to say, the boys pretty much decimated those panels over the years."

"Wow." I had thought Petsy was making up that story, but apparently the damage really had been done by children.

"Yeah." He shook his head. "Six boys with hockey sticks and lightsabers and basketballs can be amazingly destructive."

"No kidding."

"Well." Amanda adjusted her baseball cap. "In that case, I'd better get to work."

"Oh, right," Matthew said. "I'll get out of your way. But if either of you need anything, just give a shout-out."

"Thanks, Matthew," I said.

"Hey, say hi to your dad for me," he added as he was walking out. "Tell him to call me next time he's having a poker party."

"I'll tell him."

"He seems really nice," Amanda said, her tone a little wistful. I figured meeting Matthew had made her miss her father. I could totally relate to that. I still missed my mom at odd times.

Once Amanda was set up with the supplies and equipment she would need to get started, I walked outside to check on Wade and his crew. The air had grown warm and the guys were working in their T-shirts.

The ground outside the French doors was already leveled and now the guys were building a trench that would be filled with concrete, providing a base for the brick wall upon which the glass walls and steel frame of the orangery would sit.

Early in the process, the frame would be bolted to the house and the brick and mortar would be affixed to the frame.

Wade saw me coming and grinned. He pulled a handkerchief from his pocket and wiped the sweat from his forehead, then leaned his shovel against the outside wall and met me halfway. "You know we can install this thing without your help."

I gave him my sad face. "I want to help. I've only installed one of these and that was at least five years ago."

Billy piped up. "If you like shoveling dirt, we're happy to let you help."

"Who doesn't like shoveling dirt?" Todd said.

"How's Amanda doing?" Wade asked, changing the subject.

"Great. It's nice to work with someone who understands exactly what I'm saying and is capable of doing the job without constant supervision."

"It's especially nice because it'll free you up to supervise the other jobsites."

I glanced back at the house. "I hope so, but right now I don't want to leave her alone in there. Petsy could come back at any minute and freak out over something."

He snorted, then frowned. "Oh crap."

"What?"

He leaned closer. "Speaking of horrible people, here comes Scully."

"Already? I just pulled the permits last week." I turned and watched Joe Scully crossing the street and walking toward us. He was the town's building inspector and a general pain in the butt to everyone in the construction business. Scully was one of those people who enjoyed wielding power over other people and he seemed to think his title gave him that right.

It wouldn't have been so bad if he were competent, but he barely knew much of anything about construction.

"I ran into him yesterday at the hardware store," Wade murmured. "He warned me that he might come by to check on our work today."

"But nothing's been done yet."

"The trench is dug and supposedly he needs to sign off on it." Wade shrugged. "But let's get real. He just wants to harass us."

I rolled my eyes. Last year Scully had delayed one of our projects by three weeks, just to be a jerk.

I turned and flashed a big smile. "Hi, Joe."

He frowned, trying to appear concerned, but I knew he was just here to sniff around, looking for trouble. And if he couldn't find trouble, he'd *make* some. Finally he said, "This trench doesn't look deep enough."

"It's deep enough," I said mildly. "Needs to be twelve inches and I know for a fact it's more than that."

"I'll be the judge of that." Scully pulled a little tape measure out of his pocket and squatted down to measure the depth. When he stood up, he shook his head. "It's barely eleven inches."

I unclipped my own industrial-sized tape measure from my tool belt and measured for myself. I held up the tape for everyone to see. "Sorry, Joe, but you're wrong. This trench is twelve and a half inches deep."

Scully was about to dispute it, but at that moment, Petsy Jorgensen opened the French doors. "Why aren't you people working?"

Wade pointed with his thumb toward Scully. "The building inspector is here questioning the trench we dug."

She gazed at Joe Scully. "Why?"

"That's my job, ma'am."

"Well, Mr. Inspector, does it pass inspection or not?" she asked.

He gritted his teeth, knowing he was cornered. "I suppose I'll let it go."

"Thank you so much," she said, smiling acerbically.

"You're welcome." Self-conscious now, Scully coughed, then turned to Wade. "I'll be back tomorrow to make sure you got the foundation poured right." With that, he walked back toward the street.

Petsy watched him go, then asked, "Does he have to come here every day?"

"No," I said. "But he likes to feel important."

"And screw with us," Wade added under his breath.

But Petsy caught what he'd said. "Are you saying he could hold up the project?"

"Yes, he could," I said, having no problem throwing Joe Scully under the bus. "He's done it in the past."

She huffed out a breath and shook her hair back dramatically. "I'm going to call the mayor." Then she shut the door, leaving me and Wade staring at each other.

Wade looked a little dazed. "Never figured her for an ally."

"Savor the moment," I warned, gaping at the French doors. "She could turn on you like a rabid dog."

Chapter Three

Later that afternoon I drove out to the Spauldings' house to check on the kitchen rehab work. The guys had just maneuvered several large, heavy pieces of granite onto both the spacious island and the surrounding counter-tops. The hard surfaces were a stunning swirl of vibrant gold mixed with blacks and browns and whites. The colors would work perfectly with the backsplash and the new stainless steel appliances and I could tell that everyone in the family was really happy. And that made me happy, too. Nothing better than a satisfied customer to bring you *more* customers. Word of mouth was still the best possible advertising.

I drove home the long way, along Old Farm Road, where pastures still stretched for hundreds of acres, broken up only by a barn here or a silo there. It was nice to see cows and horses grazing in the fields, comforting to know that the farms continued to thrive, just as they had when Lighthouse Cove was first settled back in the 1800s.

The charming old wooden water towers and windmills that still stood in spots around town were even more plentiful out here. A few of the old towers in town had been converted to small shops or offices since we no longer had to worry about getting water pumped into our houses. But it looked as if many of the ones out here along Old Farm Road were still in working order.

I came to a stop at Queen Anne Hill Road and was about to turn right when something caught my eye. I looked up and saw that the water tower near the southeast corner had been painted a brilliant springtime yellow. Flowers painted in a rainbow of colors covered every possible spot, and the word *Marigold* was written out in letters at least six feet tall around the tank at the very top.

"Marigold?"

Was that some odd sort of "Ode to Spring" created by a local farmer? Or was it a direct reference to my friend Marigold Starling?

"Interesting," I murmured. And perfect timing, since I was meeting my girlfriends for dinner that night and Marigold would be there. I couldn't wait to find out if she was the inspiration for the mysterious water tower redesign.

Impulsively, I set the emergency brake, jumped out of my truck, and took a few pictures of the yellow marvel. Then I climbed back inside and drove away.

An hour later, I walked into Bella Rossa, my uncle's wine bar and restaurant on the town square.

"Shannon!" Jane Hennessey cried from a table in the adjoining room. "We're over here."

I hurried over to the table and circled around, giving everyone a hug. "I've missed you guys so much."

"I've missed you, too," Lizzie Logan said. "Hal sends his love."

"Tell him I love him, too," I said, smiling as I took my seat. Lizzie and Hal owned Paper Moon, the bookshop on the town square.

"So, what's been going on?" Lizzie asked. "Are you completely buried in work?"

"Pretty much," I said, feeling the underside of the table for a hook where I could hang my purse. Early on, Uncle Pete had asked for ways he could improve the room and I had pointed out that women liked to have some way to hang their purses that didn't involve draping them over the backs of their chairs where they might fall or be stolen. So there were purse hooks under the tables and under the bar.

"It's the Home and Garden Tour," I explained once I got comfortable. "It seems like everyone in town wants something done to improve their chances of winning. And I've got to admit, a few of them are hard to deal with."

"Like me," Emily said mournfully.

"No way," I insisted, laughing. "I love working on your house."

"Ghost and all?" Lizzie asked, with a gleam in her eye.

I grinned. "Of course." Last year Emily had bought the old Rawley mansion, a genuine haunted house, complete with swinging chandeliers, creaky noises, and cold spots. But ever since I'd discovered the ghost's diary while remodeling the place, things had calmed down a bit.

"The ghost of Mrs. Rawley is pretty tame these days," Emily said. "She's happy to have Gus living there."

Jane smiled at Emily. "You seem pretty happy yourself."

Lizzie giggled. "Who wouldn't be happy to have Gus Peratti around the house?"

We all chuckled at that. Gus was a sinfully handsome man, inside and out, and women loved him. Even ghostly women.

The waiter arrived with more bread and another bottle of wine, and we ordered dinner.

"So, I have a question," I said finally, after the waiter left and we'd gone around the table and shared all of our latest news. "What's with the big yellow water tower outside of town with Marigold's name splashed across the tank?"

Pulling my phone out of my purse, I pushed a few buttons and then handed it to Marigold. There was silence for a moment while she focused on my photos. Then she gasped. "Oh no, he didn't!"

"Who is *he*?" I asked, intrigued by her reaction.

The others were concerned over Marigold's distress. As for me, I couldn't tell if she was angry, embarrassed, or both.

Lizzie grabbed her arm. "Are you all right?"

"What's going on?" Jane asked me. "What did you see?"

But I was watching Marigold. She didn't look distressed at all. She looked annoyed. Okay, then. Angry.

I leaned over. "What's up, Marigold?"

"Oh, that silly man," she said, burying her face in her hands.

"Of course it's all about a silly man," Emily said, glancing around the table. I noticed her Scottish brogue was growing stronger with the wine. "It always is, isn't it?"

"That . . . that farmer!" Marigold grumbled.

"Farmer?" Jane said. "What farmer?"

"Who are you talking about?" Lizzie asked.

She clenched her teeth. "Raphael Nash."

Jane and I exchanged frowns. "Who's that?"

"He's a dolt who won't take no for an answer," she snapped, then groaned. "I just can't believe he would do this."

"Okay," Jane said calmly. "Take a deep breath; drink some wine. Then start at the beginning and tell us everything."

Marigold did as Jane said, first taking several deep breaths in and out to calm down. Then she grabbed her glass and took a big sip of wine, set it down, and straightened her shoulders. "He bought the old Jenkins property."

I frowned. "The whole thing?"

"Yes."

I glanced at Jane, who looked right back at me, and I knew we were both thinking the same thing: Raphael Nash must have had some money in the family. The old Jenkins farm was at least five hundred acres. There were open meadows and some forested areas. Coral Creek ran across the property, providing some nice spots for fishing. From what I could remember, one part of the farm spread up into the hills and from there you could see the ocean. There was a charming old fixer-upper of a farmhouse and a dilapidated barn. But those could have been refurbished easily. In truth, I'd have loved to get my hands on them.

The place had to be worth several million dollars.

"So, tell us more about Raphael," I said. "His name sounds Italian."

"Or Spanish," Lizzie added.

"He's from San Diego, and he's worth millions," Marigold said, answering my unspoken question with a blasé wave of her hand. Rolling her eyes, she added, "And he's asked me to marry him."

The silence was much longer this time.

"But that's wonderful news," Jane said, always the romantic.

"Wait," I said, tossing cold water on my friend's warm heart. "We don't even know this guy and he's already proposed?"

"Yes, he proposed."

I said, "But you don't sound too happy about it."

"Did you miss the part where I said he was a farmer?"

"Oh, Marigold," Lizzie said with a sigh. "Just because he's a farmer doesn't mean you'll be stuck milking cows for the rest of your life."

"Ah." I sat back in my chair. Puzzle solved. Our friend Marigold had been raised back east in a tight-knit, very conservative Pennsylvania Dutch community. She had grown up on a dairy farm, and as soon as she was old enough, she had left home, moving as far away as she could get, to Lighthouse Cove, where she lived with her aunt Daisy. The two of them owned the Crafts and Quilts shop on the town square.

Happily Marigold had managed in a roundabout way

to keep tabs on her Amish family and friends back home and contribute to the community's prosperity by purchasing their beautiful handcrafted quilts and toys to sell in her popular shop.

But Marigold had less than zero interest in going back to a farm. Even one complete with a husband and a bucket of money.

"Do you like him?" Lizzie asked.

She thought for a brief moment. "He's stubborn."

"And you wouldn't be able to relate to that," Jane said, smirking.

Marigold tried not to smile. "All right, maybe I'm stubborn, too. But honestly, if I never see another cow again, I'll be perfectly happy."

"If he's as wealthy as you say he is," Emily reasoned, "I'm sure he doesn't want you milking cows all day."

"That's what he'll say at first," she muttered. "But they always change their minds and then they wear you down."

Lizzie gave a knowing sigh. "Yes, they do that."

"He's impulsive and brilliant," Marigold said. "He's always inventing something."

"He sounds smart," Lizzie said.

"I guess he is."

"So, are you dating him?" Jane asked.

Marigold made a face. "I suppose."

Jane laughed. "You sound so excited."

"Jane, did you see that water tower?" Marigold asked. "The man is incorrigible."

"He sounds sweet."

"How long have you known him?" I asked, reaching for a breadstick. "How did you meet?"

"He came into the store about four weeks ago." She

smiled at the memory. "He's sort of a high-tech entrepreneur. He works with solar power. And he likes gadgets. He was interested in the wooden gyroscope my nephew designed."

"I saw that in your store window," Lizzie said. "I thought I might buy it for Taz. He's not completely plugged in to the computer yet, thank goodness. He still enjoys gadgets." Her eleven-year-old son had a birthday coming up soon.

"Taz would love it," Marigold said. "It's beautifully made and it works perfectly."

"So, tell us more about Raphael," Jane said, bringing us back to the subject at hand. "Is he nice? I mean, besides that whole cow-milking issue. Do you like him?"

Marigold smiled dreamily. "Yes, Rafe is a really nice man. I like him very much. He's kind and funny. He makes me laugh. He's tall and he's so handsome."

"He sounds . . . perfect," Emily said, looking around the table.

I met her gaze and knew what she was thinking. If this guy was so tall and handsome and perfect, how had none of us ever seen him around town before? And why hadn't Marigold told us about him?

Marigold nodded. "He's been wonderful. But then the other day he told me he'd bought a farm and was going to buy some cows and a horse and . . . well . . ." She gazed around the table, making eye contact with each of us. "I've never really talked much about my life on the farm, because it wasn't a happy time for me. So, now I finally meet this lovely man who seems so normal and nice, if unconventional. And he turns out to be a farmer. Life is so unfair."

"So, why have you kept him a big secret from *us*?" I watched her and saw the quick intake of breath.

"I just," she said, "was keeping it to myself for a while. It was so new, you know?" She frowned. "Now, though, the whole town will be talking, won't they? My name on a water tower!"

I grinned. "If you want us to get some paint and cover it up, we're here for you."

"Not a bad idea." She took a stiff gulp of wine. "Let's please change the subject. Someone else talk. Or tell a joke. Anything."

There was silence for a split second and then we all began to talk at once. Lizzie told a joke and we were laughing again. Emily mentioned that her brother might visit one of these days. And I asked Jane how the Festival Committee was holding up without me.

"I wish you were there," she said, "but I know you're too busy. We've done so many of these events, so I know it'll be fabulous. But right now it's the usual nervous rush to complete everything."

Jane and I had run the town's Festival Committee for several years with a few other ladies. The events had been so popular that our town was becoming famous for its parades and festivals. Last year our Festival Committee had taken over the running of the Home and Garden Tour and this year's tour promised to be even bigger and better than ever.

But because I was involved in refurbishing some of the houses that would be included in the tour, I'd felt it was only right to step down from my committee job for this event. Even though the general public voted for the winner of the tour, we didn't want anyone to think that my houses might somehow receive special treatment.

Jane reached for a chunk of bread. "We've commissioned six horse-drawn trolleys to take people around on the tour."

"That sounds like fun," Lizzie said. "Can I sponsor a trolley?"

"What a great idea," Emily said. "Count me in."

"I'm writing that down," Jane said, reaching for a pen from her purse. "We can have banners made up with your store names and hang them off the sides of the trolleys." She jotted down the idea. "Anyway, we'll have the usual booths set up in the town square, and because it's the garden tour, we've got three different booths selling plants and flowers."

"That's smart," I said. "I wish I could say I contributed an idea or two myself, but I'm a complete piker."

Jane flashed me a coy smile. "Well, actually, next year I was thinking we could have a DIY project booth. You could be in charge, demonstrating how to do simple construction projects. Maybe you could team up with the hardware store and give away little tool sets. We're still throwing ideas around, but I thought I'd give you a heads-up."

"I love that idea. Maybe I'll get Carla to help me. And Amanda if she's still here."

"Who's Amanda?" Emily asked.

"She's the new carpenter I hired. I think you'll all like her."

"I met her a few days ago," Lizzie said. "She came in to buy some books. Seems really nice."

"I'd love to meet her," Jane said.

I nodded. "I'll bring her around."

"Good." Jane slathered butter on her bread. "And Marigold has offered to officiate at our very first quilt show. It's going to take place at the Campbell house, which is the last house on the tour. They have a gorgeous ballroom we're using. And we'll also serve refreshments there."

"You've got it all worked out." I turned to Marigold. "And you're the perfect person to handle a quilt show."

"I hope so," she said, swirling her wine. "We've already got thirty entries and they're all beautiful. I'm kind of a wimp, though. I don't want anyone going away mad, so I'll probably give participation ribbons to everyone who enters."

We all laughed because it was true. Marigold had such a kind heart.

As dinner arrived, I made a mental note to drive out to the old Jenkins farm in the next day or two. I wanted to meet Raphael Nash and find out what a supposedly wealthy high-tech entrepreneur was doing up here, buying a five-hundred-acre farm outside of Lighthouse Cove. Did he really want to be a farmer?

But more important, what was he doing with Marigold? Not that any man wouldn't fall in love with her overnight, but did this guy really know her? Marigold had grown up very sheltered and sometimes her friends could be a little overprotective of her, but I was okay with that. Maybe this guy thought she was an easy mark.

Who in the world was Raphael Nash? Why had none of us ever seen him around town? Nash had to be a pretty common name. Was it his *real* name or a fake?

Was he hiding from his creditors? Or from the law? Okay, maybe that was a little far-fetched, but I wanted answers. And glancing around the table at the faces of my friends, I had a feeling they would want some answers, too.

The next morning, Amanda and I met at the Jorgensen house. She was wearing the same cute baseball cap from yesterday and I had a feeling it was part of her work uniform.

This time, the front door was answered by a woman around our age. She had a fragile beauty, with lovely skin and long, straight blond hair, and she wore a pretty yellow suit with two-inch ivory heels.

"You must be the construction people," she said. "I'm Lindsey Jorgensen. Come in."

"Hi, Lindsey," I said, then added, "You probably don't remember me but I'm Shannon Hammer. I went to school with Sean Brogan. I think you know his sister Amy." I said it cautiously, not wanting to get my head chewed off if she was anything like her mother.

"Oh, yes." She beamed. "I saw Sean outside a few minutes ago. It's good to meet you, Shannon."

"And this is Amanda Walsh."

"Amanda, hi." Lindsey continued to smile as she reached out and shook Amanda's hand. I started to relax. She didn't seem at all like her mother, which was a big relief.

"Amanda is a wonderful carpenter and she'll be doing all the real work in here," I explained. "I'll just be in and out, helping her and the guys outside."

"Sounds good. If you need anything, please—"

"Oh, Lindsey. Good, you're awake."

We all turned at the sound of Petsy's voice. She stood on the stairs, staring down at us with thinly veiled disdain.

Lindsey sighed. "Of course I'm awake, Mother. I have an event this morning."

"Oh." Frowning, she scanned her daughter from her shoes to her hair and back down again. "Is that what you're wearing to the fund-raising breakfast?"

Lindsey gritted her teeth briefly, then curved her mouth and said evenly, "Yes. It's comfortable and flattering and it makes me feel happy."

"Aren't you a lucky girl?" Petsy smiled tightly. "I'm off to a meeting as well. I should be back by noon." She turned and walked out the door.

With a mother like that, Lindsey didn't seem lucky at all. She let out a breath. "I presume you've met my mother."

"Yes." I stopped there, since there didn't seem to be anything else I could say without being insulting.

"I don't actually live here," she quickly explained. "I've moved to San Francisco. I have an art gallery off of Union Square, but there was a fire, so I've come home to stay for a few weeks while the reconstruction is going on."

"I'm sorry about the fire." I heard quick footsteps on the staircase and glanced up to see Matthew Jorgensen coming down. He wore jeans and a sweater and looked completely at ease.

"Hey, sweetie," he said, and gave Lindsey a loud kiss on the cheek. "You look snazzy. Going out?"

She smiled and kissed him back. "Yes, Dad. Do you have everything you need?"

"You know I do." He grinned at Amanda and me as he gave Lindsey a hug. "My favorite girl takes good care of me."

She laughed and patted his shoulder. "Because you're my favorite dad."

He leaned closer and whispered, "I wish you would move back home."

"We both know that won't happen," she murmured, then tucked her purse under her arm and glanced at us. "See you all later."

"Nice meeting you," Amanda said.

"You, too." And she was out the door.

Matthew waited until she was gone, then turned to us. "Do you girls need anything? I'm right upstairs working, so just give me a shout."

"We're good to go," I said. "Thanks, Matthew."

Once Matthew had gone, I followed Amanda into the dining room and we got things set up for the day.

After a minute, Amanda said quietly, "They both seem really nice."

"I know." I glanced around, then whispered, "Wonder what happened to the mom."

"She's so mean," Amanda said. "No wonder Lindsey lives in San Francisco."

"I don't blame her one bit for moving away. I'm only surprised she didn't go farther."

As soon as Amanda had settled into her work, I walked out the front door and went around to the side yard. Normally I hated gossiping about my clients, but

Petsy was just too awful. I couldn't believe she'd panned her own daughter's outfit in front of strangers. And it was totally uncalled-for, because Lindsey had looked great as far as I was concerned. A young business professional.

What kind of atmosphere had Lindsey grown up in? I didn't really have to wonder. It had to have been dreadful. Thank goodness she had her father to protect her. And he was a great guy, but I doubted he was strong enough to overpower his wife.

I wondered if it was his idea to send Lindsey to boarding school—for her own welfare.

"Good morning, guys," I said.

Wade grinned and held up his ever-present cup of coffee. "Morning, Shannon."

Billy looked up from adding a bag of powdered cement into the barrel of the cement mixer. "Hey, Shannon, you gonna help dig trenches today?"

"Looks like I'm too late."

"Yes, you are," Wade said. "We're almost ready to pour the foundation. Then we'll lay these concrete blocks down and wait for them to set. And while they're setting, we'll start attaching the frame to the house."

"Sounds like you've got a plan."

"We do. You sticking around?"

"I'm going to go check on the guys over at the Derry house, see how that dry rot project is going. Then I'll be back."

"See you then."

I was crossing the street when Joan Derry yanked her front door open, walked out on her porch, and began waving and pointing away from the house. "Get out."

All of a sudden Joe Scully, the building inspector, came striding out the front door. He crossed the porch and jogged down the stairs as fast as I'd ever seen him move. He turned to say something, but Joan held up her hand to stop him. "Not one word!"

"But you've got to—"

"Don't tell me what I've got to do," she shot back. "It's your fault that damage occurred in the first place."

"But, Joan—"

"Go away!" she shouted, clearly at her wit's end.

Just then, another man walked out onto the porch. "Joan, what's wrong? I heard yelling."

"It's Scully," she said scornfully. "I found him down in the basement."

"Scully? What the—?"

I assumed this was Joan's husband. He jogged down the front steps and marched right up to Scully. "You heard her, Joe. Get out of here."

Scully puffed up his chest, trying without success to appear bigger than he was. "I have a job to do."

"Not here. You should be fired—or worse. I thought we saw the end of you two years ago."

"As I told your wife, I'm—"

"I don't care," Mr. Derry said. "I know you're not a smart man, but if you were, you'd take the hint and never show up on my property again."

"Or what?" Scully countered snidely, then backed off quickly in case the man threw a punch at him. It made me think this sort of thing had happened before.

Joan ran over to her husband and grabbed hold of his shirt. "Don't tempt him, Scully. Just go away and don't come back."

"No, let him stay," Mr. Derry shouted, squirming to get loose from his wife. "Because I'm going to kill him."

"No, Stan." Joan shot Scully an angry look. "You'd better go."

Scully took off running. I slinked behind a truck parked nearby so he wouldn't see that I'd witnessed the altercation.

"Scully strikes again," I muttered to myself. Obviously the guy was hated by one and all. I had tried requesting a different inspector in the past, but Scully was in charge of the office, so he chose which sites he wanted to inspect.

I wondered if Joan and Stan would do what Petsy had done and call the mayor to complain. I hated to wish anyone ill, but I wouldn't have been sorry to see Scully lose his job.

Once Scully had driven away, I hurried up to the porch and knocked on Joan's front door. I could hear her shouting as she walked toward the door, "If you're thinking I'll let you back in here . . . Oh. Sorry, Shannon. I thought you were someone else."

"I know," I confessed. "I saw Joe Scully drive away."

"That horrible man. I'm not a violent person, but boy, I'd like to strangle him."

Because I knew she was only half kidding, I gave a nervous chuckle. "You're not alone."

"Yeah, guess you saw Stan out here." She grinned. "My husband is a poet, not a fighter, but I would've loved to see him take a swing at that nincompoop."

She glanced around, realized we were still standing on the porch, and said, "Come on in. Do you want some lemonade?"

"No, thanks. I'm just checking on my guys."

"They're doing a great job," she said as she headed for the basement door. "No thanks to Scully. That worthless . . . Sorry. Boy, I've got to get a grip."

"That's okay. He drives us all crazy."

"Nice to know he doesn't save it all for me."

"Nope."

"You go ahead down," she said, waving at the stairs. "I'll be up here if you need me."

"Thanks, Joan." I went downstairs and saw Johnny and Colin standing by the far wall, wearing gloves, respirators, and goggles.

Two steps from the bottom, I stopped and said loudly, "How are you guys doing?"

Johnny whirled around and waved, then turned back to the other two. "Keep working, you guys. I gotta go talk to the boss." He removed his respirator as he walked across the room. "Hey, Shannon. Everything's going great, but don't go over there. It's a mess."

"I can see that. Sorry you got stuck with this gig, but it's important. And I appreciate you supervising the new guys."

"I don't mind at all. The guys are cool and they know what they're doing. Colin's got some amazing tools. He brought in a great set of hand-tooled chisels we've been using for the precision work. And Joan is a kick in the pants. Not only did she read Scully the riot act, which would make me real fond of her anyway, but she keeps offering to feed us."

It was official: no one liked Scully.

"Joan's really sweet," I said. "So, what did Scully want?"

"Oh man. Scully." Johnny whistled. "She lit into him and practically dragged him upstairs by his ear."

"Why?"

He shook his head. "So, get this. He comes down here pretending he's got to inspect everything, right?"

"Yeah, I know his routine. But we're not doing anything structural down here. Just cleaning out the dry rot, replacing some boards, and coating everything with the fungicide."

"Right. So we both know he doesn't belong here. But he gets right up next to me anyway. So, I just ignore him and keep working away, scraping off the layers of deadwood. After about a minute, he starts coughing. And it gets worse. He's hacking and choking and finally he's getting so loud with his barking and wheezing that Joan comes running downstairs. And Scully yells, 'If I get sick from breathing this wood dust, I'm going to sue you for criminal negligence.'"

"You're kidding," I whispered. "It was his own fault for being down here without wearing a respirator."

"Exactly. So, he takes off upstairs and she follows him. And I go over and listen to their conversation."

"That's my guy." I patted his shoulder. "So what did you hear?"

Johnny shifted from foot to foot a little guiltily. "Well, you know we don't snoop on clients, but this was Scully and I wanted to find out if he was going to try and pull the plug on our job."

"I would have done the same thing. So, what did he say to Joan?"

He grinned and leaned in, lowering his voice conspiratorially. "So, he's whining away and finally Joan tells him to shut up. She says he has no business down here until the work's complete anyhow."

"Not even then, really. But he can't help sticking his big nose into everybody's business."

"So, then Joan starts yelling at him to get out of their house. She says that this damage never would've happened in the first place if Scully hadn't signed off on the rehab work they did a few years ago."

My stomach lurched at the news. "Scully was the inspector in charge of their basement rehab?"

"Yeah, but here's the kicker." Johnny grinned. "Scully's son-in-law did the rehab work."

I felt my mouth fall open. "No way. He must've bought the most inferior, bug-infested wood on the market if it brought on this amount of dry rot damage in such a short period of time. No wonder Joan wants to strangle him."

"I don't blame her," Johnny muttered. "What a tool."

"You can say that again." I shook my head in disgust. There had to be a way to fire that guy once and for all. "Well, thanks for the update. I'll let you get back to it. I was just checking in."

"We're good," he said.

"Oh, and if you need more chisels, I've got a pretty good set, too. I just had them all sharpened a few weeks ago."

"We should be okay, but I'll let you know," he said, waving me off. "Thanks, boss."

That afternoon in the Jorgensens' side yard, Wade had to rearrange schedules. We sent Todd to the Spaulding house to help load the appliances into the kitchen. I stayed at the Jorgensens' house, helping Wade and Sean build the base of the orangery, mixing mortar for the bricks and attaching ties that would connect to the second round of bricks. It was the calm before the storm of drilling through brick walls that would take place later in the week.

At one point, Matthew came to the French doors to check on us.

"Are we disturbing you?" I asked.

"Not at all. It's very quiet. But even if it weren't, I enjoy the racket and clamor of a construction site. It's the sound of industry."

"We like to be industrious most of the time," I said with a smile. Sometimes he spoke like a poet. "Do you work from home?"

"I do," he said. "I paint. We tore down all the walls on the third floor to make me a studio. The light is fantastic up there."

"I had no idea you were an artist."

"It's probably not something your father would've mentioned," he said jovially, then laughed. "Although I do believe he won one of my paintings in a poker game."

"He did?" I was surprised and pleased. "I would love to see your work sometime."

"You can come upstairs anytime. I enjoy having visitors. The room is sort of a shambles, what with easels and canvases and tubes of paint and palettes lying everywhere. And, oh, you know, the odd bone and shell, and the occasional fruit basket. All those crazy things painters like to paint. But please come and visit."

"I will." It suddenly made sense that his daughter, Lindsey, owned an art gallery. I wondered if she sold his paintings.

Matthew stepped out into the center of the space surrounded by the concrete foundation. "You know, this is looking good. When Petsy first suggested we put a greenhouse—er, I mean, *orangery*—here, I thought it sounded kind of dumb." He glanced around furtively. "Don't tell her I said so."

I grinned. "Your secret's safe with us."

He gave me a wink. "But yeah, this will be nice. And it's perfect that we already have these French doors right here."

"We would've had to knock out the wall and install them if they weren't already here."

"So that was good planning." He gazed around the side yard, staring up at the trees and taking in the ambience. "I never really go out into this yard. I've always thought it was too overgrown. But it's pretty. I think I'd like to paint out here."

"All those flowering bushes along the tree line look fabulous," I said.

The older man nodded absently and stuck around for a few more minutes to watch Wade lay down a row of bricks. Finally he said, "I'll get out of your way." And we watched him walk back inside.

"He's interesting," Wade murmured. "Seems like a nice guy."

"He really is," I said.

"Not like his wife."

I shook my head reflectively. "Not at all."

*   *   *

We were just about to quit for the day when Joe Scully decided to pay a surprise visit. He came sauntering onto the site as if he were taking a stroll through the park.

"What are you doing here?" I asked, and immediately regretted it. I didn't need to provoke him any further than he already had been. He would take it out on us and we didn't need that aggravation.

"I mean, we're just about finished for the day," I amended. "What's up, Joe?"

"I'm here to inspect your foundation."

"Um, okay. Sure."

Petsy must have seen him walk up, because she suddenly whipped open the French doors. "What is this all about?"

Matthew and Lindsey rushed over and stood behind her.

"What is it, Mother?" Lindsey asked. "I heard you running."

"I'll handle this," Petsy said, and pointed at Scully. "Are you here to inspect something else?"

"He wants to check the foundation," I said before Joe could say anything.

"It looks perfectly suitable to me," Petsy said regally. "A bit messy, but that's to be expected of construction workers."

"It's fine, Petsy," Matthew murmured.

"You would think so," Scully drawled. "But you're not an expert like I am."

Expert? Ugh. Where was that barf bag when you needed it?

I exchanged a look with Wade, whose expression was thunderous.

I started to say something that would stop him from blowing up at Scully, but at that moment, Amanda appeared from the front of the house. "I'm finished for the day, Shannon. Do you guys need any help out here?"

"No, we're finished, too," I said. "We're just waiting for the inspector to do his thing."

Scully made a show of hunching down to study the pattern of the concrete. It was ridiculous. The concrete foundation was perfect.

He squinted up at me. "Are you installing a water barrier?"

"Of course we are," Wade said, and I could tell he was trying not to be snide. "We'll insert a polyethylene moisture barrier when we start laying down the interior blocks."

The only layer we'd done so far was the pretty outer ring of dark red bricks that matched the house. Inside that ring, we would lay heavy eight-by-four-by-two-inch concrete bricks that would provide extra protection from the elements, but wouldn't be seen from any angle. We would drape the moisture barrier sheets around those bricks and stretch them across the ground to seal the space.

"Really, Mr. Scully," Petsy said, "what can you possibly dispute at this point in the procedure?"

"Ma'am, I told you. I'm just here to do my job."

"I don't think you are," she said with just the right touch of peevish emotionality. "I think you're here to antagonize me. I've had a long, busy day and now I have a headache. So if you don't mind, I would like you to leave."

I watched his jaw moving as he clenched his teeth. "Sorry you're feeling bad, ma'am. I'll be going now." His gaze narrowed in on me. "But I'll be back tomorrow."

Why did that sound like a threat? What had I done to him? I couldn't recall. I decided I would call Dad when I got home. Maybe he'd had a run-in with Scully once upon a time and the man was taking it out on me.

We all watched him walk away.

"What a horrible man," Petsy murmured, then turned and disappeared into the bowels of her house.

Matthew and Lindsey looked as if they might've wanted to snicker but didn't dare.

Finally Matthew broke the silence. "Well, that's enough excitement for one day. Have a good evening, everyone." And he and his daughter walked back into the house.

The next morning, Amanda and I were able to get a lot more accomplished than usual. I couldn't say why, since the workday began so pleasantly, with Petsy glaring and giving us her usual warning to get to work and stop dillydallying so much. Then she flounced past us, announcing that she had a breakfast meeting and would be gone for several hours. Watching her go, I felt a wave of relief and I imagined Amanda felt the same way.

Just before lunch, my cell phone rang and I grabbed it from the pocket of my tool belt.

"Jane," I said, after seeing her picture on the phone screen. "Hi. What's up?"

"Shannon, some guy is here saying that he wants to

inspect my garage." She was whispering into the phone, but I could understand her—and I knew who she was talking about. Joe Scully. How dared he go behind my back and harass my friends?

"I've got guests sitting in the front parlor," she continued, "and he won't be quiet. I explained that the garage renovation won't begin for another few weeks, but he doesn't seem to care. He's incredibly rude. Can you talk to him?"

"I'll try." Not that he would listen to me. Or anyone else, for that matter, I thought, clenching my teeth.

"What's his problem?" she asked.

"His problem is, I'm going to kill him," I muttered. "I'll be right there."

I jogged up to the front door of Jane's inn and walked in. The smell of baked goods and lemon furniture wax enveloped me, and despite the imminent confrontation with Scully, I smiled as I gazed around the beautifully furnished room.

Jane was talking to a guest, and when she saw me, she walked the woman over to where I was standing. The woman had wavy dark hair worn just below her shoulders. I couldn't be certain, but I would guess that her pink, gray, and black plaid business suit was pure cashmere. She exuded charm and class.

"Shannon, I wanted to introduce you to my guest. This is Loretta Samson. Ms. Samson, this is my dear friend Shannon Hammer."

"It's nice to meet you, Shannon," she said, smiling sincerely.

"It's my pleasure," I said.

"Ms. Samson," Jane said, "if you ever need a contractor, Shannon is the best in the country."

I laughed. "I wouldn't go that far, but thank you, Jane."

Jane turned to Loretta Samson. "It's true. Shannon completely renovated this building and all of the rooms. Everything from floor to ceiling. The place was about to fall apart when she took the job."

"Oh my goodness." The woman's eyes widened. "I was just telling Jane for the umpteenth time how beautiful her inn is. And now I get to meet the person responsible for all this beauty."

"That's very sweet of you. I'm pretty proud of our work here."

"You should be. It's just wonderful." She squeezed Jane's arm lightly. "I'll let you two girls get on with your conversation. I'm going to change into something more casual and take a walk to the pier."

"It's a beautiful day for a walk," I said.

"I know. I just love it here."

"Enjoy your afternoon," I said.

She waved and walked away, her low heels echoing lightly on the richly stained hardwood floor.

I turned back to Jane. "She's so nice."

"I know," Jane said. "That's why I wanted to introduce you."

I glanced around. "So, I hate to bring up a sore subject, but where's Scully, the man who was bugging you?"

She sighed. "He just left."

"What?" That didn't make sense. "Why did he leave?" I couldn't believe it. There was nothing Scully liked better than to cause grief and then hang around to watch it play out. Why would he leave before he had the opportunity to screw with me?

"I don't know," Jane said, "but listen to this. When I told him you were on your way, he got really cocky about it." She scowled. "Like he was pleased that he was causing you trouble. What a troll."

I laughed. "That's a perfect description."

"But here's what's weird. He was strutting around, pretending to be important, and he happened to glance down the hall toward the stairs. And all of a sudden it was like he'd seen a ghost."

"What did he see?"

"He saw Loretta Samson. The woman you just met. Anyway, Scully blinked a few times, then whispered, 'Loretta?' and started walking toward her."

"What did she do?"

"She was just walking her friend, another woman, to the door. Loretta noticed him and looked puzzled at first. Then she smiled and waved. But her friend just sort of glared at him."

"Did he go and talk to them?"

"No. He stopped in his tracks, then glanced around as though he'd been caught stealing something. Then he took off running, right out the door."

"Really?" I frowned. "You're right. That's weird."

"I know." Jane nodded. "It only happened a few minutes ago. After her friend left, Loretta stopped me in the front room to talk. Otherwise, I would've called right away to tell you not to bother coming over."

I scratched my head, not knowing what to think. How did Joe Scully know Loretta Samson? And who was the woman with her? Did it even matter? "It doesn't sound like Joe was afraid to see me. Something else scared him away."

"Well, you can be very frightening," she said lightly. "But I think it was more about that other woman shooting daggers at him."

"Do you know who she is?"

"No, but I could ask Loretta. It would be nice to find out who the woman is so I can thank her for getting rid of that awful man." Jane shook her head. "I don't say this about a lot of people, Shannon, but that guy is just awful."

"I'm really sorry he showed up here. He knows you're my friend and he knows I plan to renovate your garage. Since he keeps getting kicked off the Jorgensens' property, he's finding other ways to aggravate me. I'm afraid you paid the price for his lunacy."

But now I had another worry. Since Scully had been chased away from Jane's place, how did he plan to mess with my work and my crew next time?

Jane wove her arm through mine as we walked down the hall toward the kitchen and the small, comfortable space that served as a bar and lounge. Jane nodded at the two good-looking men sitting at the bar, having a quiet drink. Once we'd passed them, she nudged me and whispered, "That guy on the left is Loretta Samson's boyfriend."

I smiled at that little bit of gossip. "Good to know."

"Oh, Shannon," Jane said, "I'm so sorry you have to deal with horrible people like Scully."

"Me, too." I smiled tightly. "He's like termites. Always destructive and almost impossible to get rid of.

Scully shows up on jobsites just to make our lives miserable." And I was certain that since he'd been chased off the Jorgensens' site by Petsy, he had deliberately shown up at Jane's to get back at me. So why wasn't he here? It didn't make sense, but this was Scully we were talking about. Nothing he did made a lot of sense to me.

"I swear, people like that . . . ," she said, squeezing my arm. "Well, you obviously know him, so I don't have to say anything else."

"No, you don't. I know exactly what he's like."

"Then that's enough about that horrible man." She came to a stop outside the kitchen door. "My chef just baked a few hundred shortbread cookies. Would you like a snack?"

I smiled. "I thought you'd never ask."

Later, as I drove back to work with a half dozen of Jane's delicate shortbread cookies in a doggie bag on the passenger seat beside me, I wondered again why Joe Scully had run off so abruptly. Had he suddenly remembered that I was on my way over to smack him until he cried for mercy? Or had it been something else? It was a strange little mystery and I wanted answers.

For perhaps the first time in my life, I actually hoped I would run into Scully in the next day or two so I could try to find out what had spooked him so badly at Jane's place.

The following morning I parked in front of the Jorgensens' house. I glanced around the neighborhood, looking for Amanda's red truck, then realized that for the first time, I had beaten her to the jobsite. She always showed up early and I appreciated that quality in a worker.

Taking advantage of whatever time I would have to wait, I took a sip of my latte, pulled my tablet out, and started going over the schedule for next week. We had less than three weeks until the tour began. The Spaulding kitchen would be finished in plenty of time, and I was also feeling pretty good about the Jorgensens' projects—despite Petsy's attitude. Actually, I supposed I had her to thank for chasing Joe Scully away. He was the one person who could hold up our work schedule if he wanted to.

In the rearview mirror I saw Amanda's truck pull up and park behind me. I closed my tablet and set my latte back in the cup holder. Climbing out of the truck, I grabbed my bag and waved at her.

Without warning, I heard an earsplitting scream.

I spun around, looking in every direction to find out where the trouble was. Suddenly Joan Derry came running down her side walkway, still screaming. "Somebody help! Help me! He's dead!"

I ran over and grabbed her. "Joan! What happened?"

"He's back there!" She pointed toward her backyard. "Oh my God. He's . . . I think he's . . ." She shivered uncontrollably and couldn't say another word.

I let her go and dashed around the side of the house, reaching the backyard in seconds. Joan's lovely antique orangery glinted in the morning sunlight. There were flowers everywhere and even the trees were blooming with fragrant blossoms. It was no wonder she'd won the grand prize last year.

The orangery door had been left open and I ventured closer—and immediately regretted it. Joe Scully was sprawled across the floor with his eyes bulging out. Blood stained the sisal carpet underneath his lifeless body. I blinked once to clear my vision so I could figure out where the blood had come from, and that's when I saw the one-quarter-inch heavy-duty high-carbon-steel-bladed wood chisel sticking out of his belly.

I jolted when Amanda touched my shoulder. "Is he . . . is he . . . ?"

"He is," I said bluntly. Joe Scully was most assuredly dead.

Chapter Four

I quickly sent Amanda off to call the police and check on Joan. Then, after making sure no one else was around, I took one careful step inside the Derrys' orangery and scanned the room. The pillows from the window bench were scattered on the floor. Had Scully bumped against the bench when he fell? Or was he sitting there when the killer attacked?

I remembered that I had taken pictures of the space when Joan showed it to me Tuesday morning, so I pulled my phone from my bag to study them. There had been a plant hanging from a hook over the window bench. Now it was on the floor, too, and dirt was spread across the thickly woven rug.

And I hadn't noticed it until now, but one of the beautiful beveled windows on the opposite side was cracked. I checked my photos again and couldn't see any cracks, so I guessed that it had probably happened from Scully bumping—or being pushed—into the wall of glass. Had there been a fight?

I moved closer to study the crack and saw a minuscule spattering of blood on the glass. I stepped away, wishing I hadn't seen that.

It took me a few seconds to screw up my courage and calm my stomach before I hunched down to get a closer look at Scully. His face didn't look particularly bruised or battered, so maybe there hadn't been a fight. Had the killer surprised him? The chisel sticking out of his stomach belied that theory since Scully would have been facing his attacker. I studied the handle, a nicely sculpted dark wood. A custom-made tool. It might have been selfish of me, but I couldn't help breathing a sigh of relief that it wasn't one of my chisels.

But now I was worried that the chisel might belong to Colin or Johnny. I didn't want my guys being accused of murder simply because they'd been working in the house and someone had stolen one of their tools.

Been there, done that, I thought. It wasn't much fun.

"Oh dear," I muttered, as I suddenly realized I was way more concerned about myself and my crew than about poor old Joe Scully. The man had been reviled in life, but that didn't mean he deserved to be sprawled out on the floor of the Derrys' orangery, dead as could be.

There was a lot of blood soaked into his shirt, and more had spread out on the floor beneath him. It had to have been a fluke that whoever attacked him had managed to strike his abdominal artery. Of course, that was only a guess on my part, but given the amount of blood that had seeped out of him, the chisel had to have hit a major artery.

It was unnerving to realize how much I knew about this death stuff.

I took one last look around and caught sight of Johnny's stainless steel tool chest tucked behind the partially opened door leading into the house from the orangery. What was it doing here? I peeked around the doorjamb and saw a second tool chest sitting next to Johnny's. Did that one belong to Colin? Had Joan offered to let the guys keep their tools here overnight? If so, that was very nice of her, but it made things a little too convenient for Scully's killer. All he had to do was grab one of their chisels—or a screwdriver, or a hammer, or any number of dangerous tools we carried around with us—and kill the building inspector.

Running that scenario through my mind, I realized that the killer had to have been lying in wait for Scully. Because I honestly couldn't see someone in the heat of a confrontation casually walk over to the French doors, discover a partially hidden tool chest sitting on the floor, open it up, and select the perfect tool to jam into Scully's stomach.

And if my theory was correct, then Scully's death was premeditated murder.

Shivers erupted on my arms and shoulders and I rubbed them briskly as I left the orangery.

Thirty minutes later, Police Chief Eric Jensen appeared from the side of the Derrys' house. He stopped and sighed when he saw me sitting on the front porch. "Shannon, what are you doing here?"

I had to admit, one of the worst parts about finding a body was having to face our local police chief. Eric was usually understanding and ever since that first time had never really suspected me of being a murderer or anything. But it was just so embarrassing to always be in this situation.

I frowned at him. "If I could be anywhere else, you know I'd be there."

"Yeah, I know. Me, too." He patted my shoulder sympathetically but continued to stand, glancing around the neighborhood and taking in the scene.

I took a sip of my latte. It had gone cold, but I still welcomed the comforting mix of caffeine and milk. "I've got some of my crew working downstairs in the basement. They've got dry rot. Not my crew. The Derrys' basement."

"I got that."

"And a few of us are working across the street at the Jorgensens' house, fixing some wainscoting and building an orangery." I pointed to the grand mansion across the way.

His eyebrows arched. "You guys are busy."

"Yeah." We really were. But now we had another murder to contend with and it was *Scully*, of all people. "We've got the Home and Garden Tour coming up in a few weeks, so everyone's in a frenzy to get work done."

He nodded and leaned his shoulder against a thick post. "Did you know Joe Scully?"

"Oh yeah." I blew out a breath. No point in lying. "I knew him."

"Sounds like you didn't care for him."

"I didn't. I don't know anyone who *did*. But I didn't murder him, either."

"What makes you think he was murdered?"

"Really, Chief?" I gave him a withering look. "This ain't my first time at the rodeo, you know."

I could see him biting back a grin. It was probably a good thing he didn't actually crack a smile, given the current circumstances. Smiling would have been highly unprofessional and Eric Jensen was always professional. He played by the rules every time.

"I saw Scully," I said, rubbing my arms to ward off the chill I still felt. "He had a chisel sticking out of his gut. It wasn't a pretty sight."

"No, it wasn't." Suddenly he reached out and helped me up from my chair, then simply folded me into a comforting hug.

I hadn't even realized how badly I needed one. So I let myself relax for a minute, taking advantage of his strong arms and sense of . . . steadiness. He hugged me tightly, running his hands up and down my back. I felt completely safe.

Eric Jensen was one of the best-looking men I'd ever seen up close. When we first met—at another murder scene—I'd mentally started calling him Thor, because the guy was one of those big, rugged Viking types. Tall, with dark blond hair worn an inch too long, gorgeous blue eyes, ripped muscles, an adorable yet elusive smile. Wow. We all know that type, right?

The two of us hadn't exactly clicked in the beginning, mainly because he had been so eager to accuse me of murder. But over the past year or so, we'd managed to become good friends. I liked him a lot, even when he was scowling at me. Which was at least half the time we saw each other.

I leaned back, finally, and frowned up at him. "Did you talk to Joan? Did she tell you how he got into her greenhouse?" *Orangery,* I corrected myself silently.

Eric took a wary step back. "Are you really asking me for details about the case?"

I gave him a slight smile. "Um, maybe?"

He just shook his head. "You don't give up."

"It's a sickness, Chief."

I returned to my wicker chair. He sat down in the chair next to mine and pulled out his notepad and pen. "When did you last see Mr. Scully?"

"Yesterday, late afternoon. He came over to the Jorgensens' yard, where we're installing the orangery."

"You said that before. What is it?"

"Orangery," I repeated. "It's a fancy French name for a greenhouse. Except it's attached to the house, so it's a little different. Some people call it a solarium or a conservatory."

"Say it again," he said, so I repeated the word.

He sounded it out. *"Oh-ron-jeh-ri."*

"Very good," I said with a smile. "Think of the word *orange* and add a French accent."

He rolled his eyes at the very thought. "I might just stick with *greenhouse.*"

"Works for me."

"So, how did the conversation go between Mr. Scully and you late yesterday afternoon?"

"Not well." I described the scene, including the dialogue among Scully; Petsy Jorgensen; her husband; their daughter, Lindsey; me and Wade; and Amanda. I also told him what I'd seen at the Derry home yesterday, when Joan and Mr. Derry put on a very public display of kicking Scully out of their house.

And then I mentioned Jane's phone call in which she told me that Scully had shown up at her inn. I added that the guy had disappeared by the time I arrived. Eric had plenty of questions about that and I told him what I knew, but also suggested that he pay Jane a visit later for more answers.

"I'll do that." After writing everything down, Eric studied the notes. "Who's Amanda?"

"I'll introduce you," I said, suddenly glad that I'd suggested to Amanda that she go get started at the Jorgensens'. I wasn't sure how she would feel about being interrogated by the police so soon after seeing a dead guy. "She just moved here recently," I added. "She's a carpenter. She's the one who's working with me on the Jorgensens' wainscoting."

"I'd like to talk to her," he said, slipping his notepad into his pocket. "Along with the rest of your crew. And the neighbors, too. Including the Jorgensens. And Jane."

"Right. Just let me know when you want to see my people."

"Will do."

And I would do my best to get to them before Eric could, if only to warn them that Scully was dead and they might need an alibi. The thought depressed me.

I took another sip of my cold latte, then said, "You should probably talk to some of the other contractors around town. Scully was a thorn in all of our sides, sometimes to the point of endangering an entire project or an important timeline. And everyone knew he could be bribed. I'm just saying, someone out there could've taken it really hard."

"But not you."

I shook my head. "Not me. He annoyed the heck out

of me and I tried really hard to get him fired a few times. But I don't generally resort to murder."

"I'm grateful for that," he said, his eyes gleaming with humor.

Something else occurred to me. "While we're on the subject of people who hated Scully: you might also want to talk to the homeowners and decorators who had to deal with him."

"That sounds like it might be half the town."

"Probably. And it gets worse every year with the Home and Garden Tour. Everyone freaks out about this time, trying to prep their homes. They do everything from painting rooms to actual home renovations, and naturally it all has to be done immediately. And through it all, we've had to deal with Scully's obnoxious attitude. Someone out there might've blown a gasket, if you know what I mean."

He scratched his head. "Guess that prize money brings out the worst in people."

"It seems to."

"Is that why you do it?"

I shrugged. "I like the competition. The money goes to the homeowner, so that's not an issue for me. I'm more excited about the magazine cover."

"That makes sense."

We sat in silence for a moment; then I asked, "Have you met Petsy Jorgensen yet?"

"No." He knew me pretty well and easily surmised that I had something to say. "Tell me about her."

I took a deep breath. "She's rude and condescending. Manipulative. Basically, she's awful. And also, she's very pretty in a cold, hard way."

"So"—he nodded sagely—"not your favorite person, I take it."

"She's mean to her own daughter, Eric. And by the way, the daughter is a real sweetheart. So that's just weird to me."

"Sounds like she didn't like Joe Scully much, either."

"As much as I don't like her, I can't really hold that against her, since nobody liked him. But Petsy Jorgensen hates anything that might get in the way of her winning the grand prize this year. And Scully was getting in the way."

"Think she hated him enough to kill him?"

I started to speak, then clamped my mouth shut. I'd been accused of murder myself more than once, so I didn't like the idea of accusing someone else. But this was Petsy we were talking about. I knew she wouldn't hesitate to throw me under the bus if the situation were reversed. "Yeah, she probably hated him that much. But I doubt she did anything about it."

"Why?"

"She's very finicky. You know the type. She wouldn't want to get her St. John suit mussed.

"Meow," I added under my breath.

He laughed. "Okay, thanks for your input."

Tommy Gallagher, assistant police chief and my old high school boyfriend—and also pretty adorable, though not quite as big and rugged as the chief—walked up the front steps. "Hi, Shannon. How's it going?"

"It's going okay, all things considered." Tommy and I were still good friends, despite the fact that he was married to my worst enemy, Whitney Reid Gallagher.

It was yet another example of love being blind. And deaf and dumb in this case.

"Hey, Chief," Tommy said. "Leo's here."

Our town wasn't that big, but we had recently acquired our very own CSI unit. It consisted of only one guy, Leo Stringer, but you had to start somewhere. I supposed it wasn't exactly a happy sign when a town the size of ours needed a permanent crime-scene investigator, but we'd have to take our progress wherever we could get it.

"Thanks, Tommy," Eric said. "I'll join him around back in just a minute."

"I'll tell him." He winked at me, then jogged down the stairs and up the sidewalk.

"I'd better get back there," Eric said, standing. "Do me a favor and keep our conversation to yourself."

"Of course," I said. Did he think I would confide in Petsy? I would never do that. On the other hand, I might've said something to Wade, so maybe the request was a good thing.

Before I left the porch, I checked my phone for messages and found a text from Wade.

Hey, saw you talking to Eric. Heard about Scully. Unreal.

I texted back, **Yeah. Tell the guys Eric wants to talk to all of you.**

Wade replied, **How'd he die?**

I stared at my phone. There was no way I could tell him in a text. Instead, I typed, **We'll talk later.**

Got it, he replied. And I knew he understood.

As I crossed the street to join Amanda, I thought about the ramifications of Scully's death. It meant that we would have to be assigned another building inspector. Because as much as they were a pain in our collective butt, we still had to get our work inspected and have an official sign-off after certain jobs. But at least the next guy wouldn't be so hard-pressed to get in our faces and slow us down. I hoped.

I felt a moment of remorse for being so honest about my feelings about Joe Scully. And for thinking about my own issues with our work getting approved on time, rather than thinking of Scully's family and the grief they must be feeling right now. But in all fairness, Joe hadn't exactly gone out of his way to endear himself to anyone, let alone me.

I sighed, and as I opened the Jorgensens' front door, I made a vow right then and there to do something to help Scully's family. But that would have to wait for another day.

After walking into the foyer, I stopped in my tracks. Petsy, Matthew, and Lindsey Jorgensen were all gathered under the archway leading to the dining room, talking to Amanda. My footsteps on the marble floor caused them all to turn around.

"Hello," I said, a little suspicious of them standing there, observing my carpenter at work. Were they confronting her? What was going on here?

"You were over there talking to the police," Petsy said. It sounded more like an accusation than a statement of fact, but I figured that was just her way of making conversation.

"Yes. I asked Amanda to call them when I found Joe Scully's body."

"His . . . body?" Lindsey's face turned pale and I thought she might faint. "But . . . You mean that man who was here yesterday? He's dead?"

"Yes, Lindsey," her mother said impatiently. "That's what she's saying. The man is dead. Maybe if you didn't sleep in so late, you'd know what was going on around the neighborhood."

Lindsey took several deep breaths, clearly upset.

"Are you all right?" I asked, taking a step toward her.

"I'll be fine," she said, waving me off. "It's just such a shock. I didn't realize . . . I mean, I just came downstairs a few minutes ago, so I guess I missed the initial uproar."

"It's still going on," I said, shooting a quick glance back at the front door, knowing Eric Jensen could show up at any moment.

"It's a sad day for Cranberry Circle," Matthew murmured.

"Yes, it is," I said. "Anyway, after talking to the police chief, I thought I'd better get to work." I gave them all a small smile and started to enter the dining room.

"Wait, Shannon," Lindsey said. "You said you found the body. That must've been a terrible shock for you."

"Actually Joan Derry found the body, but I was right there after her. And yes, it was a shock." It was something I would never get used to.

"Do you mind if I ask where you found him?"

I was about to spill what I knew when I remembered Chief Jensen's warning. How much was it safe to tell them? But since Joan had seen Joe Scully's body, too, chances were good that the whole neighborhood would find out soon enough.

"He died in the Derrys' orangery," I said bluntly. "I have no idea how it happened. But naturally Joan's very upset."

"Naturally," Petsy muttered, staring up at the ceiling.

I studied her for a moment. What did she mean by that comment? I wondered. Did she think I was lying? Or did she not think Joan had a right to be upset? Did she not trust her neighbor? Maybe she thought Joan had had something to do with Scully's death. Or maybe she was just being her usual caustic self.

"But that's terrible," Lindsey said, pressing her hands to her cheeks. "Poor Joan. I'll go over there later and bring her some cookies and a bottle of wine."

"That's very thoughtful, honey," Matthew said. Slinging one arm around Lindsey's shoulders, he gave her an affectionate squeeze.

Because of the somber circumstances, I was trying not to grin. But seriously? Cookies and wine sounded like an outstanding combination that would really cheer me up if I was feeling down. Although maybe not this early in the morning.

"Shannon," Lindsey said, "can you tell us how he died? Was it a heart attack?"

"The police chief asked me not to talk about it, but since the news will be all over town within the hour, I suppose it wouldn't hurt to mention that he was most probably murdered."

"Oh my God!" she cried. "There's a murderer on the loose?"

"That settles it," Matthew said. "I don't want either of you walking around by yourselves until this crime is solved."

Petsy huffed. "I'm always watchful wherever I go, so I'll be perfectly safe. But this is outrageous. How dare anyone murder someone on Cranberry Circle?"

I glanced inside the dining room and caught Amanda's bemused yet strangely buoyant expression. Was it because she'd had the attention of the whole family for a few minutes? Had they been having a pleasant conversation or were they questioning her progress? Judging by her smile, it must've been pleasant. I would have to remember to ask Amanda what they'd been chatting about before I interrupted the conversation with my talk of murder.

"Well, we'd better let you get to work," Matthew said.

"Yes, by all means," Petsy said forcefully, then added under her breath, "Their progress is slow enough without us adding to the problem."

I squeezed my eyes shut to keep them from rolling to the back of my brain. A moment later, I opened them to see that the Jorgensens had already dispersed to other parts of the house, so I walked into the dining room. "You doing okay?"

"I guess so," Amanda said. "I've never seen a murder victim before."

"It's not something you get used to."

"No, I wouldn't think so," she murmured.

I glanced toward the archway to make sure the Jorgensens weren't nearby. "Were they bothering you?"

"Oh no, they were just asking questions, trying to get

an idea of what I'm doing." She grinned. "I explained it but I'm not sure they really wanted that much detail."

I chuckled. "Sometimes going heavily into the technical aspects is the best way to keep people from asking more questions."

"Definitely. Anyway, Matthew and Lindsey are really nice. But then Petsy joined them and, well, I'm glad you came along when you did."

I sighed and whispered, "She's just a miserable human being."

It was Amanda's turn to check the doorway; then she leaned closer. "She told Lindsey to go brush her teeth and comb her hair. I think she just says stuff like that to goad people, because Lindsey looked impeccable."

I agreed. "She looked like she was dressed for a society luncheon."

Amanda shook her head in disgust. "That woman."

"So, did they ask you anything about Scully's death?" I asked.

"Not really. Petsy said she saw you talking to the police chief, so she knew something was going on. It was hard to keep my mouth shut, but I didn't want to say anything."

"Probably a good idea," I said.

She sighed. "Oh well, I'd better get to work or I'll never finish this project."

"Amanda? Shannon?"

We both turned to see Matthew standing at the doorway. Had he heard us talking about his wife? I wondered. We'd been whispering, so I didn't think so.

"Yes?" Amanda said.

"I was hoping you'd take a minute to look at the paneling on the wall of the staircase. It's not as bad as some of the panels in here, but the color seems to be fading. Is that unusual?"

"Let's see," I said.

We followed him out to the foyer and walked halfway up the stairs. He stopped and pointed to one piece of the richly stained mahogany, and sure enough, it was lighter than the others. Amanda and I walked up several more steps to get a closer look. He took a few steps down to get out of our way.

"It's probably being bleached by the sun, which pours in every day," I suggested, pointing to the plate glass window near the threshold.

"It's not too badly damaged yet," Amanda added. "But to be safe, you might want to put a shade on the window."

"Or maybe a nice awning on the outside," I suggested. "And in the meantime, we can stain this piece."

"I would appreciate that," he said, gazing up at us. "Do you think you can match it?"

Amanda smiled. "I'm pretty good at matching wood tones."

"I thought I might be good at it, too, since I work with paints," Matthew said. "But I'd rather turn the woodworking jobs over to you."

I looked at Amanda. "Why don't you take a picture and try to match it to a few of the stains at the hardware store?"

"I will. I'll take care of it this afternoon." She started to walk down the stairs.

"Amanda, stop right there," Matthew ordered, pointing up at her.

She froze on the spot and I would've done the same. It was a shock to hear him sound so forceful.

"What's wrong?" I asked. Was he about to accuse her of something? What was going on?

He stared at her, mesmerized. Finally he shook his head as though he were trying to break some spell he was under.

"Matthew?" I said. "Are you all right?"

"Wow." With a wobbly sigh, he said, "Sorry. I was just so . . . I don't know what to say. But I want to show you both something. Please. Come with me."

He walked past us and continued up the stairs to the second floor, where he stepped into a long, wide gallery hall. I knew the house was big, but this hallway was like something out of an English Regency scene. Both sides were lined with large, fancy gold-framed paintings, mostly portraits, but also a few hunting scenes and pastorals. He led us past at least six paintings and then stopped.

"Look at this, please," he said, and gestured toward a full-length painting of a woman seated in an elegantly gilded chair, a small, fluffy dog at her feet. The woman was dressed formally, as though she were about to go off to a fancy ball, and held a yellow rose that stood out against the black lace bodice of her dress. Rather than gazing into space, she stared somberly at the observer. Despite the regal hairstyle and sophisticated dress, the lady in the painting looked so much like Amanda Walsh that I had to take a few deep breaths to maintain my balance.

Next to me, Amanda gasped.

I couldn't blame her. Facing her, I said, "Wow, that's

amazing, isn't it?" I was trying to keep it light, but Matthew wasn't helping. He stared at Amanda as though she were some alien goddess.

I tried again. "Is it just me, or do you look a lot like this lady? Except for the baseball cap," I added, smiling. Turning to Matthew, I said, "All of these paintings are remarkable. Are they all your ancestors? It must be amazing to be able to trace your family back to the Regency era."

"Uh, yes," he murmured. "But actually, we go back to the time of King Henry the Eighth."

Amanda ignored us both and simply stared at the painting. She wore a look of fear, as if the black-lace-clad woman might jump out of the canvas and take a bite out of her. I could see her shaking now. Worried for her, I moved closer and looped my arm through hers. "Are you okay, Amanda? I mean, it's weird, but—"

"It was the baseball cap that threw me," Matthew said slowly. "I fancy myself a pretty good observer of people, but I'd never really seen your full face before. You were always in shadow. But when I was standing on the lower stairs looking up at you, I could see you clearly."

Amanda seemed to realize he was talking and I could feel her tension. She coughed to clear her throat. "It—it's a fascinating coincidence, isn't it?" she said. But her words sounded so weak. Not like her at all. Or at least not as if she really believed what she was saying.

I turned to Matthew. "Do you think the two of you are related in some way?"

"I don't see how it's possible." He was still staring at Amanda and I could sense that she wasn't comfortable.

But she also didn't seem inclined to scream and race out of here and forget that she'd ever seen the painting before.

"Amanda was raised in Baltimore," I said to Matthew, still trying to keep things on an even keel, although they both looked shell-shocked. "Do you have any family there?"

"Not that I know of."

Matthew and Amanda both looked as if they'd rather be anywhere else. Neither of them was at ease, but my sympathies were more for Amanda in this. She'd been caught off guard completely and now Matthew was staring at her as if she were a ghost.

"Well," I said, feeling like a third wheel in this little drama, "we should get back to work. Are you ready?"

Amanda's shoulders jerked as if she'd just been awakened. "Uh, yes. We'd better. Thank you for showing us the painting, Matthew. It's very, um, pretty."

"You're welcome," he murmured. "I have work to do as well." He walked away first, heading to the staircase, where he jogged up to the third floor and disappeared.

Amanda and I followed him as far as the stairs and went down instead. She continued to clutch my arm for dear life and I seriously wondered what was going on in her head. Had the painting completely freaked her out? Would she be too anxious to continue with the Jorgensen job? Would she want to avoid the house and the family? I didn't know what to think, but I was going to make every effort to get her to talk to me.

As we reached the landing, I heard the floor creak

above us. Gazing up, I watched Petsy Jorgensen stride purposefully down the hall of the gallery and stop in front of the very same painting we'd just seen, of the Regency-era woman who could've been Amanda Walsh's twin sister.

Chapter Five

Once back in the dining room, I told Amanda that I thought we should go right back to work so she wouldn't have time to sit around and dwell on the fact that she'd just seen a picture of her nineteenth-century doppelgänger. Because really, that sort of thing could slow down your whole day. Work was always the best medicine as far as I was concerned, and Amanda agreed.

But before we could get started, the front doorbell rang. Lindsey ran to answer the door and I heard her murmur a few words to whoever was there. A moment later, she ushered Eric Jensen into the dining room.

"Thank you, Ms. Jorgensen," he said. "I'd like to speak with you in a few minutes, right after I've talked to Ms. Walsh."

She looked a little rattled by the statement coming from the police chief. "Yes, of course. I'll be in the kitchen. It's the door at the far end of the foyer."

"Thank you."

Lindsey nodded and walked away, and Eric glanced at me.

"Let me introduce you to Amanda," I said.

They shook hands and Eric said, "I'd like to talk to you if you have a few minutes. Shannon mentioned that you were around at the time she found Mr. Scully's body."

"I was, but just for a few seconds."

"Can we talk in here?" he asked, glancing around the dining room. He didn't wait for an answer, but pulled out a chair and indicated that Amanda should sit. She did, and he sat in the chair across from her.

I had no intention of leaving, and I started to work with one of the panels on the plywood. I heard Eric cough; then he said, "Shannon."

I looked up and saw him give me a sharp glance. I took the hint.

"I was just leaving," I lied. "I'll be on the side of the house if anybody needs me."

I hated to go, but I didn't have much choice. I just hoped he wouldn't be too tough on her. She'd been an accidental witness, after all.

Forty minutes later, Amanda walked out to the side yard, where the guys and I were laying down the inner section of heavy brick.

"Are you all right?" I asked.

"Oh, sure. It was no problem. He's in there interviewing the Jorgensens now."

I took a longer look at her. She looked pale, and her usual resilient attitude seemed to have deflated. Hard to blame her. Most people didn't show up for work, find a body, and then get interviewed by a police chief, all before lunch. Speaking of that . . .

I glanced at Wade. "Amanda and I are going to take a lunch break."

"Go for it," he said, clearly having noticed the change in Amanda. "See you when we see you."

"Let's go to lunch," I said to Amanda.

She hesitated. "I don't want to be any trouble."

"Fine. Then come with me and don't make trouble."

She smiled at that. "You're the boss."

I drove us to my house a half mile away, thinking all the while about that crazy old painting of Amanda's nineteenth-century twin. Maybe I should've been more worried about finding Scully dead a few hours earlier, but Amanda's stunned reaction to the painting had almost broken my heart. And I wasn't even sure why.

When we walked into the house, Robbie came scampering and practically slid across the kitchen floor, he was so beside himself with excitement that I was home in the middle of the day. And I'd brought a new friend with me. What joy!

Amanda knelt down on the floor. "Oh, what a precious little thing." Robbie took immediate advantage of the new girl and rolled over to get his belly rubbed.

"This is Robbie. Isn't he the cutest?" I leaned over and patted his tummy. "Yes, you are."

I stood up. "It's a little too early for wine, so I thought I would make some tea. Unless you want something cold."

She chuckled. "Since it's not even noon yet, tea sounds perfect. It's been a weird day."

"To put it mildly. And I've got tuna if you want a sandwich."

"Maybe in a while."

I started the teakettle and found some shortbread cookies. "Let's sit in the living room until the water's ready."

We walked into the living room, where Amanda sat on the couch and I chose the big chair nearby. Robbie hopped onto the couch and plopped himself in Amanda's lap. That was enough to bring Tiger out of hiding and she moved in to sniff delicately at Amanda's boots.

"You have a cat, too. She's so beautiful."

"She's a sweetie. Her name is Tiger."

"You're so lucky."

"I think so." The kettle began to scream and I jumped up to pour the water. Minutes later, I set a cup of hot tea down on the end table nearest her. The plate of cookies went on the coffee table, where we could share them.

"So," I said, sitting back down in the chair, "how are you holding up?"

"I'm fine, really," Amanda said. "He's nice. Chief Jensen, I mean. He knows I had nothing to do with Mr. Scully's murder, so it's not like I was afraid of being arrested or something."

"Of course not."

She frowned. "I couldn't really tell him much except for what I saw when I was standing right behind you. Basically, a dead man." She rubbed her arms, adding, "I won't forget that sight for a long time."

"No. Trust me, you won't."

We talked for a few more minutes about Joe Scully's murder and what it might mean to the contractors around town. Sad to say, but with Scully gone, work was going to go much more smoothly for everyone.

But this was all small talk. Before, when I'd asked her how she was holding up, I hadn't been referring to her interview with Chief Jensen or the murder. I was talking about the painting hanging in the Jorgensens' house, of the woman who looked so startlingly similar to Amanda. They could've been twin sisters. So when the conversation about murder faded, I broached the other subject.

"So, what did you think of that painting?"

She sighed heavily. "I suppose I should talk about it."

"Only if you want to." Although I really wanted her to. "It might help you sort out your feelings. I mean, it's weird, right?"

"Totally." She ran her hands through her hair and flopped back on the couch. "Believe me, I would love to sort out my feelings, but I doubt that'll happen." She sipped her tea pensively and finally looked right at me. "To be honest with you, there's something else going on. I'm not sure how to say it."

She looked a little hesitant and weary. "Something else you told Chief Jensen?"

"No, no. It has to do with why I moved here."

"I thought you moved here to work on Victorian houses."

She pressed her lips together, apparently trying to figure out how to say whatever it was she wanted to tell me. "That's only partly true."

"What do you mean?"

She winced a little. "It's a long story, and I don't want you to be mad at me."

"I love long stories, so don't worry. I won't—"

The doorbell rang just then and I wanted to scream. Jumping up, I said, "This will only take a second. I'm going to shoo them away."

"You don't have to," she said lamely.

"Yes, I do." But when I opened the front door, Mac was standing there, looking as appealing as ever. His hair was still wet from the shower and he beamed when he saw me. So no, I wasn't about to shoo him away, despite my best intentions.

"Hi," he said. "I didn't think you'd be home. I finished my book, so I cleaned up and was out driving around. And then I saw your truck. Everything okay?"

"Everything's fine," I said. "Wait. You finished your book? That's wonderful!"

"Yeah, I was hoping we could celebrate." And without warning, he picked me up and whirled me around and kissed me soundly on the lips. Nothing like a good celebration.

"Congratulations," I said, holding him close.

"Thanks." After a few seconds, he must have noticed we weren't alone. "Hey, hi."

I stepped back. "You remember Amanda?"

He chuckled. "Sure, I do. How're you doing, Amanda?"

"Oh, not too great," she said.

"We've had a bit of a shock," I said.

"Oh yeah. I made a quick stop at the drugstore and heard that somebody found a dead body. Gotta love a small town." His eyes widened. "Wait. You're the one who found him? Holy moly, girl. You're batting a thousand. Are you okay?" He pulled me into his arms again and held on. I felt warm and cozy and cherished. It was a good feeling. He gazed at me and touched my cheek. "Irish," he murmured.

I smiled. He'd started calling me that soon after we'd met, mainly because of my tangled mop of red hair.

"So, I guess we have a mystery to solve," he said.

"More than one," I said. I glanced over my shoulder at Amanda.

He got the message. "I can come back later if you're . . ."

"No," Amanda said. "It's all right. Please don't shoo him away."

Mac grinned. "I don't shoo easily."

"I know." I smiled. "Come on in and have a seat. Do you want some tea?"

"Maybe just a glass of water," he said. "You sit down. I'll get it."

"Okay."

He walked into the kitchen and I turned to Amanda. "We don't have to talk while he's here."

"No, it's past time I told you about me." She shrugged and gave me a small smile. "And I think I can trust you both."

"I promise you can."

Mac walked back in and sat in the other chair facing the couch. "So, what's going on?"

Amanda spoke up. "I was about to tell Shannon why I really moved to town."

He cocked his head in puzzlement. "I thought you wanted to live in a small town and work on Victorian houses."

"Yes, that much is true, in sort of a roundabout way," she said. "But I was actually looking for one particular house to work on. And I finally found it here."

Mac glanced briefly at me before asking, "Which house is that?"

She gave me an imploring look. "Please don't fire me when I tell you."

"Why would I fire you? You're saving my life here. I have time to do other things now that you're working for me."

"I know, but I'm still concerned."

Okay, we hadn't even gotten to the long story yet and I was wildly intrigued. Why would she be so worried I would fire her? She was terrific at her job and I really needed the help.

"Don't get freaked out," I said. "The only reason I might be mad at you is if you lied to me."

"Well, that boat has sailed," she muttered, looking so distraught that I almost laughed.

The woman really was nervous about telling me something. But now I was so curious, I couldn't wait another minute. "So you lied to me about something. It couldn't be about your experience as a carpenter, because I can see for myself that you're as great at woodworking as everyone said you were. So what is it? Did you rob a bank?"

She smiled with reluctance. "No, of course not."

"Well, then." I sat forward, impatient to hear the truth. "Come on, Amanda. I like you. What could you possibly tell me that could be so bad?"

Mac gave me a look that made me think I should be prepared for the worst.

Amanda twisted her lips nervously, then let out a breath. "Maybe it would be better if I *showed* you instead."

"Okay."

Pulling out her cell phone, she pressed a button and swiped at the screen a few times. Then she passed the phone to me. "Here. I took this photo of an old picture that my father gave me. I didn't want to lose the original somewhere while I was traveling."

I stared at the picture, then moved my fingers across the screen to zoom in. The photograph was in color, but it must have been twenty or thirty years old, because it was slightly blurred and the colors were faded.

It was a picture of an infant in an old-fashioned baby carriage, parked on a sidewalk in front of a grand old Victorian home. The baby was tiny, probably no more than a month old.

I passed the phone to Mac, who squinted a few times, trying to focus on the image. He handed it back to me without making a comment.

Again I zoomed in and out of the shot a few times, trying to study the slightly fuzzy house in the background— and finally recognized the fretwork on the brackets atop the veranda posts.

"It looks a lot like the Jorgensens' house," I said, glancing up at Amanda. "But then, a lot of the old houses look alike. Do you know whose house it is?"

She nodded. "It's the Jorgensen house."

"Interesting." I passed the phone back to her. "And your father gave you this picture. Okay. But whose baby is that?"

She hesitated. "I'm not sure who the parents are."

Mac leaned forward and spoke in a quiet voice, as if he didn't want to spook her. "Do you know who the baby is, Amanda?"

I swallowed, oddly nervous as I watched Amanda. So far she hadn't told us much, but my gut instinct told me to believe whatever she was about to say.

Her smile was tinged with sadness as she nodded again. "The baby is me."

Maybe it wasn't too early for wine after all.

My head was spinning. I went to the kitchen to make tuna sandwiches for everyone, and it gave me a few minutes to think.

How could someone whose earliest memories centered around being raised in a loving home in Baltimore have been photographed as an infant in a carriage outside a house three thousand miles away in Lighthouse Cove? There were at least two possible scenarios. Either her parents had taken a trip to the West Coast, or she had been adopted. Or maybe there was some other explanation. My mind was a jumble of odd thoughts.

I carried a tray into the living room and handed out the sandwiches along with some potato chips and more shortbread cookies. I glanced at Mac, who looked as gobsmacked by Amanda's news as I felt.

He recovered quickly and took a bite of his sandwich. "I think we're still missing some parts of the story."

"Oh, definitely," I said, turning to Amanda. "Do you mind filling in the blanks for us?"

"Are you sure you're not going to fire me?"

"Enough of that talk," I said with an edgy laugh. "I'm not firing you. You do great work and I already feel like we're friends." I waved my hands around for emphasis. "Well, except for the part where I don't know who in the world you are."

For the first time in a while she flashed a real smile.

"I'm not sure who I am, either. That's what I'm here to find out."

"Were you adopted?" Mac asked.

"Yes, although I didn't know it for many years."

"How did you find the house in the picture?" I wondered.

"It took me almost three years. I did a lot of research on Victorian mansions, getting lots of close-up photos of styles and details. During that time, I sold the family home in Baltimore and worked out my finances. Then I made a map of all the places that looked most like the house in the picture and started driving across the country. I must have made at least a hundred stops before I got to San Francisco. I spent almost a month there, driving around for hours a day, but I didn't find the house, so I drove up here. And even though Lighthouse Cove is a small town, it took me almost a week of driving around before I found the Jorgensen house."

"So obviously that's why you took this job with my crew, but how did you even find out we were working on it?"

She had the good grace to appear embarrassed. "This is where you might regret saying you won't fire me."

"Just tell me the truth," I said softly.

"I will," she said. "I promise. No more lies. But still, it's not pretty." She took a deep breath, then plunged ahead. "I staked out the house for a few days, thinking I might be able to meet one of the family members. But then last week, I saw you and Wade walk inside the house. I saw your truck with the Hammer Construction logo on the side. Just to be sure, I peeked in the truck bed and saw your tool chest and your ladder. So I realized that the Jorgensens must have been hiring a contractor to do some work."

Mac shook his head in amazement. "I've got to hand it to you. You did your homework."

"I was pretty determined," she admitted. "Anyway, I followed you around town that day, and when you went to the pub to meet your crew guys, I sat at the bar and watched all of you."

"Wow, I had a stalker," I said, only half kidding.

"It felt really weird on my end, but like I said, I was single-minded in my determination to get inside that house."

I was beginning to put the pieces of the puzzle together. "So after I left the pub, you joined Sean at the bar."

"Yes. I struck up a conversation with him and we talked about construction. I had no idea what it would take, but according to him, you were looking for someone who specialized in woodwork."

"Sean is a pretty easygoing guy."

"And I took complete advantage of him," she said, her tone remorseful. "I admit it."

"Well, I asked for the truth."

"The thing is, I never heard from him again. After a few days I was starting to panic. I followed you again and saw you working at another house on the other side of town."

"The Spauldings' house."

"Yes. I didn't know if you'd gotten the Jorgensen job or not, but then I saw you pulling permits over at City Hall. As soon as you left, I went into the office and asked the building inspector about you."

"Whoa," Mac said. "You talked to Joe Scully about the permits Shannon pulled?"

"Yes."

"Did you mention this to Chief Jensen?" I asked.

Her eyes widened. "Oh my God. Do you think that makes me look guilty of murder?"

"Maybe," Mac said. "You could've wanted to shut him up. Or maybe he tried to blackmail you."

She looked completely baffled. "But why?"

Mac shrugged. "I know it's weak, but what the heck? Motives come in all shapes and sizes."

"You're scaring her, Mac," I murmured. "Don't tease."

Mac grinned. "Sorry. Go ahead with your story, Amanda."

"You are kind of freaking me out."

"It's a gift," he said lightly.

"Don't mind him, Amanda," I said, smacking Mac's knee. "Go ahead."

She blew out a breath. "Okay, so, meanwhile, I realized I needed a job, so I took on some freelance construction work. And somehow, you happened to hear about my work from one of the guys on the site."

"Bob the brick guy."

"Yeah. So in the end, I got exactly what I wanted. I think."

"Yeah, I guess you did, and I'm glad." I paused, then added, "I'm not so glad that I got played."

"I know you're angry."

"Angry?" I thought about it. "Not really. I'm mainly just wondering why you thought you had to lie to me."

She grabbed a potato chip, but then just stared at it instead of eating it. Finally she gazed at me and Mac.

"I've been alone and desperate for almost three years, ever since my father died. When I finally found the Jorgensen house, I didn't know which approach to take. I thought about going right up and knocking on their front door and asking them, point-blank. But I couldn't. How do you ask someone if they're your real mom or dad? How do you ask them why they gave you up? I had actual stomach pains just thinking about it. So when I saw you show up with Wade that first day, the pain went away and everything came into focus. I had a way to get in there that I hadn't counted on."

"Do you think the Jorgensens are your parents?"

It was her turn to pause. "To be honest, I didn't think so until Matthew showed us a portrait of one of his relatives from a few hundred years ago. She looked just like me, so that's when I started to believe it might be true. Except . . ."

"Except it would mean that Petsy is your mother," I muttered. "God help you."

I realized what I'd said and covered my mouth in horror. "I'm so sorry. I mean, if she's your mother, I'm sure you can learn to love her. I'm not sure how, but she might grow on you and . . . I mean . . . Oh God. Never mind. I'm not thinking."

"Don't be sorry, Shannon," she said quickly. "You're right. It would be terrifying to have her as a mother. Look at Lindsey. She's practically downtrodden when Petsy's around, but otherwise she's pretty and smart and successful."

"This woman doesn't sound like much of a mother figure," Mac said.

"She's not." Amanda shook her head vigorously. "Not

at all. And besides, I already have a mother. Even though she's gone now, my mom was amazing, like some kind of dream mother. She loved working at home and taking care of the house and my dad and me. She insisted on making a big breakfast every morning and she always had dinner on the table when we would get home from work or school. She was the most thoughtful person and so smart. Nobody will ever take her place in my heart."

Mac nodded. "Of course not."

She gave me an imploring look. "I need you to tell me the truth, Shannon. Do you see the slightest resemblance between us?"

"Between who? Oh. You and Petsy?" I took my time and studied her face, then had to blink and look away.

"Oh my God." Amanda's eyes widened. "I can tell by your reaction that you do."

"Wait," I said hurriedly. "No. Okay, yes. I guess there are some superficial similarities. You both have dark hair and a similar facial shape. But other than that, it's hard to say, because I know you're nothing like Petsy. You're nice and funny and smart. And Petsy is just evil. I mean, talk about the mother from hell. So no, I don't see much of *her* in you, if that makes sense."

Her shoulders relaxed slightly. "It does. And thank you. Seriously."

"Do you feel anything when you're around her?" Mac asked.

"You mean, like some kind of mother-daughter connection?"

"Yeah." He winced a little. "It sounds clichéd, but those things have been known to happen."

"I'm sure they have," Amanda said, "but in my case

it's a big *no*. The only thing I felt in that house was sorry for Lindsey and Matthew for having to live with that woman."

"Me, too." I took a bite of sandwich and munched for a moment while staring at Mac. "I wish there was a way for you to meet Petsy. I'd love to hear your opinion of her."

"That's easy," he said, with a rascally grin. "I'll just follow her."

"She wouldn't like that," Amanda said.

He grinned. "She wouldn't know."

I smiled. Mac had been a Navy SEAL for years before turning to writing thrillers. His protagonist, Jake Slater, was a SEAL, too, so Mac's mind was always focused on stuff like this.

"If nothing else, she's quite a character," I said. "You could make her a bad guy in one of your books."

"I've got to meet this woman." Mac reached for a cookie, then turned to Amanda. "So, let me ask you this. What did you hope to learn by going to work in their house? Were you planning to search for some documentation or something?"

She made a face. "You'll think I'm crazy, but I was hoping I could find some of their hair in a hairbrush and have a DNA lab run it against my own."

"Not a bad idea," Mac mused.

With a firm shake of her head, she said, "No, it's ridiculous. Who would I give it to? The police? I don't know any private crime-scene investigators. And even if I did, don't those tests take forever?"

"You don't need an investigator," I said. "Just a good lab."

Mac spoke up then. "I have a friend at a forensics lab in San Francisco. It usually takes about four weeks."

I leaned forward and rested my elbows on my knees. "Why don't we just go the direct route and ask Matthew if he and Petsy had a child that was given up for adoption? He showed us the painting, so he must be curious about you."

"I wasn't prepared to take the direct route," she admitted. "But maybe if I'm working there for another few weeks, we might develop a rapport."

"He likes you," I reminded her. "Or he wouldn't have shown you that painting." But then I frowned. "Oh."

"Oh?" Mac repeated. "That doesn't sound good."

I glanced at Amanda. "I was so distracted earlier that I forgot to tell you something."

"Oh no." Amanda said. "You're scaring me."

"It's nothing," I insisted. "It's just that after you and Matthew and I walked away from the painting, I looked up and saw Petsy march over and stare at it."

"You think she overheard the conversation?" Mac asked.

"It's entirely possible," I said. "Those old hallways with their arched ceilings can sometimes create an echo chamber."

"Oh great." Amanda sighed. "What if she thinks I'm Matthew's love child or something?" She buried her head in her hands.

Mac leaned forward. "But what if you *are* his love child?"

She raised her head and moaned, "Oh God. My life is suddenly a soap opera."

"Look on the bright side," he said cheerfully.

"There's a bright side?"

"Sure. If it's true, it means that Petsy isn't your mother."

It was just the right tack to take. A short, sharp laugh shot from Amanda's throat before she slapped one hand across her mouth as if to hold back budding hysteria. Her shoulders began to shake and I could imagine that she was close to reaching her breaking point. Oh boy.

I jumped up and rubbed her shoulder in sympathy. "It'll be okay. Please don't cry."

"Oh, Shannon. You're so sweet." She glanced up at me and that's when I saw that there were no tears in her eyes, except maybe a few tears of laughter.

"Ah, you were laughing. Okay, then. Good." I sat down, feeling a little silly. On the other hand, I was pleased to know she wasn't the type to burst into tears, even when she had every reason to do so. "Glad you're taking this well."

She laughed again. "Honestly, I'm not. But you guys are so great to humor me and show me the upside of this situation. I'm not sure how I'll ever thank you, but I really appreciate it."

"Always here to help," Mac said with a wry smile.

She turned to me. "I feel so lucky I met you. I don't know what I would do without you."

"Well, you won't have to find out," I said staunchly.

Mac sat back in the big chair. "So, what do you know about your adoption?"

"Not much, to tell the truth," she said. "I was raised by a wonderful mom and dad who never told me I was adopted. My mother died when I was nineteen and I stayed home to keep my father company. I guess I could've moved out, but I never felt like I wanted to. My dad and I always had fun. He was smart and talented and was always trying to make me laugh. And we worked together. He taught me everything I know about carpentry and construction."

"He sounds like a good guy," Mac said.

"The best. But about four years ago, he got sick. I thought he would recover, but he never quite did, even though he was in remission. Then he relapsed and had to stop working altogether. When he realized he was close to dying, he called me to his bedside and gave me that photograph."

"Did he tell you anything specific about it?" I asked.

"He said that the lawyer who handled the adoption gave it to him and my mom. Other than that, I don't have any details. Mom never wanted me to know I was adopted. She was afraid she would lose me, but she wouldn't have."

"Of course not," I murmured.

"I understood her feelings, though," Amanda said. "They were a little older and had never had any luck having children of their own, so when I came along, they were ultracareful about everything. But not in a stifling way. They loved me so much. We laughed a lot. Oh dear."

And that's when she burst into tears for real. I jumped up to grab a box of tissues and put them next to her on the couch.

"I loved them," she said, sniffling. "They were good people, you know?"

"I do. Mine were the same. I still have that same sort

of relationship with my dad that you described having with yours, so I can relate to your feelings."

"Mom was also afraid that I'd worry that I hadn't been loved enough by my birth parents. She thought I would get a complex or something." Amanda balled up a tissue in one hand and shook her head. "They loved me enough to prevent any kind of complex, for heaven's sake. Dad said it couldn't be true that I hadn't been loved, but I have trouble believing that. I mean, why else would someone give up their child?"

"There are plenty of reasons," Mac said. "It might not have had anything to do with loving you. They might've been too young, with no money. Maybe their parents forced them to give up their child. You'd have to have some sympathy for them if that was the case. Then again, maybe they were just horrible people and didn't want you. Who knows? But look, whatever the reason, by giving you up, they made it possible for you to have the life you've had."

She thought about his words for a moment, then nodded. "That's true enough, I guess."

"Look," he continued, "I've got a million platitudes I could spout, but the bottom line is that you got lucky with the people who adopted you. Not everyone is that lucky."

"That's for sure."

Mac leaned forward. "We touched on it before, but seriously, why don't you just ask the Jorgensens if they gave up a baby for adoption? That way, you get your answer without having to go through all that DNA rigmarole, and then the ball is in your court. You can decide to be friends with them or never see them again."

She pondered his words. "The ball's in my court. I like that."

"But wait," I said. "What if Matthew didn't know there was a baby? If you bring up the subject, it could get ugly."

Mac perked up at the idea of intrigue. "So you think Petsy could've had a child out of wedlock and given it up before Matthew found out. I like it." He flashed Amanda a sheepish grin. "I can get a little carried away with my theories."

"I don't mind at all," Amanda said. "But I was thinking. They call that house the Jorgensen house, right? So doesn't that mean that Matthew's family has always lived there?"

"Yeah," I said, recalling that the place had been known as the Jorgensen house for as long as I could remember.

"So if Petsy had a baby by another man, I wouldn't be related to Matthew."

"True."

"So then why do I look so much like his ancestor?"

"Wow," Mac said, grinning. "Good deduction. I'm impressed."

"Me, too." I pursed my lips as I thought about it. "That never even occurred to me, but you're right. You would have to be Matthew's daughter."

"That wouldn't be so bad," she said quietly.

"He's a lovely man," I said. "I have no idea how or why he ever hooked up with Petsy."

"Does Matthew have a brother?" Mac asked.

Amanda gasped, then clapped her hands. "Good question."

Mac grinned. "Thank you. Thank you very much."

"And not a bad Elvis impression, either," I said, laughing with him. After a moment, I sobered. "I don't remember if Matthew has a brother, but it would be easy enough to find out."

Then I remembered something. "Petsy said that Matthew's nephews destroyed the paneling in the dining room. And Matthew told us that he has three siblings. One of them could've given up a child for adoption."

"Maybe he's got a sister," Mac said. "She could've given up a child for adoption for any number of reasons."

I frowned. "I guess I could find out the names of any siblings and track down where they're living now."

"If it matters," Mac added.

"Right. We could still be talking about Matthew."

We sat with our own thoughts for a moment; then Mac said, "Not to change the subject or anything, but do we know who killed the building inspector?"

Amanda winced. "I've been so hung up on my own problems, I forgot all about the murder of that poor man."

"Your problem is important," Mac assured her.

I gazed at Mac. "No, we don't know who killed Joe Scully." Turning to Amanda I added, "But we need to think about your situation, too."

Especially since Joe Scully was already dead, while Amanda was very much alive. And as far as I was concerned, her problem was much more intriguing.

"So, we've got to find out who your parents are," I continued. "And we've also got to find a killer. And as usual, we've got too many questions and not enough answers in both cases."

"As usual," Mac murmured.

Amanda looked a little puzzled by that comment so I hastened to explain as discreetly as I could. "Over the past few years, there have been one or two unexplained deaths that Mac and I have taken an interest in solving."

Mac seemed surprised by my explanation, but I refused to increase the number of bodies. I figured that if Amanda knew the real body count, she wouldn't want to hang around with me anymore.

"What should we do now?" Amanda asked.

"Good question. There's so much going on." I walked over to the sideboard and pulled a notepad and pen out of a drawer. "I think it's time we made a list."

Chapter Six

Okay, maybe making a list wasn't the most exciting activity I could've proposed. But ever since we first met, Mac and I had somehow been involved in many of the murder cases that had occurred in town. It just seemed natural that we would get together and brainstorm motives and suspects and try to figure out who had the most to gain from the victim's death.

It wasn't as if our lives revolved around solving horrible homicides, but hey, after being suspected of murder on more than one occasion, I'd taken a real interest in coming up with alternative theories. Plus, Mac made his living by devising elaborate mystery plots and then laying down clues for his readers to try to unmask the killer before the end of the book. And in the case of Joe Scully, since the murder had occurred in my new client's orangery, and since I was one of the first people to find him, and knew many of the people who might've held a grudge against him, I was eager to figure it all out.

Problem was, I had just now realized that I didn't

want to talk about any of it in front of Amanda. I had three reasons to keep her out of the loop. First of all, she was too new to Lighthouse Cove, and while I liked her, I barely knew her. Second, she was essentially my employee, so I didn't want her to get the wrong idea about me as I delved into grisly topics such as murders and weapons and suspects and motives.

And third, I had no choice but to consider Amanda a suspect. I really didn't want to, because, as I mentioned before, I liked Amanda. But again, she was new in town, and frankly, she seemed to have a lot of secrets. Plus, she had talked to Joe Scully in order to get information about me. Knowing Scully, I wouldn't have put it past him to turn around and insist on payback from her. Would that be enough to drive someone like Amanda to murder? I doubted it. In fact, I couldn't see Amanda killing anyone ever. And yet, I still had to circle back to the fact that I barely knew her. Yes, I liked her. I even trusted her, sort of, despite all the ways she had been less than truthful with me.

The bottom line was that I wanted to wait until Mac and I were alone before enthusiastically digging into the reasons why certain people deserved to be on our suspect list and what their various motives for murder might have been.

Truly, we knew how to have a good time.

After I'd brought out more cookies and chips, I picked up my pen. "First, let's figure out how we can broach the subject of baby Amanda and the Jorgensens."

"There's no way I can talk about this with Petsy," she said firmly, with a shake of her head for emphasis. "She's just too formidable."

I had to agree with her. I didn't want to talk to Petsy about the weather, let alone something private. The woman was scary.

"But you could talk to Matthew," I said.

She took a deep breath. "I'd have to build up to it."

"We could do it together," I offered. "Find a way to start a conversation about Baltimore or families or children or, I don't know. But somewhere in the middle we could casually mention that you were adopted."

"I'm not sure how a subject like that would come up naturally."

"What if I brought it up?" I said. "I could say something like"—I struck a pose and began—"'Matthew, it's so interesting that Amanda looks like your ancestor in the painting. Did you know she was adopted? Maybe the two of you are long-lost relatives. Wouldn't that be remarkable?'" I glanced at the two of them. "How does that sound?"

Mac grinned. "Not awkward at all."

I laughed. "Okay, fine. But you get the idea."

"Sure. You're just trying to start a conversation."

"Exactly."

"And that could work." He turned to Amanda. "What do you think? Would you be comfortable with that approach?"

Another deep breath, then a halfhearted smile. "Nothing about any of this will be comfortable, but at least the conversation will be started."

"What about talking to the daughter?" Mac asked. "Think she knows anything?"

"I doubt it," I said, and glanced at Amanda.

She gave a clueless shrug. "I don't think so, either.

She's kind and friendly, but she seems a little removed from the family dynamic. And who could blame her?"

"How do you mean?" he asked.

"She moved away to San Francisco," I explained. "And when she was younger, they sent her to boarding school."

"By her request?" he asked.

"Possibly," I said. "If Petsy were my mother, I'd be begging to go away to school."

Amanda said, "But Lindsey and Matthew are great together. They talk and laugh and enjoy each other's company. Then Petsy comes around, and Lindsey clams up. It feels like it's a pattern they've been following for years. Can't blame Lindsey for that, either."

"Agreed," I said. "She's probably spent a lifetime being slapped down by her mother."

"In that case," Mac said, "it sounds like Matthew would be the best person to start a conversation with."

Amanda thought for a moment, then nodded. "I think so, too."

"Okay," I said. "I'll get the conversational ball rolling if you want me to. And I'll try not to embarrass you."

"You couldn't," Amanda insisted, reaching out to squeeze my hand. "I'm just so grateful for your help."

There was a break in the conversation and we all reached for chips and cookies. A moment later, Mac said, "You know, I'd like to revisit the DNA angle. But first, I'm wondering if you have a strict time limit set for finding out if you're related to these people."

Amanda frowned at him. "What do you mean?"

"I mean, were you hoping to find a long-lost relative in order to get a kidney transplant or something?"

She chuckled. "No. I don't need any kidneys right now. I just want to know who I am. I'd like to get to know my birth family. I want to know where I belong."

I glanced at Mac and could tell what he was thinking. *Be careful what you wish for.* I didn't say it aloud, but I totally agreed. Especially after meeting Petsy Jorgensen. I would never want to learn that she was my mother.

"In that case," Mac said, "I think you should go ahead and try to find one of their hairbrushes. I'll take it to my buddy in San Francisco and we'll get the analysis done."

"You'd do that? Thank you so much."

I wrote *hairbrush* on my list. Because making lists was one of the great joys in my life.

"When you find the brush," Mac said, "try to pick out strands of hair with the root attached. Otherwise, it's not much use."

"Okay," she said. "Are there other ways to get DNA?"

"There are dozens of ways." He grinned. "Want to hear them?"

"Sure."

"Some are a little grisly."

Amanda made a face. "I figured, but give me some ideas anyway. I might not be able to find anyone's hairbrush."

"Good idea. So, you can also look for chewed gum, or dried blood, fingernail clippings, a used tissue, a toothbrush, even a sweaty T-shirt. You want more? I can get into bodily fluids."

"You should probably stop right there," I said. "We don't want to get totally grossed out."

"I'm already there," Amanda said, grimacing.

"Sorry," Mac said, but he looked rather pleased with himself.

"I just realized," I said, glancing from Mac to Amanda, "we should probably try to find two different hairbrushes."

"Good thinking," he said. "We should analyze both Matthew's and Petsy's DNA."

I frowned. "And you know they probably sleep in separate bedrooms."

"So how am I supposed to sneak into both of their rooms?"

"We might be able to do it on different days," I suggested. "Or we could ask Matthew or Lindsey for a tour of the house."

"I could see asking Lindsey. As long as Petsy isn't home."

"Absolutely," I said. "None of this happens unless Petsy's out of the house."

"Matthew's already offered to show us his studio."

"Oh, that's right. And while we're up there, one of us can beg to use the bathroom."

"And while we're in the bathroom, we scout around for some hair," she said, rubbing her hands together.

I was glad to see her finally getting into the spirit of the search. And that reminded me of something. I jumped up and jogged into the kitchen, grabbed what I wanted, and returned. "Here are a few Baggies," I said, handing them to Amanda. "You can carry them with you, put whatever you find in there, zip it up, and stick the Baggie back in your pocket."

"That's so smart." She stood up and shoved them into her back pocket. "Thank you."

Mac grinned and nodded. "I think you're good to go."

With our new plan of action worked out, Mac and I drove Amanda back to her truck parked on Cranberry Circle.

I glanced at my watch. "It's almost quitting time. You might as well take the rest of the day off and save your energy for tomorrow and the next day."

"Sounds good to me, boss," she said with a grin and, after thanking me again, jogged to her truck.

As soon as she started the truck's engine, Mac slowly drove off.

As we turned onto Main Street, something occurred to me. "Would you be willing to drive out to the old Jenkins farm before you go home?"

"Where's the Jenkins farm?"

"It's about two miles east of town."

"Take Main Street?"

"Yes. Then turn right on Queen Anne Hill Road and go for another mile or so."

"Who are the Jenkinses?"

"The farm belongs to someone else now. It's some guy who wants to marry Marigold."

I must have sounded annoyed, because he flashed me a look. "Are you opposed to the idea?"

"I'm not for or against it. Yet. I've never met him before. None of the girls have met him. In fact, we've never even seen him."

"Sounds suitably suspicious," he said. "Let's go check him out."

On the way out of town, we talked about Amanda.

"I don't want her working alone inside the Jorgensen house," I said. "I think Petsy overheard our conversation in the hall with Matthew and I have no idea what she'll do."

Mac scowled. "Do you think Petsy would try to hurt her?"

I thought about it. Amanda was young and in great shape from the kind of work she did. Petsy was thin and probably worked out regularly, but she didn't have the kind of agility and strength that Amanda had.

"No," I said finally. "She wouldn't be able to hurt Amanda physically. But she can be cruel and I refuse to give her the opportunity."

And if she did try to attack Amanda, I would pull my crew off the job and walk away. But I doubted it would come to that. Petsy was rude and imperious with me and my crew, but I couldn't picture her being violent with anyone. In any event, I would be sticking close by most of the time, so Amanda and I would present a united front.

Fifteen minutes later, Mac turned into the long driveway leading to the farmhouse on the old Jenkins property. I was surprised to see three gigantic wind turbines standing several hundred feet away where the Jenkins property began to rise slightly higher than the rest of the land.

These weren't the old wooden windmills that the town was famous for. No, these were modern, streamlined steel towers topped by blades that looked more like powerful propellers than the fan-shaped blades of an old-fashioned windmill.

"Marigold told us he's a wealthy entrepreneur," I said. "I guess he's into alternative power sources."

"Wait a minute," Mac said. "Is this Rafe's farm?"

I gaped at him. "You know this guy?"

"I met him a few weeks ago when I went to the pub for a beer with Eric. Great guy. Really smart. I mean, like, genius smart. I told him I wanted to pick his brain sometime."

"Because Jake Slater might have to save the world from an errant wind turbine?"

He grinned at me. "It could happen, right?" He parked the car in front of a three-car garage that had seen better days. "Let's go see what's going on."

"Wait, Mac," I said, grabbing his arm. "I know you won't say anything, but try not to make this look like I'm here to check Rafe out. Marigold really likes him but she says she won't marry him because he's a farmer. She doesn't want to milk cows for the rest of her life."

"Who does?"

"It's just that she was raised Amish . . ."

"Ah. So she's had enough of cows?"

"Yes. But if he's a nice guy, I don't want to offend him. I just want to meet the guy who's apparently crazy about one of my best friends."

"I'll be cool." He leaned over and kissed me. "Promise."

Of course he would, I thought. Still, a little cloud of guilt continued to hover over me.

As I jumped down from Mac's SUV, a man walked out of the farmhouse and stood on the front porch. From where I stood, he looked tall, dark, and handsome. Three lovely qualities in a man.

The house was another matter, though. It was utilitarian, to put it nicely, and the pale yellow paint had faded and peeled until the house looked parched and sickly. The porch roof leaned precariously and I worried that it might collapse on top of its good-looking owner at any moment.

I'd looked up the house online after dinner with Marigold the other night, so I knew it was a small three-bedroom home with one bathroom. The place needed refurbishing badly, if not a complete renovation. At the very least, the wiring and plumbing had to be updated soon. And add a powder room for heaven's sake. No one should have to live with only one bathroom.

The man waved. "Mac, is that you?"

"Yeah, it's me, Rafe. Thought I'd take a drive out to see how you're doing."

"That's awfully nice of you." He walked down the steps toward us.

"This is my friend Shannon Hammer."

"Shannon Hammer." He held out his arm and we shook hands. "You're the contractor?"

"Yes, I am," I said, surprised that he knew who I was.

"It's great to meet you," he said, holding on to my hand. "Marigold has told me all about you. I can tell she has terrific friends."

"Thank you. She's pretty terrific herself."

"She's fantastic," he said softly.

I glanced around. "So, are you living out here now?"

"Temporarily," he said, grinning dolefully. "The house is tiny and needs a ton of work done to it. I was living at the Inn on Main Street for a few weeks, but decided I needed to be out here to take care of business. So I bit the bullet and made the move."

I wondered what kind of business he was taking care of out here, but I kept my mouth shut for now.

"I was actually going to call you this week, Shannon," Rafe continued. "But I got distracted. I've been fiddling with a new idea out in the barn and I tend to get wrapped up and forgetful when I'm working on something new."

I stared at him. "You were going to call me?"

"Yeah. You come highly recommended by Marigold. I guess it's obvious I need to renovate this house. Are you available?"

Wow, just a minute ago, I'd been thinking about what needed to be done to the place and here was Rafe, offering me the job. I was caught just a little off guard. "Uh, wow. Yes, of course. I'd be happy to help you. You might want to get another opinion or two, but I'll be glad to look things over and give you an estimate." I rummaged through my purse and handed him a card.

"Great." He smiled then, and I could see what had attracted Marigold to him. The man was pretty darn gorgeous. And tall. His skin was a beautiful, smooth shade of café au lait with a shot of warm brandy added to it. His dark hair was cut short and his eyes twinkled with intelligence and humor. But it was his smile that won me over.

"Hey," he said suddenly, "you guys want to see my new toy? Come on."

He sounded like an excited kid about to try out his new model race car. He didn't wait for us, just led the way to the barn. Mac and I both followed, of course. His excitement was infectious.

The house was a wreck, and from the outside, the barn didn't look much better. But *inside*, things were different. The barn had been transformed into a warehouse filled with large vehicle parts and, along the sides, stacks of boxes apparently filled with smaller vehicle parts and lots of electronics. There was stuff everywhere, but it was all laid out precisely. So there seemed to be some sort of method to Rafe's madness.

"Here it is," Rafe said, pointing to the heavy-duty contraption in the middle of the space.

"Wow," I said, studying the machine with absolutely no clue what I was looking at. "What is it?"

He grinned. "It's a solar-powered tractor. I built it and now I'm modifying it to fit a front-end loader and a backhoe. I could go out and buy one fully equipped, but what's the fun in that?" He gave the top of one of the wheel wells a friendly tap. "It's got solar panels on the cab roof and over the wheels. The cab is air-conditioned, too."

"Good selling point," Mac said, nodding in approval as he moved around the vehicle, checking out every inch of it in a very male way.

Rafe continued to describe the thing and I was glad Mac was paying attention, because I had lost track of the conversation back at *solar-powered tractor*. It wasn't because his words weren't interesting, but because I was more fascinated by Raphael Nash, the man himself, than by his latest invention. After all, if things fell into place, he might someday marry my friend Marigold. I considered it my sacred duty to make sure that he lived up to the high standards any friend would demand for her girlfriend.

So far, I liked him.

Mac couldn't resist taking a ride on the tractor, and then we spent another half hour chatting while Rafe showed us the farm.

"How are the wind turbines working for you?" Mac asked.

"They're awesome. It's only been a few weeks and I'm almost completely off the grid."

"They're huge," I murmured, staring up at a shaft that had to be at least sixty feet high.

"They have to be tall enough to catch the wind without anything blocking them. You want your wind tower to be the tallest thing on your land. And generally speaking, the higher the tower, the more kilowatts you can collect."

"I didn't realize they were so loud." We had all begun to raise our voices to be heard over the sound.

"That's why I put them all the way out here," he said. "I didn't want them in the pasture, disturbing the animals, or anywhere near the house. I can't hear them when I'm inside the house or the barn."

"You're right," I said, gazing back at the barn and gauging the distance we had walked. "I didn't actually hear them until we got closer."

"See?" He grinned, then added, "I'm working on something that will reduce the noise."

"I'd be interested in hearing about that," Mac said, "but not this afternoon. We've taken up enough of your time."

"I don't mind at all. I'm glad you swung by."

"I am, too," I said, as Rafe led the way back toward the house.

"Next time you visit," he said as we walked, "I'll introduce you to some of my cattle."

I turned around, looking for signs of animals. "You have cattle?"

"Nothing yet," he said. "But they should be arriving in the next few days. I figured since I have a farm now, I should have some farm animals."

"Sounds fair," I said carefully. "What kinds of animals?"

"Ten milking cows and three horses."

"Will you also be hiring a farmhand or two?" Was I being too obvious? Maybe I was pushing it, but I was dying to know how he intended to milk all those cows. I wanted to assure him it wouldn't be Marigold doing the work, but I figured the two of them would have to talk it out by themselves.

He grinned. "Don't you think I can handle it, Shannon?"

"Oh, I'm sure you can. I just . . . hmm."

He chuckled. "I was teasing you. Don't worry. I plan to hire someone who actually knows what he's doing. He'll start next week, setting up a mechanized milking parlor. Then when the cows arrive, they'll be good to go."

I let go of a breath I didn't realize I was holding on Marigold's behalf. "That sounds great. Ten cows will produce a lot of milk."

"I know." He grinned again. "Someone suggested that I only needed one cow. But I have so much land and I didn't want the one cow to get lonely, so I ended up with ten of them. I'll have way too much milk for just me, so I'll either give away the excess or go into the ice cream business or something."

I was so bowled over by his concern for lonely cows that it took me a few seconds to realize he had uttered the words *ice cream*. "I'll be glad to do some taste testing for you."

"I'll take you up on that," he said with a laugh.

We all shook hands and I gave him a welcoming hug, and then we took off. I couldn't wait to call my girlfriends to let them know I had met the mysterious Raphael Nash. And big surprise, I liked him a lot. Especially since I could now report that he was going to be hiring himself an honest-to-goodness cowhand. Or maybe he was called a cow milker? I really had no idea. Either way, it was good news for Marigold. And for me, too. Hello, ice cream? Who wouldn't love a guy like that?

Driving back to town, Mac wanted to talk about Joe Scully. "You didn't say much about Joe while we were talking with Amanda."

"No. I decided I didn't want to say anything while she was sitting there with us. She's my employee, so I didn't want her to see us going on and on about suspects and motives and murder."

"I get it." He flashed a cockeyed grin. "We have way too much fun talking about murder."

"I know." I laughed. "It's weird."

"No way. Perfectly normal. Anyway, now that we're alone, what can you tell me?"

"He was stabbed in the abdomen with a sharpened quarter-inch chisel."

"Oh man. You got a good look at the body?"

"Oh yeah. The wound. The weapon. The blood."

"Lucky you," he said flatly. "Usually a lot of blood with an abdominal wound."

"Tell me about it."

He reached for my hand and held on to it as we drove. That connection felt warm and comforting and I was able to let the blood-soaked memory of Joe Scully fade from my mind.

"Instead of going out," he said after a moment, "why don't we stop and pick up some steaks and potatoes?"

"That is a fantastic idea."

"I do come up with them," he said, smiling as he came to a stop at Queen Anne Hill.

"There's Marigold's water tower," I said, pointing out the sunshine yellow tower—not that I needed to show him. The thing was like a neon beacon in the sky.

"Kind of hard to miss, isn't it?" He stared at it for a moment, then proceeded to turn onto Main Street. "We can talk more about the murder while we make dinner."

"I can't think of anything I'd rather do with you."

He laughed. "Well, I could always paint a water tower for you."

"That would be nice, too," I said, squeezing his hand. "But I'd much rather spend our time figuring out who killed Joe Scully."

Still grinning, he pulled into the supermarket parking lot. "Steaks. Wine. Candlelight. Murder. Just a couple of romantic fools."

Chapter Seven

While the potatoes baked, I did a little predinner gardening in order to fill our salad bowl. I plucked two ripe tomatoes, cut off some leaves of romaine from the larger head, and grabbed a clump of green onions from the dirt.

Mac seasoned the steaks, then poured a glass of wine for each of us. He sat down at the kitchen table and played with Robbie and Tiger while I washed the veggies and cut up half a cucumber to add to the salad.

I gazed at him. "I'm still flummoxed about Scully's murder. He was found at the Derrys' house, but I can't believe either of them would kill him. Especially Joan. She's so nice."

"It's always hard to believe that anyone we know might be capable of murder." Tiger jumped up onto his lap and he stroked her soft fur. "But it happens. How many times have I had a nice person turn out to be the killer in one of my books? Nice people make great killers."

"Good to know. I'll never look at my friends the same way again."

"I'm here to help." He grinned. "Do you know how well the Derrys knew the victim?"

"Pretty well. Scully's son-in-law remodeled the Derrys' basement."

Mac stopped in midstroke. "Interesting." He picked up his wineglass and swirled it a few times. "So it sounds like they were friends."

"It's hard to picture anyone being friends with Scully, but I guess it's possible." But the more I thought about that argument the Derrys had had with Scully out in front of their house the other day, the less likely it seemed. I described the incident to Mac. "So yeah, they might've been friends once upon a time, but at this point, they're not even *friends adjacent*."

"That is an interesting concept."

Now I smiled at him. "It works for this situation."

Mac set Tiger down on the floor and walked over to the sink to wash his hands before joining me at the chopping block, where I was prepping the salad. "How about if you tell me everything that happened this morning?"

"Okay." I mentally retraced my steps. "I parked in front of the Jorgensens' house. A few minutes later I saw Amanda arrive. I jumped out of my truck to greet her, and that's when Joan Derry came running around the side of her house, shrieking that someone was dead."

"That got your attention."

"You bet it did." I chopped the green onions, then added them to the salad bowl. "I dashed across the street and grabbed Joan. She pointed toward the backyard and tried to get the words out, but she was too rattled to speak, so I just took off running up the side of the house. I noticed that the orangery was open, and when I got closer, I saw the body. I didn't even realize Amanda was behind me until that moment. Suddenly she's there and asking me if he's dead."

"Freak you out a little?"

"Yeah, a little." That was putting it mildly, but I didn't want to sound like a complete wimp.

Mac grabbed a small chunk of cucumber and popped it into his mouth. "So, then what happened?"

"I asked Amanda to go call the police and begged her to try and get Joan to calm down."

"So Amanda went off to make the call and find Joan, leaving you alone outside the orangery. What did you do?"

Before I answered, I glanced around the room nervously, as though someone might've been listening in. "I walked into the orangery."

"That's my girl," he said, grinning. "What did you see?"

I pictured the scene in my mind. "One of the glass panes was cracked. Some pillows that belonged on the window bench were on the floor. A plant had fallen and some of the dirt was spilled on the carpet."

"And Joe Scully?" he prompted.

I sighed heavily, hating to remember but unable to forget. "He was lying in the center of the room, completely dead. His eyes were open."

"His eyes were open?" He grimaced. "Gross."

"Totally gross." I rubbed my stomach, feeling unsettled by the memory. Honestly, was I ever going to get used to stumbling across bodies? I kind of hoped I wouldn't. "And the chisel handle was sticking out of his stomach."

He exhaled slowly. "Wow."

"Yeah." I concentrated on drying the lettuce leaves and breaking them into bite-sized pieces.

"Tell me about the chisel handle."

"It was a good one," I said after a moment. "Not some cheap tool. I could tell at a glance that the handle was made of expensive hardwood."

"Not one of your tools, I hope."

"No," I said, letting out my own relieved breath. That was something I didn't want to go through again.

"Do you know who it belongs to?"

"I'm almost afraid to say it. But it might belong to one of my guys. I had two of them working full-time on the dry rot problem."

He grimaced. "Okay. Don't think about that right now. Let's get back to the orangery. What else did you see?"

I flicked him a quick glance. "Well, this is kind of fortuitous. But while I was looking around, I suddenly remembered that I had taken pictures of the room earlier in the week."

He grabbed his wineglass. "How did you happen to be there taking pictures?"

"I had gone there to talk to Joan about her dry rot problem. When we were finished surveying the damage to her basement, I asked if I could see the orangery because we were about to build one for the Jorgensens." I shrugged and never stopped chopping. "I wanted to see how they'd built the brick base and also check on the way it was connected to the outside wall of the house."

"So you took pictures of the same room a few days ago. Yeah, *fortuitous* is the right word."

"Right?" I gave him an approving smile. "So when I saw all the damage, I got my phone out to compare things. For instance, I wanted to make sure that the glass wasn't already cracked before."

"Was it?"

"No."

"So it must've happened during some kind of scuffle or fight with the killer."

"That's what I thought. Same goes for the pillows and the plant on the floor."

"Anything else?"

I sighed again. Couldn't seem to help myself. "I found Johnny's tool chest just inside the door leading to the rest of the house." I pulled Dijon mustard and wine vinegar from the refrigerator to make a vinaigrette for the salad.

"What was his tool chest doing there?"

I frowned. "I think Colin's was there, too. He's one of my new guys."

"So both tool chests were stored near the door leading to the orangery? How do you know they belonged to your guys?"

As I reached for the olive oil on the counter near the stove, I explained about Johnny's distinctive stainless steel case. "I assumed when I saw the two cases that maybe Joan had offered to let them store their tools in the house while they're working there."

"Makes sense."

"I'm not sure it does. Why didn't they just keep them in the basement instead of all the way upstairs?" I leaned back against the counter and munched on a baby carrot. "Then again, maybe there was too much dust down there and they wanted to keep them clean. Or maybe they'd already carried them upstairs when Joan suggested that they keep their tools there."

"Either of those possibilities works for me."

"The best thing would be to just ask Johnny."

"Right. So, are you thinking the murder weapon belongs to one of your guys?"

I had been trying really hard *not* to think that, but the thought kept popping back into my head. "That's what I'm afraid of. But I've seen Johnny's chisels. I think they're the same brand as mine, which means the handles are a heavily reinforced plastic. They're really strong."

"But they're not wood," Mac said.

"Right. I was wondering if Colin's are made of wood. I hope not."

"Maybe we should find out."

"I'd better start another list." I really didn't want to think one of my guys was a murderer. It felt . . . disloyal even considering it.

"You're making salad. I can start the list." He walked over to the kitchen table, sat down, and wrote a reminder down on the notepad I'd left there. "Okay. Now you won't forget to ask them about the chisels."

I gazed at him as I added ground pepper to the vinaigrette. "I've got to assume that Eric already covered this issue."

"Since it's the murder weapon, you're probably right. He's pretty good at this stuff."

"I know. I just hope he didn't harass my guys. They're not killers."

"Of course not." Mac leaned back in his chair and shook his head. He knew all of my guys pretty well now, so having him back me up felt good.

"I probably would've heard if he arrested one of them."

"In this town?" He grinned. "You'd hear within thirty seconds."

The stove timer went off and I jolted.

"Easy there, partner," he said. He got up, walked over to me, and wrapped me in a hug. Just what I needed apparently because in an instant, the jitters faded away and I was warm and relaxed and happy.

After a moment, he stepped back and touched my cheek. "Okay?"

"Yes. Thanks." I rubbed away the last of the goose bumps on my arms. "I don't know why I'm so jumpy."

He laughed shortly. "Seriously? Anyone else would probably be jabbering in a corner by now. It's all this talk about weapons and murder and picturing the victim with his eyes bulging open."

"Thanks for that reminder." I couldn't help but laugh. Mac always took such macabre pleasure in discussing the gory details of murder.

"I'll check the potatoes." I grabbed a fork and carefully opened the oven door. The blast of heat was powerful and I waited a few seconds before moving closer to stick a fork into one of the potatoes. "Potatoes are done. They can sit in the oven until we're ready to eat."

Closing the door, I turned off the oven and set the fork down on the counter.

"I'll go start the grill," he said.

"Okay. And I'll figure out what else we need to add to this list."

"You can wait for me if you want. I won't be long."

I smiled at him. "I'm much better now."

When he returned two minutes later, I had added a new column titled *Suspects* to the list. Under that heading, I'd written down eleven names: Petsy, Matthew, and Lindsey Jorgensen; Amanda; Joan and Stan Derry; Wade; Colin; Johnny; Sean; and me.

I imagined there were dozens more people around town who had wished Scully dead at one time or another. Or if not dead, at least forcibly retired. Mac always liked to have a long list of suspects to choose from. But the problem with having lots of names was that we then had to come up with motives for each of them. When it came to someone like Joe Scully, though, it wasn't hard to find a motive. The guy was as corrupt as the day was long and had always been willing to take bribes for granting favors. And I didn't exactly know it for a fact, but I wouldn't have been shocked to find out that he'd been involved in some blackmail schemes in the past.

I had added my own name to the list, along with my crew, because we all had a motive. We'd all been victims of Scully's contemptible business practices over the years. As I'd explained to Chief Jensen that morning, Scully was universally despised by contractors, construction workers, and homeowners alike.

"What have you got there?" Mac asked when he came back inside.

"Suspect list." I handed it to him.

He leaned his hip against the kitchen counter and read what I'd written. "I understand why you've got your name here, but it's probably not necessary. We both know you didn't kill him."

"I know, but it felt right. If I'm putting my guys on the list, I should be there, too. Besides, if the police had heard me cussing out Scully these past few days, they would definitely consider me a suspect."

"Well, I'm just going to ignore your name for now. Let's go alphabetically down the list and start with Amanda."

I smiled. "You did that on purpose."

"You'd like to clear her name quickly, right?"

"I would. But speaking of Amanda, I have a question." I inhaled and let the breath out slowly. "Do you think I'm being played?"

"By Amanda?" He thought about it. "No."

"Okay, good. Let's move on."

"Don't you want to know why I don't think so?"

"I trust your instincts."

He smiled and gave me a wink. "And I trust yours. But I'll tell you anyway. I think that even though she lied to you and withheld information, she's basically too transparent to actually *play* you. To me, that idea of being played means someone's a user. A grifter. They're scheming to get your money or property, or they want to destroy you in some way. And Amanda doesn't want anything from you except access to the Jorgensens' house."

That was sort of what my own mind had been telling me, but it was good to have it confirmed by Mac.

"I think you might be right, but how can you know for sure?"

"I ran her story through my Baloney Meter and it checks out. And add in the fact that she's a really bad liar." He leaned over and patted my cheek. "Kind of like you."

"I'm not a . . ." I scowled. "Okay, fine, I'm not a very good liar."

He laughed. "Don't look so down. That's a good thing."

I supposed he was right, but why did it not sound like a compliment? "Wait. Baloney Meter?"

"Everybody has one."

I laughed and shook my head as I reached for my wineglass. Honestly, just talking to Mac settled my nerves and made me feel as if everything was going to be all right. "Okay, back to Amanda. Let's face it: the story she told is just bizarre."

"True, but stranger things have happened." He grabbed his wineglass from the chopping block and sat down at the table with me. "Let's work backward. Let's start with the premise that Amanda is the killer. Why did she do it? And how?"

"She did it because she was asking Scully about me, and once she realized what a jerk he was, she was afraid he would reveal that she'd been following me."

"Would he really try to blackmail her over that?"

"Because she asked him about me?" I shook my head. "Let me put it this way. He might try, but she wouldn't go for it."

He grinned. "Exactly my thought."

"Okay. Shall we move on?"

"Let's figure out how she could've done it first." Mac rubbed his hands together gleefully. He really did enjoy this too much.

"I have no idea," I said. "Did she lure him into Joan's orangery?"

"Does she even know Joan?" he asked.

"She first met Joan the day we checked out the dry rot." I took a sip of my wine. "But while I was taking pictures of the orangery, she went back to her truck, so she never even saw it, as far as I know."

"All right," he said, disappointed by my answers. "Guess we should let her off the hook."

"I agree. She's innocent." I checked her name off the list.

"Good." He stood. "I'm going to put the steaks on and we can talk about the rest over dinner."

We sat at the dining room table, where I'd dimmed the chandelier in favor of candlelight. The steaks were rare, the wine was yummy, and the company was delightful. Everything was perfect, except for all this talk of murder. But even that was enjoyable with Mac.

After toasting happy times, Mac got back to our earlier conversation. "What do you think about Colin?"

"I like him. I just hired him last month and he seems like a good guy and a really great worker. He lives in Flanders and he's worked all over the area, so it's possible that he's had to deal with Scully before. But I can't see how he would've had a serious run-in with him. He's not the one who would've dealt with the building inspector."

"He sounds innocent," Mac admitted, "but you should find out whether his chisels are made of hardwood."

"I will." I took a bite of steak and savored the flavor for a minute before glancing back at the list. "Looks like Joan is up next."

"Tell me everything you know about her."

"Honestly, she and her husband are the most suspicious ones on the list."

"Because it was done on their property?"

"Well, yes."

"Do they seem guilty to you?"

"To tell you the truth, I only just met Joan and I'd never even seen Stan until two days ago, when I happened to be there to watch him shout at Scully to get the heck off his lawn."

"So he has a temper."

"To be fair, everyone who runs up against Scully has a temper." I took a sip of wine. "He's such a jerk, you can't help but start seething with indignation when he's around. Once, I seriously considered running him down in the street."

"Seriously?"

"Well, sort of seriously."

"He sounds like a really good victim."

"This is going to sound harsh," I admitted, already starting to feel guilty. "Even though I'm not happy that Scully's dead, I have to admit that his death makes my life easier."

"It probably does that for a lot of people."

"No doubt." Which didn't really help with the guilt, but I appreciated his saying so.

"So, what about this temper of Stan's?" he said.

"Since I don't know him, I wouldn't want to hazard a guess. But Joan is just a darling woman. She's friendly and funny and kind. Her home is beautiful and she makes lemonade from scratch."

"Definitely suspicious."

I chuckled. "I know, right? Seriously, though, I can't picture her coming at Scully with a weapon."

"But you saw her yelling at him."

"Yeah, I did." While I arranged my thoughts, I took a bite of salad and appreciated the crunchy freshness of veggies straight from my garden. "She really let him have it, but he deserved it. And yelling at somebody is way far removed from stabbing them with a chisel."

"True. So you're saying she was fighting fairly."

"Exactly. I see her as the type that would yell at him or even sue him, or call the cops on him. But kill him? I just can't see it."

"But we can't say the same about her husband."

"No, like I said, I saw him for the first time the other morning." Frowning, I took a sip of wine. "For all I know, he could be Jack the Ripper. God, was it really just two days ago? This has been the longest week in history and it's not over yet."

"You've had a lot going on."

"It makes me a little dizzy."

"Well, any day that starts with finding a dead body is not going to be the most relaxing day of the week." He paused to reflect on his words. "That was amazingly philosophical, wasn't it?"

"Plato would be proud," I said, smiling at him.

He laughed. "Thank you."

We both took a minute to eat a few more bites of steak and potato, and sip our wine.

"So, what about your pal Petsy?" Mac said finally.

"No more alphabetical order?"

"Life is short. I think we should skip to the juiciest suspects."

"Good idea." But the thought of Petsy drove me to take another gulp of wine. "She's thoroughly unpleasant, to put it mildly. She's probably the most capable of anyone on the list of killing another human being. Actually she's the perfect suspect. But I don't see how she could've done it."

"Why not?"

I thought about it. "When I got to the Jorgensens' house this morning, we talked a little bit about the murder. I mentioned Joan's name and Petsy seemed frankly contemptuous of her. So why would she ever have gone to the Derrys' house for any reason?"

"What better reason than because she hates her?" He patted his mouth with his napkin as he considered my question. "It's a great way to spit in Joan's eye, metaphorically speaking. She kills someone on Joan's property and lets her take the fall. It's kind of perfect."

I nodded slowly. "And she's vicious enough to find that scenario appealing. But it still seems too far-fetched to be real."

"So you don't think she did it?"

"Unless she had some personal reason for killing Scully, I don't see it. I can't tell you how much I wish she was guilty, but I'm not seeing the means and opportunity. Did she arrange a meeting with him? And how did she get into the orangery? Does she have a key? Seems unlikely since she and Joan despise each other."

"Well, darn. As she's our most capable and likely suspect, I hate to move on from her so soon. But so be it." He glanced back at the list. "Her husband and daughter are just too nice, right?"

"They're really nice. They're polite and friendly and calm."

He waved his hand in the air for emphasis. "Which makes them both perfect suspects."

I laughed. "Of course it does."

"What if one of them looked out their window late last night and saw Scully tiptoeing up the walkway to the Derrys' backyard?"

I could picture it. "Go on."

"They stopped to throw on a bathrobe and then took off after him."

"To kill him or just talk to him?"

Mac considered. "They just wanted to have a word with him. Maybe even warn him that Petsy was on the warpath."

"And in the middle of the conversation, something went dreadfully wrong."

"Clearly," he said, his mouth curved in a half grin. "Question is, would they have brought a chisel with them?"

"That's where we go off track," I said, pointing at him with my fork. "Why would any of them bring a chisel along? Or did they just pick up the chisel from one of the guys' toolboxes? But I don't know that the chisel was one of theirs, so that's a big question mark. I think they had to have brought it with them."

"Why? You tell me."

"Hmm. Maybe it's something they carry around for general self-defense."

"Like a can of mace?"

"Exactly."

"Because everyone needs a sharp weapon when traversing the mean streets of Lighthouse Cove."

"Especially in the middle of the night."

"Okay," Mac said, chuckling as he reached for his wineglass. "So they always have something with them in case they have to defend themselves."

"Plus, Scully's a creepy guy," I added. "If they happened to see him skulking around, it would have been smart to bring a weapon along, knowing they might need to threaten him a little."

"Okay," he said, nodding. "Go on."

I frowned. "I have no idea where to go from here. But whoever it was, I can't see them casually rummaging through Johnny's or Colin's tool chest while they're in the middle of an argument with Scully. So they must've brought the chisel with them."

He speared a lettuce leaf with his fork and took a bite. "You said Matthew is a painter. He might have a set of chisels."

"You think?"

Mac shrugged. "Sure. Painters sometimes apply thicker paint with a sculpting tool. Or maybe he actually does some sculpting as well as painting."

"Hmm. Maybe." I absently ran my finger around the rim of my wineglass. Here was yet another reason for taking a tour of Matthew's art studio. "Is that likely?"

"Absolutely. Plenty of artists work in multiple types

of media. Look at Leonardo, or Picasso, or Calder. Matthew could, too. Have you seen his studio?"

"Not yet. I'm hoping we'll get a look at it tomorrow."

"Good. Take pictures. And notes. Find out if our painter is also a chiseler." He took a beat before adding, "See what I did there?"

"I did," I said, laughing. "You are brilliant."

He sighed dramatically. "It's both a gift and a burden."

Chapter Eight

I had assured Mac the night before that I would check out Matthew's studio with Amanda sometime today. But it was getting close to noon and we hadn't even seen him yet.

Earlier Lindsey had come to the door to let us in and mentioned that both of her parents were out at meetings this morning. My first thought was that Petsy went to a lot of meetings. I figured it was just her way of getting out of the house and I would bet money that Lindsey and Matthew didn't mind at all. And I would readily admit, I didn't, either.

"I'm going to take a lunch break," I said to Amanda, setting my tools down on the tarp. "I have to meet a friend. Will you be all right on your own?"

She smiled. "Of course. Please don't worry about me, Shannon. I can fend for myself just fine."

"Of course you can," I said. "I'm just concerned because of, well, you-know-who."

She glanced toward the doorway and lowered her

voice. "If Petsy comes home, I'll just go outside and visit with the guys. Or I'll go for a walk. I'd rather not be around her, frankly."

"I don't blame you. And on the off chance that there's any trouble, just yell for Wade or Sean. They would be happy to kick Petsy's behind if she causes you any grief at all. And you can call me if you need anything."

"My heroes," she said with a grin. "But I don't expect any trouble, so go enjoy your lunch and I'll see you in a while."

"Okay." But as I left the house, I couldn't help feeling like a mother hen worried about her new chick. Especially after learning Amanda's big secret. Even though we'd planned it out and I'd given her a supply of Baggies to collect DNA, I really hoped she wouldn't go snooping around the house while I was gone. Snooping was *my* job.

I drove to the town square a half mile away and parked on a side street, then walked to Emily's tea shop. I felt a little guilty that I hadn't asked Amanda to join us for lunch, but I made a silent promise to make it up to her in the next few days. Today, though, I wanted to tell the girls about my visit with Rafe. And frankly, I also needed a little downtime away from work and stress and all the talk of murder that had overwhelmed my life for the past twenty-four hours. I needed some girlfriend time.

I had called earlier to let Emily know I was coming and she had promised to contact the rest of our friends. Sure enough, when I walked into her charming little tea shop, with its mint green walls and bright, pretty decor, Emily greeted me and led me straight back to her small private dining room, where our friends were already gathered around a lovely table covered in flowers and teapots and pastries.

"There you are," Jane said, jumping up to give me a hug. "When Emily called to say you wanted us to get together, I knew you had something to tell us. Is it about that horrible Joe Scully?"

I went around giving hugs to everyone. "I suppose you've all heard what happened."

"We heard you found him dead," Emily said, slinging her arm around my shoulders. "You poor thing. How many bodies does that make now?"

My eyes widened. "Emily!"

She grinned, completely unrepentant. And this was why I had needed to see my friends. Who else could make me feel better about being a death magnet?

Emily squeezed my shoulders affectionately. "Well, really, Shannon. It must be some sort of record."

Just what I'd been thinking, though I hadn't tried to add them all up. For someone so prone to making lists, I had yet to write down the names of the murder victims I'd discovered. "I haven't been keeping track."

"I have," Lizzie piped up. "This one makes nine."

"That's not possible," I whispered. Was it? Nine dead bodies? I started to do a mental body count, then gave it up. I really didn't want to dredge up the memories. I would accept Lizzie's number, horrible or not.

"I thought it was eight," Marigold said as she sipped her tea. "Oh, but I forgot to count that fellow who used to come here for vacations. What was his name?"

Great. I'd become a parlor game. "Come on, you guys!"

Jane pushed my chair back. "Sit down, Shannon. We're just teasing you."

"Yes, sit." Marigold reached for the teapot. "After all, it's not *your* fault you find dead people. We all have gifts."

"Gifts?" I stared blankly at her, then grabbed for my teacup when she'd filled it.

"Sure," Marigold said. "Some people sing. Some paint. Some fix things. And some answer the call from the universe when a dead person needs help. That's you."

Marigold had managed to make it sound almost poetic.

"Poor Shannon," Marigold said softly. "You must be completely stressed out. Drink your tea and have a pastry."

"I have to check on the kitchen," Emily said, giving my shoulder a pat. "But I'll be right back."

"Will you be able to join us?" Lizzie asked.

"Yes, I promise." She patted my arm. "Just hold off telling your news for a few minutes."

"I will."

While we waited for Emily, we thankfully got past the references to my "gift" and regaled one another with favorite pet stories. I told them of Robbie's shenanigans and Lizzie recounted her kitty's latest trip to the vet. We all loved our pets, and since none of us but Lizzie had kids, they were as neutral and happy a topic as we could find.

I piled my plate with Emily's amazing savory pastries and finger sandwiches. Her wonderful tea was a special blend made for her by the Colonnades in Edinburgh and I swore I could've finished an entire pot all by myself.

I ate slowly, knowing that once I cleaned my plate, I would get to move on to the sweet pastries. It was a ridiculously decadent way to spend my lunch hour, but so worth it.

"I'm back," Emily cried softly, and plopped herself down at the table. She poured herself a cup of tea and turned to me. "Now, Shannon, tell us everything."

"I'm not here to talk about the murder," I warned.

"So it was murder," Lizzie whispered.

"It's always murder," Emily murmured.

"And if you've ever met Joe Scully," Jane said dryly, "you would know for sure it was murder."

Marigold turned to me. "Was he awful, Shannon?"

"Absolutely, yes, but I don't want to talk about him."

Jane reached for a miniature gâteau. "What did you want to talk about?"

I turned and smiled at Marigold. "I want to talk about your friend Raphael Nash."

"Raphael?" She frowned. "Why?"

I flashed them all a devilish smile. "Because I met him."

Marigold paled. "You did?"

"Shannon, where did you meet him?"

"How?"

"What does he look like?"

"Spill the beans!"

Everyone was speaking at once, but Lizzie's voice predominated. "Start talking. What did you think of him? Tell us everything."

"All right, all right." I was conscious of Marigold sitting on the edge of her seat, so I reached over and squeezed her arm. "He's a sweetie."

She seemed to relax and so did I. I told them about

the spur-of-the-moment decision to drive out to the Jenkins farm with Mac.

"That was smart, to bring Mac along," Lizzie said.

"I thought so, too." I told them about the dilapidated farmhouse and the barn, and how I would love the chance to renovate them both. I mentioned the wind turbines and the solar-powered tractor. And I told them how handsome I thought he was and so nice and sweet.

And then I mentioned the cows.

"And we've come to the end of the story," Marigold grumbled, her forehead riddled with frown lines.

"No, we haven't," I insisted, laughing. "He says he's going to hire a guy who's an expert with cows. He knows how to set up a milking parlor and he'll be doing all the work."

"Yay!" Lizzie cried.

"There, Marigold," Jane said. "Isn't that great news?"

Clearly nervous, she twirled her napkin tightly in her lap. "If only I could believe it."

"Why wouldn't you believe him?" I asked. "I believe him. He seems way too honest to ever tell a lie."

"Maybe she's been lied to before," Emily murmured.

"Haven't we all?" Lizzie said with a worldly shrug. "You get over it and move on."

"I'm telling you, he's a good guy," I said. "There is no way that Rafe would have Marigold out milking cows. Besides, if he tried, you're completely capable of saying no."

Marigold sucked in a deep breath and let it out slowly. "That's true of course, and yes, he really is sweet and he has the most beautiful eyes. And I never doubted his honesty."

"It's just his desire to have cows," Emily said.

"*Ten* cows," Marigold emphasized. "He mentioned he might buy a few, but what's he going to do with ten cows?"

"Rafe says that if he gets too much milk, he'll start an ice cream company." I took another bite of a tiny sandwich and sighed happily. Honestly, between my friends and good food, I could feel my worries draining away. For now.

"My hero," Lizzie said with a sigh.

In fact, there were sighs heard all around the table. I wasn't sure if they were meant for Rafe's beautiful eyes or his idea of starting an ice cream company. But I had a feeling.

"That was my very thought," I said, laughing. "The man is a hero." Then I turned to Marigold. "I don't blame you if you don't trust my opinion on the subject. What if I ask Mac to come over and vouch for him? He believes in Rafe completely and Mac is no pushover. He's a hard-nosed, cynical Navy SEAL who's dealt with the absolute worst dregs of humanity in his career." I wasn't sure Mac would appreciate that particular description of himself, but I hoped he would consider the circumstances.

"That's a great idea, Shannon," Lizzie said. "Marigold, would you like to talk to Mac about it?"

She made a waving motion with her hand. "I don't want to bother him about something so trivial."

"Your future is hardly trivial," Jane insisted.

"Mac cares about you, Marigold," I said. "He cares about all of you. This town is his home and he loves it here, and he considers you all his friends. He would never allow someone to hurt any of us."

Jane sniffled and I knew I'd breached her soft heart with my words about Mac. But I kept my gaze on Marigold. "If you don't mind, I'll ask him to stop by your shop later this afternoon or maybe tomorrow. Is that all right?"

"Well, if it's not out of his way."

Emily chuckled. "It's not out of his way."

Lizzie laughed then, and finally Marigold smiled. "All right. Thank you."

"And really," I added as an afterthought, "Rafe might find that he hates having cows around. They don't smell wonderful, for one thing. He might get rid of them despite the ice cream dreams."

"That's possible, too," Marigold mused.

Jane leaned forward. "Okay, we've heard about the farmhouse and the wind turbines and the possible ice-cream-giving cows, so now tell us all about Rafe."

"He's just adorable," I said, smiling broadly. "Tall, dark, and handsome. And genius smart. I couldn't understand half of what he said, but I enjoyed hearing him say it."

As the others chatted about everything, Marigold reached over and grabbed my hand. "Thank you."

I squeezed hers back. "The fact that Mac and I like him doesn't mean you have to run off and marry him. We just want you to be happy, whatever you decide to do."

"I know, and I appreciate it so much." She gazed around the table, her eyes glistening. "I'm so lucky to have such good friends in my life."

"We're all lucky," I said, and reached for a mini cream puff topped with hot fudge, just to prove it.

"I'm back," I said as I walked into the Jorgensens' dining room. "How's it going?"

"I've been dying for you to get back," Amanda whispered.

"Why?" I asked, alarmed. "What happened?"

"Oh, nothing important," she murmured. "It's just that Matthew is home. I still haven't seen Petsy yet."

"Well, then, everything is perfect." I almost rubbed my hands together eagerly, but I thought that might be a little over the top.

She grinned. "I was thinking the same thing."

"Did he stop in here and talk to you?" I asked.

She shrugged. "He just said a quick hello and mentioned that he would stop by later to chat."

"I guess we'll have to be satisfied with that."

"I guess."

"I really want to get up there today," I said, staring at the ceiling as though I could see through to the attic.

"Me, too. The wait is killing me."

"Oh, that reminds me," I said, pulling a small box from my bag. "I met my friend Emily at her tea shop, so I brought you a couple of pastries."

"Oh, I've been in there," she said. "It's charming. So you know the owner?"

"Yes, the Scottish woman."

"She's been so sweet to me."

I smiled. "I'll bring you along next time and introduce you."

She blinked twice and I worried that she might start

to cry. "Shannon, that's so nice of you. I don't know what to say. I've only known you a few days but you've already been such a good friend to me."

I shrugged, a little embarrassed by her glowing words. "I just figure that if you're going to live here, you'll want to meet some nice people."

"I've met a few, but believe me, I can use all the friends I can get. So thank you again."

"You're very welcome." I wanted to add that I already considered her a friend, too. So what held me back? Was I still suspicious? Did I really think Amanda could've killed Joe Scully? I thought about it and realized the answer was no.

She took a bite of the mini napoleon pastry and moaned. "Oh my God. This is fantastic."

I grinned. "Yeah, Emily knows what she's doing."

"She's a goddess. Thank you for thinking of me." She held up her hand. "I need a moment of silence."

I laughed, but stopped immediately when we heard footsteps on the staircase. "Do you think that's Matthew?"

"I don't know."

"Are you ready for this?"

"Absolutely." But she was taking deep breaths, clearly not as calm and collected as she wanted to be. But neither was I.

Seconds later, Matthew walked into the room. "How are you ladies doing today?"

"Couldn't be better," I said with a smile.

Amanda had to swallow the pastry before she could reply. "Just great. How are you, Matthew?"

"I'm super."

"You were gone all morning," she said, with concern in her voice. "Is everything all right?"

"Everything is fantastic. I spent the morning at an art gallery showing and sold two paintings. Oh, and I received a commission to do a third."

"Wow, that's wonderful."

"It's pretty darn great," he said, nodding. "So, since I'm too wound up to work this afternoon, I thought I would invite you both on a tour of my studio."

"I would love to visit your studio," I said. "Amanda?"

"Absolutely. I've been dying to see your work."

"Well, then," he said jovially, "I'll lead the way."

As we followed him across the foyer to the staircase, I said, "Your house is so beautiful. Would you mind if I ask questions as we go?"

"Not a bit."

Glancing up, I said, "Your coffered ceiling is gorgeous. Did the same person design the entire house or have you had more work done over the years?"

"The overall design and decorative elements are the work of the original owner. But of course we've updated the bathrooms and kitchen and expanded a few closets, that sort of thing."

"Well, the overall design is just stunning."

"Thank you," he said, turning to smile at me. "I agree, although Petsy would love to trash most of it."

I was taken aback by his words, although I shouldn't have been surprised, given Petsy's antagonistic nature. But still, who wouldn't want to live in this incredible home?

"Would you say she has more of a modern sensibility?" I asked, searching for ways to sound neutral when it came to discussing his evil wife.

"No, she likes the classic style well enough," Matthew said. "Maybe it's just this house that she has a problem with. She calls it a dusty old mausoleum." He chuckled. "I suppose we do have a little dust, and yes, maybe it's old. But I love it."

"I do, too," I said fiercely. "I specialize in Victorian home construction and restoration and yours is one of the most elegant examples of the period that I've ever seen." I ran my hand along the wall as we climbed the stairs. "These panels are spectacular. Oh, that reminds me. Do you still want us to stain this faded panel? I'm sorry it slipped my mind with everything that's been going on lately."

"We have had a few busy days around here," he said lightly. "It's no wonder we've all forgotten this and that. But yes, I would love to have it fixed whenever you can get around to it."

"I'll work on it tomorrow," Amanda said.

She and I exchanged a look and I made a mental note to arrange time to shop for stains. I thought we might again broach the subject of purchasing some sort of a shade for the window that was responsible for the fading.

We continued climbing up to the third floor. On the way, Matthew pointed out several landscape paintings that one ancestor or another had purchased over the years. As we passed the second floor I glanced down the hallway where the portrait of the Regency woman hung. I looked at Amanda and wondered if she was thinking of the face of that beautiful woman displayed on the canvas. It was too bad that woman couldn't talk to us and tell us her story. Maybe then we wouldn't have to go to such lengths as sneaking DNA-encrusted hair roots out of the house.

On the third floor, the staircase opened onto the massive studio. I took a few steps into the room and gazed around. Everywhere I looked, there was something to admire or to surprise us. As Matthew had promised, the light was indeed wonderful. At the far end of the room, four steps led up to the round tower room, with its circle of bay windows. Several easels were set up in that area, probably to catch as much light as possible.

"This is . . . amazing," Amanda murmured as she turned around to take it all in.

"It's a beautiful room," I said.

Along one long wall were shelves that held hundreds of books on all kinds of art and architecture, on perspective and home design and portraiture. In and among the books were oddities. A miniature model of the Eiffel Tower, the bleached skull of a horse, a clear box filled with starfish. All types of dried flowers were hung in bundles from the rafters. There was a peculiarly shaped vase that held wooden spoons. A life-sized model of a hula dancer stood in one corner, her grass skirt fluttering in the breeze coming from an open window. It was such an incongruous sight in the midst of all this artistry that it made me laugh. Matthew seemed happy with my reaction.

One round table in the middle of the room held jars of paintbrushes. A large square pot held several dozen twisted tubes of oil paint in every color. Cans and bottles held more brushes and tools of all kinds. Small palettes were stacked neatly in an old woven basket.

Around the edges of the room were a number of easels with canvases of different sizes. Some were finished paintings and some appeared to be works in progress. And from where I stood, they all looked stunning.

Matthew Jorgensen was a master artist. I wasn't sure why the realization surprised me. Maybe because he was such a genial man that I didn't expect to find such depth of talent. Or maybe because Petsy's personality was so stridently negative that I didn't believe any true genius or talent could survive and thrive in the same house.

As I walked around, I noticed that Matthew didn't seem to specialize in any one style of art, such as still life or portraiture. He did it all. There were landscapes and seascapes and desert rock formations. He painted eerie tree skeletons and colorful fields of flowers. There were several beautiful portraits of women and a few of men. Lindsey was featured in numerous works and it was clear from each of those depictions that he loved his daughter very much.

"You are so talented," Amanda said softly.

"It's a shocker, right?" Matthew laughed.

"Not at all," she said. "If my tone made it seem like I felt that way, it's just that I'm always a little awed when I'm surrounded by so much talent and beauty."

I was surprised. She sounded so formal, all of a sudden.

But Matthew beamed. "That's very sweet of you to say."

She continued walking slowly around the room until she stopped at an elongated dancing figure standing on a pedestal. "What's this? Did you sculpt this? It's beautiful."

"I did. Thanks." He shoved his hands into his pockets

and moved toward the pedestal. "I like working in clay and wood, but I don't get the chance very often. Unfortunately I'm always painting." With a grin, he added, "Although it's really not unfortunate at all, is it?"

"No, it's a very good thing," I said, secretly dismayed to see a work of sculpture that he'd done. That meant he had sculpting tools, such as a chisel, hiding here someplace. I loved uncovering new clues, but hated the possibility that Matthew might be a killer.

Matthew chuckled. "Well, it certainly pays the bills."

"I'm glad." I moved around the room, taking it all in. "You've got so much light pouring in. No wonder you love it up here."

"That's what it's all about for me," he said.

I stared out of the bay window on the west side of the room. "Your view is sensational."

"You should see the view from the widow's walk," he said, pointing toward the tower room. "I wanted to connect this space to the tower because it's got doors that lead out to the roof."

He crossed the room and we followed him up the steps to the tower room. A set of French doors led right out onto the widow's walk and I stared out the windows at the rectangular space. The flat surface was about twenty feet long by ten feet wide, surrounded by a clean white railing. Two white Adirondack chairs sat in the center of the platform, facing the ocean. It was incredibly charming and one of the picturesque elements that made this house such a classic Victorian.

He smiled dreamily. "I sit out there once in a while and paint the coastline. We can walk out there if you'd like."

"I would love to see it," Amanda said.

"I would, too," I said, but glanced around nervously. "And I really want to spend more time in your studio. But would you mind if I used the bathroom first?"

"Not at all. I've got a little one to the left of the door. Or you can run down to the second floor and use the bigger one. If you turn left, it's the second door on your right."

"If you don't mind, I'll go downstairs. Thanks. I'll be right back." I gave a quick glance at Amanda, who nodded, and then I took off. I figured I would have a better chance of finding hairbrushes if I used the larger bathroom on the same floor as everyone's bedrooms.

I found the bathroom, walked in, and locked the door. Only then did I realize there was a second door, leading to another room. I locked that one, too, and began to search. It took me only a few seconds to find someone's hairbrush. I was a little disappointed to discover that this was Lindsey's bathroom—the strands of hair left in the brush were long and blond. Would it be useful to test hers as well as her parents' hair? Maybe but I was still more interested in finding the brushes that belonged to Matthew and Petsy.

Did I dare venture farther down the hall? Petsy was still not home and I hadn't seen or heard Lindsey since I got back from lunch. Was she home? Was I crazy? Maybe, but I had to take the chance and look while the time was right. Besides, I wasn't worried about Lindsey finding me. Petsy was another issue altogether. There was no way I wanted her to find me down here. Even so, I figured I had a few minutes' leeway to do a quick search.

I left the bathroom and walked quickly down the hall. I opened the third door on the opposite side of the hall and glanced inside. It was very obviously a lady's bedroom, with a huge bed and a very puffy comforter, with pillows of every size and shape. It had to be Petsy's bedroom. I wondered where Matthew slept, because I had no doubt that they did not sleep together in the same bedroom. As a couple, they just didn't have that . . . connection. The one that said to the world that these two people were close. A unit.

I stepped inside the room, closed the door behind me, and then scurried over to the door most likely leading to the bathroom. Instead it was a large walk-in closet, so I opened the other door, noting that so far, no two doorknobs I'd tried were the same. That gave me a thrill, although I acknowledged that I shouldn't have been wasting time admiring doorknobs. But these were so special, made of an anodized copper, and each had a different curlicue pattern on the surface. That was another Victorian detail that would've delighted me even more if I weren't currently on a covert mission to find discarded strands of hair.

I tried the door and found the bathroom. It was all pinks and purples—and not in a soft, pretty way. No, this room was loud and gaudy, with outlandishly girlie froufrous everywhere.

On the built-in vanity there were several dozen brands of moisturizers and lotions and potions mixed in with sprays and tubes and jars of perfumes and balms and crèmes. On the wall, there were paintings that depicted nursery rhymes, of all things. Little Bo Peep and her sheep. Little Miss Muffet and her tuffet. The childish paintings were so far removed from my imaginary picture of Petsy's style that I started to laugh. To each her own, I supposed.

I quickly sobered and began opening drawers in the cabinets beneath the sink counter. Nothing was orderly; everything was a jumble. Again, not what I'd imagined I'd find in Petsy's rooms.

Finally I found an old cracked hairbrush with plenty of dark strands still attached. I grabbed as many as I could, all the while wishing I had thought to bring gloves with me. Because yuck. This was Petsy's old hair.

I quickly stuffed the hairs into the small Baggie and then took another moment to glance around. In the pink trash can under the sink I saw used tissues. I grimaced, but I knew it would be smart to gather up whatever I could find that might contain enough DNA to run the tests for Amanda.

I used the inside of the Baggie itself to grab a few tissues and quickly tucked them inside. I zipped the bag shut, shoved it in my back pocket, and tiptoed to the door leading back to the bedroom. Glancing out, I saw nobody standing around, waiting to arrest me, so I sneaked across the bedroom and back into the hallway.

I had made it as far as Lindsey's bathroom door when I heard footsteps on the stairs. Someone was walking upstairs from the first floor. I wanted to run in the opposite direction, but instead I took a deep breath and tried to hold on to my cool and calm attitude. And keep walking. A moment later, the person stepped onto the hallway carpet.

Naturally it was Petsy. She couldn't have given me fifteen extra seconds to escape this confrontation? Of course not.

I had obviously startled her, because she stopped abruptly. "What do you think you're doing here?"

"Hi, Petsy," I said oh so casually. "I was upstairs in Matthew's studio and had to use the bathroom. He suggested I use the one down here, so I did. And now I'm going back upstairs for a few more minutes."

"This is ridiculous," she cried, genuinely outraged. "Why aren't you working? I'm losing money by the minute."

"I appreciate your concerns, but you're not actually paying my crew by the minute, or even the hour." I smiled gently as I spoke, as if I were afraid of upsetting her too badly. Which I wasn't, of course. "You're paying us for the entire job. And believe me, you're getting more than your money's worth. Now, if you'll excuse me." I breezed past her and headed for the staircase.

She harrumphed. "You are the rudest—"

That was enough. I turned back to her. "I beg your pardon?"

"Never mind," she griped. "Just go. And don't let me catch you up here again."

I felt my temper rising and knew I had to stand my ground or forever walk around with my tail between my legs. Besides, what could she do to me? At the very worst, she could search me, but all she would find was a bag of hair and tissues.

And if she tried to search me, I swore I would tell the world about Little Miss Muffet.

"You didn't *catch* me up here, Petsy," I said evenly. "I was simply using the bathroom."

And before I started shaking, I turned and walked away. I could hear her sputtering and I felt her eyes following me. But she didn't say another word, and by the time I reached Matthew's studio on the third floor, I was sagging with relief. I wasn't sure why. Again, what was the worst that could have happened? I suppose Petsy could have fired us, but that really would not have been the worst thing. In fact, Wade would be delighted if we got fired from this job.

No, it was just Petsy herself that freaked me out. The way she thrived on cutting a person down and making them feel like less than a human being. I had no idea why she thought she had to behave that way, but I knew I could hate her forever because of it.

Chapter Nine

I returned to the third-floor studio and spent another half hour with Matthew and Amanda. I did a casual perusal of the table where all of Matthew's tools were stored in odd cans and jars. There had to be a dozen different chisels of varying sizes and shapes, along with other tools of the trade. We ventured out to the widow's walk and admired the amazing view. And we talked about painting and other arts. I enjoyed listening to Matthew talk about everything.

When I asked if Lindsey painted, too, he chuckled fondly. "My daughter loves to paint, but readily admits that she's not very good. But she's fantastic at *selling* art, so that makes up for it as far as I'm concerned. Believe me, that is an art in itself."

"Does Petsy have an artistic bent as well?" I asked casually. I didn't want to pry, but . . . Oh, who was I kidding? I wanted to know every possible detail about the Jorgensens.

"She used to," Matthew said. "Back in school, she

was very interested in her art and drama classes, but as the years went by, she lost interest. You know how it is. You grow up and get distracted by other things. Money, status, all those things that make the world go round." He said it tongue in cheek, but I could tell this was a painful subject for him.

"You two went to school together?" Amanda asked.

"We did," he said, a soft smile on his face. "I fell in love with her the first time I saw her walk into my third-grade class." His gaze drifted off as his mind seemed to wander back to those old days. "I know she might seem a little harsh sometimes, but she was a beautiful little girl and she grew up to be a lovely young woman."

A little harsh? Was he kidding? The woman could give piranhas lessons in aggression. But maybe he wasn't kidding, since he sounded very much like a man who was still in love with his wife.

"She's still beautiful," Amanda said kindly.

"Yes, she is," he agreed, then added quietly, "Although you can't always see it when she goes on one of her tirades."

"She does seem a bit . . ."

His eyebrows rose. "Cranky?"

"I was going to say *overly concerned*," I said, although it was a lie. I just wanted to keep him talking.

Matthew sighed. "I've learned to live with it. She's mild compared to her mother, though. That woman was always so petty, so wrapped up in appearances, it was like a sickness. Petsy tried to break free from that mindset, and she was doing pretty well for a while. We got married and we were happy, but then Lindsey was born and Petsy seemed to turn into her mother all over again.

I think the baby made her so nervous that she fell back on those negative attitudes and behaviors she grew up with."

"A baby changes everything," I murmured.

"Yes," he said. "So, you've obviously noticed that Petsy can be overly critical. Just like her mother, she's very concerned about superficial things like what someone's wearing or the way they speak. I try to ignore it, try to recall the girl I fell in love with, but . . ." He shrugged, then suddenly grinned. "What can you do?"

I was taken aback by his abrupt change of mood. It was understandable, though. He'd probably had enough of trash-talking his wife, so I didn't ask any more questions. We went back to the subject of art and painting and had a short but fun chat about our favorite artists.

None of us mentioned the painting Matthew had shown us the other day, of the woman who looked so much like Amanda. It was as if it was a forbidden topic and I wondered why. If we could just have an open, honest discussion about it with Matthew, we might be able to put an end to our great search for dirty old hairbrushes. But, then, I'd had so much fun, why would I want to stop?

Amanda and I left Matthew to his work and returned to the dining room to continue ours. She leaned in close so we could talk quietly. "That was interesting, wasn't it?"

"It was," I whispered. "I never thought I'd actually feel sorry for Petsy, but hearing Matthew talk about her made me a little sad."

"Me, too."

"And I wanted to bring up the adoption, but he was

going on and on about Petsy and I couldn't find the right moment to switch gears."

"I know," she said. "We can try to talk about it the next time he comes around."

"By the way, I found Petsy's bathroom and got a bunch of hair from her brush."

"Fantastic!" Amanda said.

"Yeah, but Petsy found me up there and she was really annoyed. So if you were thinking of snooping around this afternoon, you might want to wait until sometime tomorrow, when she's out of the house."

"Good idea. The last thing I want is a confrontation with her."

We went back to work, but a few minutes later, my phone rang. It was Carla, asking if I could run over to the Spaulding house to check on a problem with the new soffits above the kitchen cabinets.

"I'm not sure I'll make it back here before the end of the day," I said to Amanda. "Do you want to meet at my house after work to commiserate for a while?"

"Absolutely," she said. "I'll bring a bottle of wine."

I smiled. "Not necessary, but always appreciated."

The whole time I was gone, I worried that Amanda might try to sneak upstairs and hunt down Matthew Jorgensen's hairbrush. I'd warned her about my run-in with Petsy, but what if Amanda got a bee in her bonnet anyway? What if Petsy caught her in Matthew's bathroom? What if Petsy or Matthew called the police? What if Amanda confronted them both with the ever-growing probability that they were her parents?

My mother-hen analogy was at work again, making me anxious and distracted. I had to get back and find out if Amanda was all right. But as I drove home, I thought about the situation and finally came to my senses. I really had to let these worries go. Amanda was a grown-up, just like me. She had been making her own decisions for years. She was talented and savvy and knew what she was doing. If she couldn't handle a little hairbrush espionage, she shouldn't have signed on to the job.

And lest I forget, she had pulled a pretty slick number on me to get the Jorgensen job, so it was probably downright silly of me to worry about her now.

Still, I hovered over the speed limit most of the way home.

I spotted Amanda's red truck as soon as I turned onto my street. And in spite of all my best intentions to quit worrying, I breathed a sigh of relief seeing that truck parked outside my house. Fine. I admit it. I should start a chapter of Worriers Anonymous. *Hi. My name is Shannon. I'm worried.*

After parking my own truck in the driveway, I watched as Amanda jogged over to join me. I led the way through the gate and into the kitchen. Amanda played with Robbie while I poured us each a glass of wine and put together a little plate of cheese, crackers, olives, and almonds for munching purposes.

As soon as I sat down, she pounced. "So, tell me everything that happened. You found Petsy's bathroom. What did you do? And when did she catch you? I've been so nervous, just thinking about that confrontation. We didn't get much of a chance to talk."

"I know. I'm sorry I had to run out, but we can talk

now." I raised my wineglass. "But first, cheers. Let's drink to gathering hair for a good cause."

"Cheers," she said, laughing as I hoped she would. "But seriously? Ugh. What a horrible way to get answers."

We each took a sip of wine, and I said, "It was pretty gross. I kept wishing I'd remembered to bring rubber gloves."

"Next time, for sure."

"For sure." I told her the scary details about Petsy suddenly showing up while I was trying to escape the second floor.

"Didn't you almost die?" she asked, with a shudder and shake of her head. "I know I would've. She freaks me out."

"I did just about die," I admitted. "But then I got mad. She irritated me so much that I gave her an earful before finally walking away." I told her the gist of the conversation with Petsy. "I'm surprised she didn't fire me right then and there. Actually it would have been a relief to get out of doing any work for her. But I've thought about it and I'm afraid she's got something else in mind."

Amanda propped her elbows on the table. "What do you mean?"

"Doesn't she seem like the kind of person who would plot her revenge and strike when you least expect it?"

"Oh, absolutely. So what do you think she'll do?" She took an enthusiastic sip of wine and sat back to hear more drama. I was surprised she didn't clap her hands excitedly and I suddenly wondered if maybe I should've made popcorn. And really, how lucky was it that Amanda and I had hit it off so well? Bonding over a horrible woman.

Petsy. The woman made every story seem almost operatic in scope. She was the epitome of a drama queen. And rude to boot.

I knew that Petsy would be planning some kind of revenge for my wandering around her house unaccompanied. I just couldn't figure out what it might be, probably because I wasn't a psycho and couldn't read her crazy mind. I grimaced. "I don't know, but I know she's going to come after me in some way. I'll just have to watch my step around her and wait to find out what she does."

"I'm not sure I would've been as brave as you were. You handled her so well."

"I was brave on the outside, but my stomach still hurts when I think about it."

"But what you said to her was the truth," Amanda insisted. "You were just using the bathroom."

I laughed. "Both of us know that's not really true, but Petsy didn't need to know that."

"I owe you," Amanda said, shaking her head. "If I'd known you were going to take so much heat from Petsy, I'm not sure I would've let you do it."

"Don't worry about it," I said, reaching for an olive. "Anyone who comes into contact with Petsy has to know they'll take some kind of heat. But look on the bright side. We'll have a story to tell our grandchildren, and that's always worth it."

She was silent for a few seconds, then took a sip of wine. "Can I be honest?"

"Of course."

"Whenever I have to deal with Petsy, it makes me wonder all over again whether I really want to find out the truth or not."

"You mean, you might not want to discover that she's your actual birth mother?"

"Would you?" she countered, shuddering for effect again.

"Oh, no. Just thinking about that woman as a mother is enough to terrify me."

"Me, too," she said. "I almost can't believe what Matthew said, about how she used to be nicer, before Lindsey was born. I can't picture it, but I guess it's possible. Having a kid can freak some people out."

"And if she really is your birth mother, it means that she had to give up a child at some point. Maybe the combination of giving you up and then having another baby sent her right over the edge."

"I hadn't thought of that." Her shoulders slumped. "It's kind of an icky situation, isn't it?"

"Sorry, but yes, it's icky," I said. "Still, if it's true, it's not written in stone that you have to have a relationship with her."

"I know. But she would know and I would know, and it would be weird. You know?"

I chuckled. "I actually followed that reasoning."

"I'm glad someone did." She laughed lightly, then grabbed an olive and munched absently for a moment. "It would be nice if Matthew was my father and Lindsey was my sister."

"The three of you would make a lovely family," I said.

"I think so, too. Of course, Lindsey and I couldn't look like sisters if we tried." She gave me a wry smile and a shrug.

I stared at her face and nodded. "That's true. You two are like night and day. But at least she's a nice girl."

"It's the one part of the equation that I don't get. If the Jorgensens really are my parents, how did those two people give birth to both of us?"

I shrugged. "I have a sister who's blond, but we still look enough alike to be part of the same family. But you and Lindsey? Not so much. Anything's possible, though. Who knows what their parents and grandparents look like?"

"Good point." She sighed. "You know, if I find out she really is my sister, I'd want her to stay in Lighthouse Cove."

"You mean, not go back to San Francisco?" I thought about it. "I'm not sure you'll get your wish there."

"I'm not, either," she said, frowning.

We nibbled on nuts and cheese and sipped our wine for a moment; then Amanda sighed again. "Families can be so bizarre."

The tone of her voice made me wonder. "You're not second-guessing yourself again, are you?"

She glanced at me. "Do you mean, questioning whether I want to find my birth parents?"

"Yeah, because I've got a bag of hair in my pocket that says you need to have some faith in the process."

She laughed and then nodded resolutely. "No way am I changing my mind. I'm in this to the bitter end." She made a face. "And if Petsy turns out to be my mother, it'll *really* be bitter."

I smiled sympathetically and sipped my wine, hoping like heck that the bitter end wouldn't be *too* bitter. But knowing was better than not knowing, right?

It was almost dinnertime and I was heating up some of my homemade chicken vegetable soup when Jane called. "Shannon, you've got to get over here."

Normally Jane was cool and calm and about as dependable as the sunrise. At the moment, though, she sounded frantic. "I can tell you're upset. What's wrong?"

"Oh God, Shannon." Her voice dropped to a throaty whisper. "One of my guests is . . . She's dead."

I shook my head, unsure if I'd heard her correctly. "What? That can't be true. Who's dead?"

"Mrs. Samson," Jane said, sniffling between words. "The woman you met."

"What?" I couldn't believe it. She had been so full of life when I met her. "Did you call the police?"

"Yes. I spoke to Eric. He said they'd be here soon, but could you come over now?"

I turned the fire off under my soup. "Are you all right?"

"Not really. You always handle these things better than I do."

Well, of course I did, I thought. Because I had found, according to my friends, nine dead bodies. Sigh. "I'll be right there."

On the drive over, I considered Jane's statement that I always handled these things better than she did. It made me wonder all over again. What did it say about me that my friends thought I was comfortable around a dead body? It wasn't true! On the other hand, I reminded myself, my friends thought me a strong, capable woman. So that was good, right?

The fact that they kept track of the dead bodies should've been a clue that they might've been considering my proclivity for finding murder victims some kind of bizarre superpower. I knew they'd been teasing me at lunch, but still . . . I was getting a reputation. Pretty soon, nobody would want to be my friend, because everybody knew I seemed to attract trouble. Who wants to hang around someone like that?

I was thoroughly depressed when I pulled to the curb in front of the Hennessey Inn. Taking a few deep breaths, I mentally slapped myself to snap out of it and jumped down from the truck. I didn't see any black-and-white police cars around and I wondered where they were. I ran to the front door and walked inside and saw Jane immediately. I could see her fighting to maintain a calm exterior and knew it was for the sake of her other guests.

I gave her a quick hug. "What happened?"

"Oh God." Glancing around at the half dozen guests in her front parlor, she murmured, "Not here. Let's go to my room." She pulled me upstairs and into her suite, where she began to pace the floor.

"And where are the police?" I asked.

She shook her head. "Eric called again. There's a pileup out on the highway."

"Oh, that's terrible." But not unexpected. Tourists flocked to this part of California all year long, and some of them were so busy looking at the scenery, they weren't watching the road. Every local I knew drove their car so defensively, they were ready for anything.

"Tommy called after I spoke to Eric. He said they would get here as soon as they can. But meanwhile, Shannon, my guest is dead. It's so awful."

Okay, I had to calm Jane down enough so that I could get some information. If it was wrong of me to be a little glad that I'd beaten Eric here, well, no one else had to know that.

"Tell me what happened."

"You know how I installed those cute little televisions in each of the bathrooms so my guests can watch their favorite shows while taking a bubble bath?"

I smiled. "Jane, I helped you install them, remember?"

"Oh, that's right. I'm not thinking straight." She waved her hands in the air as if to change the energy. "So, anyway, apparently Loretta was taking a bath and somehow both the hair dryer and the TV fell into the water. I don't know how it happened. I guess she somehow yanked on the cords or they got caught on something, because both of them went tumbling in."

A TV *and* a hair dryer fell into a tub? What were the chances of that kind of accident happening? I was getting a bad feeling here. "How did you find out?"

"She had asked for some recipes from my chef, so I went up to give them to her. I knocked on the door and she didn't answer, but I hadn't seen her go out. I just knew she was in there. So I opened the door and called her name. There was no response so I walked in."

I winced. Now I understood why the usually unflappable Jane was, well . . . flapped. "And you found her."

Dismayed, Jane pressed her hands to her cheeks. "Shannon, she was electrocuted in the tub."

I had to stand up and take a few breaths myself.

Hearing about it was one thing. Hearing it from my friend while looking into her teary eyes was another. I could actually *feel* Jane's distress and share it. "That's just too horrible to contemplate. I'm so sorry."

But the more I thought about it, the more my construction site training kicked in and I realized something wasn't right about Jane's story.

"I'm so glad you're here," she said, looking exhausted as she leaned against the wall. "I just wish Eric would get here. I don't know what to do. I hate to leave her there in the bathtub. I mean, it's such an indignity."

I hesitated, then asked, "Do you mind if I take a quick look around?"

She stared at me. "You mean, you want to look around her bathroom?"

I knew it sounded ghoulish, but honestly, being able to check out a potential crime scene before Eric showed up was a big deal for me. Besides, I had helped build this place and I knew it from top to bottom. Maybe I could figure out what was bothering me and help out the police at the same time. "Yes, I do. Just for a minute. I'll be out of there before Eric shows up."

"Um, okay, I guess. I just feel bad that . . . well, she's dead. And, oh God. I mean, she's naked."

"I understand," I said gently. "I'm not going to be looking at her. But I took extra precautions when I installed that TV and I want to see how in the world it ended up in the tub."

And that was true. I remembered how extra careful we had been to tuck the TV into its own special place on the counter. At an early age, I had learned how potentially hazardous it was to have electrical appliances near a bathtub. But these days, things were different. Jane had actually tracked down waterproof TV sets that swiveled. I had suggested mounting them on the wall, but she thought having them on the counter would allow her guests to watch their favorite shows from wherever they happened to be in the bathroom.

"Okay, let's hurry," she said.

We scurried down the hall to the Ophelia suite. It spoke to Jane's romantic nature that she had named each of her rooms after Shakespeare's heroines. I had a grim thought that the Ophelia room was suddenly living up to its name.

Jane unlocked the door, walked in, and crossed the room. The bathroom door was open.

"Is this how you found it?" I asked, pointing toward the bathroom. "Was that door open?"

"Yes."

It might not mean anything, I thought. Some people probably didn't care. But if it were me, even if I were alone in my suite, I would close the bathroom door to take a bath. You never knew when housekeeping might walk right in to put a piece of chocolate on your pillow.

And then I remembered that Loretta Samson had been staying here with a man. Were they sharing this suite or did he have his own room? Either way, I had to wonder where he had gone off to.

I stepped into the luxurious bathroom and glanced around. It was impossible to avoid the sight of the dead woman in the beautifully restored claw-foot tub, but I tried, staring instead at the outlet where the television set was still plugged in. The hair dryer was plugged into a different outlet, closer to the tub.

Had she lost her balance and pulled at the cords?

Why would the hair dryer be plugged in so close to the bathtub? It wasn't as if she were going to blow-dry her hair *while* she was bathing. The more logical plug to use would have been the one closer to the mirror.

Shaking my head, I wondered if she'd planned to use the hot air to keep warm while she dried off. It was something I'd seen a friend do in college. I still thought it was a little weird, but maybe I was in the minority.

Water was puddled on the floor and the bath mat was damp. Had there been a struggle of some kind? Could the police get a footprint off of the rug? With that possibility in mind, I avoided stepping on it, then braced myself and took a look inside the tub.

There had been bubbles, but most had dissipated, with just a few remnants around the edge of the tub. Finally I couldn't help it. I looked at Loretta Samson. She lay on her back, her face just beneath the surface of the water. Her long, wavy hair floated on top of the water, creating an eerie, undulating halo effect. She was still lovely, even in death. I recalled our conversation and how much I'd liked her. There was rarely a good way to die, but this was definitely a bad way.

The hair dryer cord was wrapped loosely around her neck. Had it been used to strangle her? *What an odd choice*, I thought. The TV lay upside down and cockeyed by her knees.

Two electrical appliances in the water? And yet she probably died of strangulation. I stared at the unnerving scenario for a few more seconds, then murmured, "Let's go."

Jane breathed a sigh of relief beside me.

I followed her out of the bathroom and across the small living room, but stopped when I noticed a woman's purse on the chair and what looked like an appointment book on the end table. "Jane, wait."

Using the tweezers I always carried, I gingerly opened the book to today's date. There were no afternoon or evening appointments listed. Just two big dollar signs. Was she planning to receive a check from someone today? Was there some deal in the works? Was she buying or selling property? Was she stealing government secrets?

My imagination was flying free and I had to shake it off before I went nuts.

"We need to get out of here," Jane whispered.

"Right." I carefully closed the book and followed her out. "I'll meet you back in your room," I said. "I want to check to see if the circuit breakers were tripped."

"I'll make us some tea."

"Sounds good." I jogged downstairs and into the kitchen, where the main electrical box was kept. Even though the bathroom plugs were equipped with ground fault circuit interrupters, or GFCIs, I was still concerned that someone might have deliberately tripped a breaker in order to electrocute Loretta Samson. But everything looked hunky-dory—no breakers had been tripped—so I closed the box and ran back up to Jane's suite.

She had made us each a cup of tea and pulled out a few cookies to snack on. My stomach growled and I realized I was hungry. I thought longingly of the pot of homemade soup sitting on my stove. Cookies would have to suffice for now.

"Tell me more about Loretta Samson," I said.

"You saw how nice she was," Jane said. "Very friendly. And don't you think she's gorgeous?"

"She's beautiful."

Jane sighed. "Curvy, with big blue eyes and the sort of dark, wavy hair that you just wash and wear, you know? Sort of like yours."

"I don't wash and wear mine," I said ruefully. "It takes me an hour to dry it enough to barely manage it."

"Oh, but you know what I mean. I think all those curls are so sexy. Anyway, she's really smart, too. She might be some sort of high-powered businesswoman. She dresses beautifully."

I knew Jane didn't realize she was describing the woman in the present tense, but I wasn't going to mention it. She was upset enough as it was.

"You don't know what she does for a living?"

"No, I never asked and she never told me."

"You said she was here with a boyfriend. Were they sharing the room?"

"No. They had separate rooms, but they were traveling together. His name is Mr. Winesap. He's very attractive." She blinked. "Oh, we saw him downstairs at the bar the other day. Do you remember?"

"I do. Wasn't he sitting with another man?"

"That's right. He was sitting with Mr. Greenfield, another guest. Mr. Winesap is here for the first time, staying in the Juliet room."

"But Loretta has been here before?"

"That's right." Jane smiled. "She stayed here once before with another man, but they must've broken up, because Mr. Winesap is new."

"How long has it been since she was here?"

She considered. "It was about this time last year."

"Did Loretta and the two men all travel here together?"

"Oh, no. Loretta and Mr. Winesap arrived together." Jane closed her eyes and thought for a second. "Mr. Greenfield's by himself. I think Mr. Winesap and Mr. Greenfield just happened to be at the bar at the same time the other afternoon."

This was why Jane was such a great innkeeper. She remembered her guests and made it a point to learn everything she could about them without prying.

"Was Loretta here as a tourist?" I asked. "Or did she come on business?"

Jane frowned as she thought about that. "It's hard to say. Both times she's been here, she's only stayed for three days. And she books one of the larger suites because, she told me, she planned to have meetings in her room." She glanced at me. "That sounds like she was here on business."

"Do you know who she meets with?"

She shook her head. "I've never seen anyone go up to her room."

"What about that other woman she was with the day I came looking for Joe Scully?"

"Oh." Jane looked puzzled. "I forgot about her. They seemed like friends, not business acquaintances. Anyway, I don't know if she went up to the room or not. Sorry, Shannon."

"That's okay," I said. "I was just wondering. Does Mr. Winesap stay for the meetings?"

"No, he's here as more of a tourist. He dresses very casually and leaves every morning to go out and see the sights."

"Do you know where he is right now?"

"I have no idea." She grimaced. "It's going to be a terrible shock when he gets back." She gasped. "Oh God, *shock*. I shouldn't have said that. Oh, this is awful."

"Yes, it's awful," I said. "But Loretta didn't die of electrical shock."

"But the hair dryer—"

"It was used to strangle her."

Jane seemed to gasp for air. "Oh my God. How do you know these things?"

"I put GFCI outlets in all the bathrooms to prevent that very thing. And both the TV and the hair dryer have trip switches. Neither of them would've killed her if they fell into the water."

She brushed her hair back, clearly exhausted by the ordeal of finding the dead body. "I don't know how I'll ever explain all that to Mr. Winesap."

"You don't have to explain anything," I said gently. "That's Eric's job."

"That's another reason why I wish he would show up."

I was wishing Winesap would show up, too. I checked my watch. It was past dinnertime. Maybe the man had come back earlier and murdered his girlfriend. He could have been long gone by now.

"Let's go downstairs and wait for Chief Jensen," I suggested. The sooner Chief Jensen arrived, I thought, the sooner the cops could track down the mysterious Mr. Winesap.

*   *   *

Chief Jensen and Tommy arrived ten minutes later and went to work in Loretta Samson's suite. I stayed around a while to make sure Jane would be all right. It was going to be a long night at the Hennessey Inn, but with both men working the scene, along with several uniformed officers and Leo the crime-scene investigator, I knew she didn't need me sticking around any longer. And I wouldn't have to worry about Jane, because Eric would take care of her.

As I drove home, I thought about everything I'd seen in Loretta Samson's room, and knew that something felt wrong. I replayed the entire scene in my head, but couldn't figure out what I was missing. I had a sinking feeling that it would keep me awake that night.

I paid bills, reviewed schedules, and took care of other work stuff all weekend. Then, early Monday morning, I walked over to the Cozy Cove Diner on the town square to meet my dad and Uncle Pete for breakfast. We usually met on Saturday mornings, but the guys had had a business matter to attend to. I wondered if it'd had something to do with the boat Dad had been eyeing the last time I saw him.

"Hi, Shannon," the waitress at the front counter said when I walked in. She held up a coffeepot. "Coffee?"

"Definitely. Thanks, Cindy." I would need the whole pot to get me awake after spending most of the night tossing and turning. Seeing a dead body in a bathtub could do that to you.

"Shannon," Dad called. "Over here."

I walked over to the booth by the front window and

gave Uncle Pete a hug. Dad moved over so I could slide into the booth and he wrapped his arm around my shoulders and squeezed.

"Hi, Dad," I murmured.

"Hi, honey. You working today?"

"We sure are. We're over on Cranberry Circle, at the Jorgensen house. They want an orangery installed in their side yard and we're redoing some of the wainscoting in the dining room."

"Busy girl." Dad gave my hair a playful tug. "What else is going on?"

I carefully avoided any mention of dead bodies and instead chatted about the Spaulding renovation and the Derrys' dry rot. I mentioned that Carla and two of the guys were working on Emily's tower roof today and that we had several other jobs around town. He asked a few questions, as always, and we talked about the work in general. Even though he was retired, he liked to keep up with the company news.

"So, are you two official yet?" I asked, smiling. "Did you buy the boat?"

Uncle Pete looked up from his paper and grinned. "Pulled the trigger yesterday afternoon."

"All right! Congratulations!"

Cindy walked over right then and poured me a cup of coffee. She took our orders and strolled back to the front counter.

I held up my coffee mug. "Here's to the new yachtsmen."

Dad snorted. "Hardly a yacht. But she's a beauty."

"Do I call you Skipper now?"

"You can call me Captain." He glanced at Uncle Pete. "He's the Admiral."

"Impressive," I said with a laugh.

"Hey, I won the bet," Uncle Pete said with a shrug.

Dad rolled his eyes. "It means I do all the work. He drinks beer and snoozes in the sun."

"Nice gig."

Uncle Pete winked at me, then continued reading the paper as Dad and I chatted.

"I heard about Scully," Dad said. "Can't believe it."

I knew why he hadn't said something about it right away. He was letting me settle in and relax by talking about the ordinary. My guys. Our jobs. His new boat. Now that he'd given me time, he was easing me into the subject. That was my dad. Was it any wonder I was nuts about him?

"I can't believe it, either," I said. "He was a big jerk, but he didn't deserve to die like that."

"He always was an irritation," Dad grumbled. "Like a splinter of wood under your thumbnail. Painful and always in the way."

That pretty much summed up the man.

"Was he bugging you about anything specific?"

"Yeah. In fact, I tried to call you about it last week, but you were away."

He winced as if regretting not getting back to me, but it was too late now. "I got your message but I figured we'd see you today, so I decided to wait."

"That's okay. I called to ask if something happened between you two that made him hate me so much."

Dad sighed. "The easy answer is yes. I'm afraid you're taking the heat for what I did to him ten years ago."

Dad looked guilty, uncomfortable, and definitely uneasy. Oh, I so didn't like to see that.

"What did you do?"

He took a sip of coffee, then sat back in the booth. "I got him fired."

"You're kidding." I almost smiled at the thought. "You did something I've dreamed of doing forever. What happened?"

Dad's warm brown eyes narrowed in remembered outrage. "He accepted a bribe from a competitor and I busted him. Sherman fired him, but then he got reinstated when Sherman died."

Sherman Sweet had been the head of the building department. His name said it all. He was the sweetest old guy I'd ever met. It was a real shame when he passed away and Scully took over.

Frankly, I often wondered why the mayor put up with him. It wasn't as if Scully had been elected. And there had to have been hundreds of complaints about the man over the years. Why not just fire him and hire someone else? Heck. *Anyone* else.

"I always wondered if it was my imagination." I shook my head. "I guess he really was out to get me. But you know, that somehow makes me feel better. At least I know there was nothing I could have done to win him over—not that I ever tried."

"Sorry about that, honey," Dad said. "I hate that he took his bitterness toward me out on you. But Scully had a lot of enemies and it looks to me like someone finally had enough."

"Yeah. Well, he started coming around every day at the Jorgensens'. Mrs. Jorgensen called the mayor to complain, but Scully still came around. And then he had the nerve to show up at Jane's place and throw his weight around. I know he did it just because he knew I was the contractor."

"He was a toad, rest his soul."

I nodded. "Jane called me about it and I raced over there, but he was already gone. And then the next day, he was, well, *really* gone."

"Why was he at Jane's place?"

"I told you we're renovating her old garage, right? Well, I pulled the permits for that job a while ago and Scully decided he'd show up and check things out. We haven't even started that job yet, but that didn't stop Scully. He just did it to rile me."

"He wasn't just a jerk," Dad grumbled. "He was an incompetent jerk."

We drank our coffee in silence for a moment until Uncle Pete began folding the newspaper. "Did you see this story?"

Dad set down his coffee mug. "Which one?"

Pete handed the paper to Dad. I could see the full-color picture accompanying the story. It was a photograph of Loretta Samson when she was alive.

Dad stared at the photograph. "She looks familiar." He began to read the article.

"Sure, she does. It's Loretta Beeman," Uncle Pete said. "Don't you remember her?"

Dad glanced more closely at the photo. "Oh, yeah. Loretta. She's still a beauty. Or she was. Sorry. It's been so long, I almost didn't recognize her. Didn't you date her, Pete?"

Dad knew Loretta? Uncle Pete had dated her? How was that even possible?

"I sure did," Pete boasted. "She was a pistol."

"Wait," I said. "When did you date her?"

"Oh, years ago," Pete said. "You were just a baby."

"The newspaper is calling her Loretta Samson," Dad said. "She must've remarried." Dad gave me a sideways glance. "Says here, she died just last night. And she was staying at Jane's inn."

I nodded. "It's true. Jane called me. She was so distressed about finding the body, she asked me to keep her company."

Dad dragged one hand through his hair, clearly frustrated. "Honey, I don't like you being in the thick of all these deaths."

"Believe me, neither do I. And I don't do it on purpose, Dad," I argued. "Jane was really upset, so I stayed with her until the police arrived."

"So you didn't see the body," Dad said.

I avoided looking at him and instead glanced down at the paper for a moment, and then gazed toward the counter. Where was my order of French toast and bacon? I really needed a distraction right about now.

"Shannon," Dad said sternly, "you saw the body? I don't get it. Why can't you leave this stuff up to the police? You found Scully's body, too. Honey, I'm worried about you."

"We should cancel our trip," Uncle Pete said immediately. "Stick close to town until things blow over."

"No way," I insisted. I wanted these two to go ahead and live their lives and enjoy themselves without worrying about me. Besides, if they did stick around, they'd stick to *me* like glue and maybe they'd end up in danger. I couldn't risk it. "You're both going fishing. You don't have to worry about me. This is just some weird coincidence. The death at Jane's inn had nothing to do with Scully's murder."

And yet, Scully had been there the other day and had seen Loretta Samson. And right after that he went tearing out of the place. What was the connection? I chewed on my lower lip until I realized that my dad was watching my every move.

"Here we go," Cindy said, carrying three plates on one arm with the ease of a circus juggler.

I breathed a monumental sigh of relief. "Yay, food."

Cindy set our plates down and started to walk away, but stopped and turned back. She stared at Uncle Pete's newspaper, still folded to show Loretta's picture. "Hey, she looks familiar."

"You've seen her before?" I asked.

"Sure. She's been coming in here once a year for as long as I can remember." She read the headline and frowned. "Oh no. That's a shame. Poor woman. She was always so friendly. That's too bad." She glanced around the table and her smile returned. "Well, you all enjoy your breakfast. I'll bring coffee around in a minute."

"Thanks, Cindy," Dad said.

We all began to eat and stopped talking for several blessed minutes, thank goodness. It gave me a chance to think. Loretta Samson had been coming here for years, Cindy said. The last two years she'd booked a room at Jane's inn. I wondered where she'd stayed before that. Probably didn't matter. I wondered what she did while she was here, besides walk to the pier. Did she have friends in town? Or business? I took a sip of coffee and then brought up the subject again.

"So, Uncle Pete, you said you dated Loretta. How did you know her? Did she once live here?" Frankly, I was dying of curiosity. My father and uncle had both known the dead woman, and yet Jane had been under the impression that Loretta had only visited Lighthouse Cove twice in the last two years.

Uncle Pete glanced at Dad as if he might be seeking his permission to speak. Dad rolled his eyes. "Might as well tell her. She won't stop bugging you until she knows all the answers."

I laughed. "I'm not that bad. Just curious. This woman was a regular visitor in town and she ends up dying last night. And this morning I find out that you both knew her. It's intriguing, don't you think?"

"She was an interesting woman," Uncle Pete said.

"Pete knew her better than I did," Dad confessed. "I was a happily married man at the time, but he was footloose and fancy-free."

"And Loretta was a beautiful woman," Pete said, sounding a little misty at the memory. "Smart, too. She had a way with money. Always working a deal."

I frowned. "What did she do for a living?"

"She was a housekeeper back when I knew her."

"A housekeeper? But she was always working a deal? Did she make money on the side?"

"Not much. Believe it or not," Uncle Pete said, "back then, housekeeping was a decent middle-class job."

"That's true," Dad said with a sly grin. "I should know. After all, I was just a construction worker, but I did okay."

I almost laughed. My father had made a boatload of

money building and renovating the houses of the rich and powerful. But if you asked some people around town who didn't know better, they might say he was just a working-class guy living on social security.

Funny thing was, Dad would probably agree.

Uncle Pete sat back with his coffee in his hand. "Loretta grew up here."

"She did?"

"Yeah. Gosh, she was a pretty gal. Remember, Jack?"

"I remember," Dad said. "Didn't she end up marrying what's his name?"

"Ernie," Pete murmured. "Can't think of his last name."

"It wasn't Samson," Dad said.

"Ernie?" I said. "Who's Ernie?"

"He worked for the Jorgensens," Uncle Pete said. "Did a little bit of everything. Chauffeur. Handyman. Gardener. Even did some cooking."

His words sank into my brain. "Wait. Wait. Wait. Did you say he worked at the Jorgensens' house?"

"Yeah. So did Loretta."

"Right. They worked together," Dad said, nodding. "I used to see Loretta when Matthew and I got together over at his house, which was pretty often. His parents had just died and the house had been bequeathed to him since he was the oldest son. We were great friends back then. Well, we still are friends, but I don't get a chance to see him too often."

"Unless there's a poker game," Pete said, grinning. "He likes to play poker."

"Did you know he's an artist?" Dad asked. "A good

one. We have one of his paintings in the hall, unless you moved it."

"The pasture scene?" I said. "With the horse?"

"Yeah." Dad nodded. "I always liked that picture."

"I do, too. It's still there." I had thought that Dad had one of Matthew's paintings but I couldn't believe it was the one hanging in my hallway. So, we owned a genuine Matthew Jorgensen painting. I couldn't wait to tell Amanda.

"When did Loretta leave town?" I asked. "And why? Did Ernie go with her?"

"I'm not sure." Uncle Pete scratched his ear. "Do you remember, Jack?"

"Ernie stayed here when she left," Dad said. "I remember thinking it was a shame their marriage didn't work out. Then Ernie died."

"Wasn't that just a few weeks after Loretta left?" Pete asked.

"Yeah. Tragic, really. He was so young. And Loretta never returned."

My head was reeling from all of this information. Loretta had worked for the Jorgensens. She'd married poor Ernie and then left town. But Dad was wrong. Loretta *did* return. At least twice. And ultimately she came home to die.

"So Loretta and Ernie got married," I prompted, "and then Loretta left town. Do you know why?"

"Nope."

I sighed and tried a different angle. "Did you know Ernie well?"

"Not as well as I knew Loretta," Pete said. "But he was a nice enough guy."

"And Loretta was the housekeeper?"

"Yeah," Pete said. "Anyway, she and Ernie got married and had a baby, and then all of a sudden she left town. Took the baby with her."

"Wait." I shook my head a little to make sure I was hearing correctly. "Loretta had a baby?"

"Yeah."

"And when she left, she took the baby with her? And then Ernie died after that?" I had to repeat everything because I couldn't quite believe what I was hearing.

"Yeah." Uncle Pete squinted, trying to think. "Didn't he fall from the roof?"

"That's right," Dad said. "He was up there repairing the chimney and he fell."

I felt my stomach tumble at that news. "He fell from the Jorgensens' roof?" I had been staring out at that very roof the day before. I shivered at the thought.

"Yup," Pete said. "Sad way to end your life."

"You can say that again," Dad muttered.

I couldn't agree more. "Did Ernie and Loretta live in the house with the Jorgensens?"

"Oh yeah. The third floor was the servants' quarters, and since it was just the two of them, they had the entire floor to themselves. Well, until the baby came along."

I frowned, trying to picture it, since I'd had a tour of that floor just yesterday. "The attic is Matthew's studio now."

Dad nodded. "I remember when they blew out the bedrooms and turned the whole space into one big studio. I bid on that job, but Greenwich underbid me."

"Who took care of the baby while Loretta and Ernie were working?"

Uncle Pete and Dad exchanged a glance; then Dad shrugged. "I don't know."

Too many pieces of the puzzle were falling into place, and I still had no clue what they all meant.

Pete tapped his finger on the photograph of Loretta. "Only one problem with this picture. Her hair is all wrong."

"What do you mean?" I asked. "She's a brunette."

"No," Pete said, grinning as he wiggled his eyebrows. "She had thick, wavy blond hair and she was a real looker. What we used to call a blond bombshell."

Chapter Ten

On my walk home after breakfast, I gave Mac a quick call and was relieved when he answered the phone. "I have so much to tell you."

"Why don't you come over? We can watch the waves and talk."

"I'd love to," I said. "I'll see you in about twenty minutes."

After I hung up, I called Amanda to let her know I would be coming to work late.

She chuckled. "You're the boss, you know. You can show up whenever you want to."

I laughed with her, but it faded quickly. I had so much on my mind, so much I wanted to say to her, but couldn't. "Please be careful. Don't do anything dangerous, okay?"

"Don't worry. I'm just going to sit in the dining room and carve pretty flowers and grapevines."

"Perfect. I'll see you later."

The winding drive to Mac's new home, otherwise

known as the lighthouse mansion, was downright nostalgic. My parents used to take us to the beach out here. Chloe and I would climb up the sandy dunes and use a folded newspaper to slide down the other side. Dad taught me how to skip a stone across the surface of the water. And of course, we used to love to climb up to the top of the beautiful old lighthouse. I never dreamed back then that I would be the one who refurbished the famous lighthouse mansion—for the equally famous thriller writer MacKintyre Sullivan.

Mac, holding two cups of coffee, greeted me on the wide front porch. "I thought we could sit out here for a while."

"That sounds so nice." We sat in the comfy patio chairs and I took a sip. Even though I'd had two cups at the diner, I was ready for one more, especially the rich, dark French roast that Mac always used.

"I hope I haven't interrupted any writing," I said.

"I'm just waiting for revision notes from my editor. So you actually interrupted me trying to reorganize my files."

"Ooh, good times." After another sip, I asked, "How do you like your new home?"

"It's fantastic. I love what you did in the master bedroom. And the kitchen is pure joy. Those French doors are beautiful."

I beamed with pleasure. "Just following orders."

"I think you've got a real future in the construction business, kiddo."

"Gosh, I hope so," I said, laughing. Taking another sip of rich coffee, I stared out at the horizon, marveling at how peaceful it was.

Mac studied my face for a moment. "You look worried. I know you wanted to talk. Something happen I don't know about yet?"

"You could say so." I proceeded to tell him everything I could remember of what my dad and Uncle Pete told me about Loretta Samson and her husband, Ernie, who died so tragically. I told him about the baby that Loretta took with her. And then I told him what happened last night at Jane's inn. How I saw Loretta lying dead in the bathtub.

"I read about that in the paper," he said softly. "I'm sorry. I was going to ask if you wanted to go see Jane and commiserate. But it sounds like maybe you took care of that last night."

Was it any wonder I liked Mac so much? I mean, he had slid into life in Lighthouse Cove as if he'd been born here. And he was generous and kind enough to know that both Jane and I could use a little commiseration time.

"I spent several hours with her last night, but I would love to go over there sometime today and see how she's doing."

"I'll go with you." But he was still frowning. "Are you all right?"

I took a few deep breaths. "You know, I guess I'm a little shaky. It's been a weird couple of days."

"I can't believe you went into a bathroom where a woman was dead in the water." He studied me for a long moment. "What were you hoping to find?"

"I'm not sure, really. But I installed those outlets and that TV, Mac. I had to get a look at the scene." I sipped my coffee. "I've worked on every room in that house, so I guess I thought I might be able to spot something out of place or jury-rigged. Something wrong or suspicious."

"You are one amazing woman."

I couldn't help but laugh. "You have very low standards."

"On the contrary," he said, smiling, "they are impossibly high, but you meet them in every way."

He met and exceeded all of my standards, too, so I knew how he felt. "Thank you."

He watched me for a moment. "So, it was pretty awful."

"I'd never seen a dead body in a bathtub," I murmured. "And now that I have, I wouldn't wish it on anyone."

"Of course not." He stood up and reached out, grabbing my hands and lifting me up and into his arms. He held me and I leaned into him, relishing the hard strength of his chest muscles. I was strong enough to take care of myself and do what needed doing, but I was also woman enough to enjoy having a strong man to lean on when I needed it. I was pretty sure I would've collapsed if he hadn't been holding on to me.

After a long while, I felt steadier. I leaned back. "Thanks. I needed that."

He smiled. "I did, too."

We stared out at the ocean for a moment; then Mac nudged me. "Let's go for a walk."

"Sounds wonderful."

We left our coffee mugs on the small table between the porch chairs. Holding hands, we walked down the steps and headed for the shoreline.

"So, Loretta Samson—or Beeman, if that's her real name—had a baby, and then she left town," Mac mused. "What does it mean?"

"I don't know. But then Ernie died tragically a few weeks later."

"Huh. He and his wife work for the Jorgensens. His wife and baby leave town and he dies shortly after that. Coincidence?"

At the water's edge, I absently picked up a rock and tried skimming it across the calm surface. It plunked and sank and I chuckled. I definitely needed more practice. "What do you think?"

"You know what I think about coincidences."

He didn't believe in them. We'd talked about that before. "Okay, since there are no coincidences, what do we think about Scully? Where does he fit in?"

"Scully's death is a mystery," Mac said, shaking his head as he found a smooth stone on the sand and skimmed it perfectly across the water. "Everybody hated him, but enough to kill him?"

"Someone did."

"Definitely. And knowing what I do about him now, I would say his murder smells like he either knew too much, or heard something he wasn't supposed to hear, or worse."

"Worse? As in blackmail or a bribe?" I told him what my father said about getting Scully fired over a bribe.

"So he wasn't your everyday, average jackass," Mac said. "He was a really evil jackass. Whoever killed him must've reached the end of his rope."

"Like Mr. Derry, maybe?" I tried a second time and the stone skipped merrily across the water. I was ridiculously exultant.

He thought about it. "Maybe."

We headed for the breakwater and began to climb

the rugged rocks that led up to the flat surface of the jetty. The stretch of concrete and rocks extended one hundred yards into the ocean. At the end of the jetty, there was a flashing warning light that signaled to any boats that were moving too close to the shore.

As I climbed, I pulled my jacket collar up to protect my neck from the crisp breeze. "So, what if Scully really did see or hear something he shouldn't have?"

"If he did," Mac said, "his fatal error was in trying to bribe or blackmail that person."

I scowled. "It sounds like his kind of sleazy move."

"So, let's play it the other way. How does Loretta's death relate to Scully?" Mac held out his hand to pull me up to the top of the jetty. It was windier out here and it felt glorious, but my hair was blowing every which way. This was an ongoing problem, especially if I wanted to see where I was going. I reached into my jacket pocket and found a scrunchie—I never left home without one—and wrapped it around my hair.

"Call me self-absorbed," Mac said with a grin, "but I usually wind up bringing everything in life back to my writing. So, if this were my story and I had two people die under suspicious circumstances within a day or two of each other, there would have to be a connection. We just have to figure out what it is."

"There was a third suspicious death," I reminded him.

"Right." He nodded. "Can't forget about old Ernie. Of course, he died more than, what? Thirty years ago?"

"Something like that." I grimaced. "He fell off the roof while he was fixing the chimney."

"That's an ugly way to die," Mac muttered.

I glanced at him. "Is there a pretty way?"

"I'd like to go when I'm sound asleep in bed, around age ninety-five. That's about as pretty as I can imagine when it comes to death."

"You'd be a *healthy* ninety-five, right?"

"Of course. No hideous illnesses and no medications that make you constipated and cranky."

I smiled. "A natural death."

"Exactly." He shoved his hands into his jacket pockets. "So, back to murder. Have we figured out the connection here?"

Frowning, I said, "Well, for one thing, both Loretta and Scully were at Jane's inn at the same time the other day."

"What were they doing there?"

I couldn't seem to shake the frown. "Loretta was minding her own business, being a guest. And Scully was traipsing around, sticking his nose where it didn't belong."

"A sure way to get it cut off," he murmured.

"There has to be a connection between the two deaths," I said. I explained what Jane had told me about Scully being shocked to see Loretta and the other woman glaring at him.

"Who's the other woman?" he asked.

"That's a mystery so far."

"Did you talk to Eric? Do we know if Loretta's death was actually a murder?"

I gaped at him. "Don't we?"

"Let's talk it out," he said genially. "You've got a television and a hair dryer in the tub. There's a very slim chance that it was an accident, but I seriously doubt it."

"Me, too." I slipped my arm through his when we

reached the end of the jetty. The ocean was fairly calm, but the wind was still blowing. I took a deep breath and felt my lungs fill with healthy sea air. I felt so lucky to be here, close to the ocean, with this man. "What are you thinking?" I asked.

"I'll just throw this out there. It could've been suicide."

I thought about it. "No way."

He nodded. "I agree with you, but I was playing devil's advocate for a minute. Trying to electrocute oneself is not the way most women would choose to commit suicide, statistically speaking."

"Of course not. No woman would want to be found naked in the tub with her hair wet, all sprawled out and—" I broke off because I seriously didn't want that sad image in my brain again. "Not that I would ever consider it," I went on, "but I suppose if I were going to kill myself, I would take some pills, or something nonviolent like that." The very thought of wanting to kill myself made me shiver, which was getting to be a habit, by the way.

"As we both know, the new small appliances they're making have a cutoff switch to prevent electrocution. So the hair dryer was never going to electrocute her."

"But not everyone knows that." I glanced over at him. "But you do."

"I do." He flashed me a tight grin. "Have to stay current with all the latest murder ploys. For research purposes only."

"Good to know." We turned and headed back to the shore. I tried to picture the grim scenario in Loretta's bathroom—without focusing in on Loretta. "So, I imagine the killer tossed the hair dryer into the water and when nothing happened, he got frustrated, grabbed the TV, and tossed it in."

"That's my theory."

"So, when the hair dryer fell into the water and didn't kill her, why didn't Loretta scream or yell for help?" I asked.

"Maybe she did," he said, giving me a sideways glance. "But I think in that moment, her main goal would have been to get out of the tub. Maybe she and the killer were screaming at each other. Maybe she grabbed the hair dryer out of his hands, and they tussled with it. Then it dropped into the water, and nothing happened. The killer was furious."

"I would have been, too," I said. "If I thought the hair dryer was going to be my murder weapon and then I watched it poop out on me, I'd have been more than a little irritated."

"Fair enough," he agreed. "So, does he immediately go for the TV?"

"There was water all over the floor," I mused. "And meanwhile, Loretta might've been standing precariously, fighting for her life. In an enamel-coated tub filled with soapy water and bubbles?" I winced as I pictured myself in the same position, slip-sliding around, scrambling to escape from a dangerous, deadly situation. It wouldn't be pretty. "She's lucky she didn't slip and hit her head." I cringed. "Well, not *lucky*, considering the final outcome."

"However you look at it, it was a terrifying spot for anyone to be in."

"Just imagining it gives me the creeps."

"Yeah." He scowled and I appreciated it. It was good

to know we were on the same page. "So you saw the cord wrapped around her neck. Was it pulled tight enough to strangle her?"

"It had loosened by the time I got there."

"The killer must've been going crazy by now. None of the electrical appliances had done the job, so he was forced to get up close and personal with his victim. Meanwhile, Loretta was fighting him off. He grabbed the only thing within reach, the hair dryer. He wound the cord around her neck and pulled. When the job was done, he let it go. Loretta slipped back into the water, and he let go of the cord."

I shivered once again, and Mac pulled me close. I leaned my head on his shoulder as we walked. "I'm still trying to figure out how Scully and Loretta knew each other."

"You have some ideas."

"Yeah." I did a quick calculation in my head. "They're both around the same age as my dad and Uncle Pete, who both knew Loretta."

"And your dad and Pete both knew Scully, too."

"Right. So maybe Scully and Loretta knew each other."

"Did Scully grow up here?" Mac asked. "Maybe they went to school together."

"Here in Lighthouse Cove? I never even thought about that, but it's possible. I can ask my dad."

We climbed down off the jetty and trudged across the sand to Mac's property line. Staring back at the water, I grabbed my phone from my jacket pocket and was about to push Dad's number on speed dial when something else occurred to me. "Matthew Jorgensen grew up here, too. And he's around the same age as my dad."

"I wonder if your pal Petsy did, too."

"She did, according to Matthew." I grimaced. "You still haven't met her, but she would make the most perfect villain."

"Which means she's the least likely to be guilty," Mac said cheerfully.

"But it would solve everything." I shook my head. "There's something else we haven't talked about."

"I know," Mac said thoughtfully. "Loretta was working for the Jorgensens when she had a baby."

"Yeah. What if that baby was Amanda?"

"It's possible." Mac paced a few steps forward, then turned and faced me. "What about this? Matthew and Loretta have an affair. She gets pregnant. Matthew pays the good-natured Ernie to marry her."

"Oh man . . ."

"And," Mac continued, "Loretta couldn't stay in a fake marriage so she left with the baby. Once she was gone, there was no reason to keep Ernie around when he knew so many secrets, so one quick tumble off the roof and problem solved."

I sighed. It made sense and I hated that. "He could've just slipped and fallen. But if he was pushed, I really hope that Petsy is the bad guy here. I like Matthew."

"That's the kiss of death, right there," Mac said, and gave me a quick, hard hug.

"It's possible that none of that is true and Loretta and Ernie were very happy together."

"You think?"

I gave him an incredulous look. "No."

"That's my girl." He gave me an elbow nudge. "Let's go back to the house. You can call your dad and we can find out who knew whom back then."

Ten minutes later, sitting in Mac's spacious living room, I disconnected from the call with Dad and gazed at Mac. "You heard him. They all knew one another. Scully, Loretta, Matthew, and Petsy."

"And your father and Uncle Pete."

"Right."

Mac seemed lost in thought for a few seconds. We had moved on from coffee to water and he took a long sip. "What he said about Loretta being a whiz with money is interesting. She was a housekeeper years ago. What is she doing these days? Didn't you say she had dollar signs in her appointment book?"

"Yes, and Jane agreed that she seemed to be a smart businesswoman. I was thinking she might've been in town to work some deal." I grabbed my pen and notepad and started a brand-new list with my top four suspects. Then I stared at the page for a moment. "Don't you think Stan and Joan Derry fit in here somewhere?"

"I've never met them, but you have." He shrugged. "The only thing we have on them is Scully's body being found at their house."

"That's kind of a lot," I said.

"Are they about the same age as the others?"

"Stan looks about my father's age, but Joan might be a little younger. I could find out." I tapped my pen against my notebook. "And, you know, it might not even matter. Scully's killer might be some contractor on a completely different job, totally unrelated to any of our suspects. Or it could be a family member of his."

"Right. And Loretta Samson could've committed suicide."

I looked at him wryly. "But we don't believe that, either."

He grinned. "Nope. Because why would some unknown contractor or family member drag Scully over to the Derrys' orangery and stab him with a chisel?"

I chuckled lightly. "Good question. Okay, back to Stan and Joan."

"If I recall what you told me, Joan kicked Scully out of their house. And then Stan had a very loud, very public confrontation with him."

"Right." I sighed. "And as you said, Scully's body was found on their property."

Mac pointed to my list. "Okay, that's two big strikes against both Stan and Joan, so they stay on the suspect list. For now, anyway." He reached for his glass of water and took another drink, emptying the glass. "This is thirsty business. Do you want some more? Or I've got iced tea in the fridge."

"Water's fine," I said.

He grabbed both of our glasses and walked into the kitchen. A minute later, he was back, setting the glasses on the table and sitting down next to me on the couch. "Let's take each of the principals and go over them, one by one."

"Okay. I'll start with Loretta." I began ticking off everything I'd been told about her. "She had blond hair years ago. Now it's darker. Big blue eyes. Good with money. Married Ernie. Housekeeper. Worked for the Jorgensens. Left town with her baby." I frowned at Mac. "Why did she leave? And why didn't Ernie go with her?"

Mac's lips twisted as he thought about that. "We've got one theory that says Ernie wasn't the baby's father."

"But he could've been. Then again, if not him, who else?"

Mac grinned. "Not Scully."

"Oh dear God, no. And it wasn't Uncle Pete," I muttered. "I'll bet my life on it."

"Who else could it be?" Mac said. "It's got to be Matthew Jorgensen. He's the only one that makes sense."

"I hate that it might be Matthew. He seems so solid and sweet and devoted. But if you're right, then he was cheating on his wife with the housemaid. And even though his wife is the evil Petsy, that's just tacky."

"It might not be Matthew."

"Yeah." I was getting dizzy from all the possibilities. "Let's stick with Loretta's story for now. So, where did she go when she left Lighthouse Cove? What did she do?"

He shrugged. "She traveled across the country, and when she got to Baltimore, she gave the baby up for adoption."

"So you're set on thinking that Amanda's mother is Loretta."

"We're just hypothesizing here, but it makes sense. Especially when you take that photograph into consideration."

"I almost forgot that little detail. Amanda has that picture of herself as a baby in front of the Jorgensen mansion."

"A very significant little detail."

I sighed. "So, why would someone kill Loretta?"

"We don't actually know what she was doing in town."

"Maybe she followed Amanda from Baltimore to the West Coast."

"*Or*"—he emphasized the word—"maybe Amanda was following *her*."

"You really think Amanda tracked her here and killed her?" Having said it out loud, I was anxious now and stood up to pace around the room. I really didn't want to think Amanda was a murderer. And the harder I tried to convince myself that she might be, the less the possibility worked for me. Amanda just didn't ring any of the "danger" bells. After a few circuits, I stopped pacing and stood in front of Mac, ready to make my case. "That's a really good theory about Amanda, but I hate it anyway. I just refuse to believe that Amanda killed Loretta, especially in such a gruesome way."

He reached out and took my hand. "I agree, so let's come up with a better theory."

I nodded and blew out a relieved breath. "Okay. Let's not forget that this wasn't Loretta's first visit here."

"That's right," Mac said, reflecting on that for a moment. "Cindy at the diner said she's seen her a bunch of times, right?"

"That's right. She stayed at the Hennessey Inn for her last two visits. I wonder where she stayed before that."

"Does Loretta have family in town?" he wondered aloud. "Wait. Maybe she came back to visit Ernie's family."

"Oh." I thought about that possibility. "That would be nice."

"If Amanda is her daughter, she actually might've

followed her out here this time. Maybe Loretta has always kept tabs on her, but never let her know it." Mac took a drink of water. "So, now she's out here, and maybe the deal she's working on is a house. If Amanda's moving here, then Loretta wants to be close by."

"I like it," I said, nodding. "But why does she bring a different boyfriend each time? I mean, if she's on business, why would she bring a date? Although I can't blame her for wanting someone around when the business part of her day is over."

"I'm not even going to go there," Mac said, shaking his head. "No man alive can figure out what women are actually thinking or what makes them do the things they do."

"I don't know. I think you do a pretty good job of figuring us out most of the time."

"Sure, maybe I get it right once in a while, but not on a regular basis."

I laughed. "I like that you think we're mysterious."

"I will say that I've noticed that some women like to have a man around the house. Or the inn, as the case may be."

I frowned. "It doesn't really matter if she had a boyfriend with her. I was just being judgmental."

"It only matters if the boyfriend killed her."

"That's true." I took a big sip of water. "There are just too many questions. Was Matthew having an affair with Loretta? Was Amanda his daughter after all? Did he pay Loretta to leave town with the baby?"

Mac had a few questions of his own. "Are you sure Jane didn't see anyone visiting Loretta over the last few days?"

"Just that one woman I told you about. And Jane still doesn't know who she is."

"Okay, but what about the other people on her staff? Or her other guests?" Mac spoke quickly as different thoughts occurred to him. "Have the police questioned Loretta's boyfriend?"

"Mr. Winesap," I murmured. "You know, he belongs on the suspect list."

"Absolutely."

"I'll give Jane a call right now and you can ask her your questions." I picked up my phone and hit Jane's cell number. A moment later, she answered.

"Hi, Shannon."

"Sorry to bother you," I said, "but I'm here with Mac and we have a few questions about Loretta. Do you mind?"

"Not at all," she said. "I would love to find out what happened."

"Okay, I'm putting you on speakerphone."

"Hi, Jane," Mac said.

Jane chuckled. "Hi, Mac."

I smiled. "First we wanted to know if the police questioned Mr. Winesap."

"Only for a few minutes," she said. "He has an alibi. He was at Uncle Pete's wine bar with the other guest I told you about."

I frowned. "Mr. Greenfield?"

"Yes. They've gotten to be friends in the short time they've been here."

"That's nice," I said. *And convenient, too,* I thought. "So the police must have questioned Mr. Greenfield, also."

"I don't know for sure, but I would guess so," she said.

"Now, you said you didn't see anyone visiting Loretta, but did you happen to ask your staff about it?"

She paused. "No, I didn't think to ask anyone else."

"Did the police question them?"

"They did. They were here for hours last night, asking questions and investigating." She paused, and her voice dropped a little as she added, "I'm hoping my guests find this exciting and not horrifying. I know that sounds awful, but I'd hate to lose potential future guests because they were grilled by Eric."

"I'm sure he was tactful," I said, and mentally crossed my fingers. "Eric's pretty thorough about these things."

"He is," she said. "He even wanted to take a look at my guest amenities—you know, the bath soap and shampoo and things we set out for guests."

"How come?"

"Apparently there was a shower cap floating in the tub, and he wanted to know if it was part of our amenities package."

"A shower cap?" I glanced at Mac, who gave a clueless shrug. "That's really interesting."

"I thought so, too."

Mac held up his hand to interrupt our train of thought. "How about if we take some pictures over to show to Jane's staff? Maybe they'll recognize someone."

"That's a great idea. Did you hear that, Jane?"

"Yes, Mac. Come over anytime. I'm here all day."

"Thanks, Jane. We'll see you in a while."

I ended the call and looked at Mac. "How do we get pictures of the suspects?"

He thought about it for a moment. "The Jorgensens and the Derrys are fairly wealthy and probably give money to some local organizations. Wouldn't their pictures be in the newspaper occasionally?"

"Yes. That's brilliant."

"I'll get my computer." He jogged down the hall and was back a minute later. Having set it up on the coffee table, he went online and found the website for the *Lighthouse Standard*, our local newspaper. A search for Petsy's name turned up a recent column describing the Volunteer Guild's annual fund-raising gala. There was a good picture of Petsy and Matthew in formal attire and he printed it out.

Joan and Stan were a little harder to track down, but we finally found a photo of them taken at a high school football game last season. They were all bundled up, but I could still see their faces. Mac printed that photo, too.

"I guess we should bring a picture of Amanda," I said.

"Why don't we wait on that?" Mac said. "Neither of us thinks she had anything to do with this, so let's not push it."

I breathed a sigh of relief. "Okay. Thanks."

"Should we find a picture of Scully?" he asked. "Maybe one of Jane's staff saw him with Loretta. His reaction to seeing her was so striking, there may be more to the story."

"Not a bad idea," I said. Mac searched for the photo of Scully the paper had printed after his death. Then he walked back to his office and pulled the pages he'd printed.

"These came out pretty good," I said, when he showed them to me.

"Yeah. I think we're good to go."

On the drive over to Jane's I kept going back to the grisly scene in Loretta's bathroom the night before. Something had been bugging me and it had kept me awake most of the night.

When he pulled to a stop at a red light, Mac reached over and squeezed my hand. "What's going on? I can hear you thinking all the way over here."

I shook my head in frustration. "I was missing something, but I'm getting closer. I've almost got it figured out."

"It's because there are too many pieces to this puzzle," he said. "We can't keep them all straight. Why don't you go over your list again?"

"Good idea." I pulled the notepad from my purse and flipped it open to the list. I'd jotted down all the details I could come up with for each person. I started with Loretta. Wavy blond hair back when Uncle Pete knew her. Brunette now. Beautiful. Big blue eyes. Smart. Married Ernie. Left town. Baby. Businesswoman?

I gazed up at Mac. "Uncle Pete said Loretta was a blonde back when he knew her. But her hair was darker when she died. Did she color her hair to disguise her appearance?"

"It's possible." Mac watched the light turn green and he continued driving down Main Street.

I turned in my seat and smiled happily at him. "I figured out what I was trying to remember."

"Great. Let's hear it."

"Okay. I met Loretta and she had big blue eyes and her dark hair was thick and wavy. Jane called it 'wash and wear.'"

"Yeah? Where are you going with this?"

"Here's the thing. Trust me on this: with all that hair, she probably wore it pinned up last night when she got into the tub. It's just a theory, but that's what I would do. I know some women wash their hair in the bathtub, but I don't like it. It's too hard. You've got to shampoo and then rinse it under the tap. It's a pain. But that's just me. Some women do it all the time."

"If you say so."

"I do. My point is, if she wasn't washing her hair, she wouldn't have needed a hair dryer."

"Ah. Very good point." He grinned. "And it goes to our theory that she didn't commit suicide."

"Exactly. But then along comes that stupid shower cap and blows my theory away."

"No, it doesn't. It corroborates your theory."

"I know. It's just that, well, my brain hurts from obsessing over hair and shampoo, and the shower cap was there all along." I shook my head.

He laughed, grabbed my hand, and squeezed. "You're funny, Shannon Hammer."

"My only excuse is that this case is making me crazy."

"Right there with you, babe."

As Mac drove, I stared at the suspect list, absently twisting a thick strand of hair around my fingers as I did so.

"You never play with your hair," he said lightly. "Is something else on your mind?"

I should've known he would be able to read my mood. "Yes, but it's probably stupid."

"There are no stupid theories," he intoned with the seriousness of a college professor.

I laughed. "This one might be the exception to that rule. But here goes. Loretta had wavy blond hair and big blue eyes, according to Uncle Pete. And me. I mean, I didn't see blond hair, but I saw her eyes."

"You told me that."

"A dozen times, right?" I smiled. "Sorry. I'm trying to work all this out."

"Go for it."

"Okay, so, Loretta is a blue-eyed blonde. Amanda has brown hair and brown eyes."

"What about Matthew?"

"Dark hair. Dark eyes."

"Interesting."

"I know that blond women can have dark-haired children, and I know that blue eyes are a recessive trait, but here's the thing. I just can't find *any* physical similarity between Loretta and Amanda. There's nothing. Loretta was curvy; Amanda's got more of a boyish figure. Loretta's face was heart shaped while Amanda's is more narrow. And Amanda has a longer chin. There's more, but I just can't . . ."

"What is it?"

As I stared out at the passing trees, my gaze began to blur. "Oh my God," I whispered. "Oh my God."

Mac drove around a curve and then took the turnoff into town. Without warning, he pulled the car over and parked on the side of the road. Then he turned to face me, wearing a patient smile. "I don't know what's going on in your head right now, but you're practically shaking the whole car. What's up?"

"Sorry," I said, laughing again. "But it's so off the wall, I'm not sure I should even say it out loud."

"Are you kidding? You can't leave me hanging." He ran his hands up and down my arms. "Just say it, Shannon. I'm dying to know what you're thinking."

I had to take a couple of deep breaths before I uttered my next thought aloud. "Okay. We know Loretta had blond hair and blue eyes. Do you know who else has blond hair and blue eyes?"

"No. Who?"

"Matthew and Petsy's daughter, Lindsey."

Chapter Eleven

Instead of being properly dumbstruck, Mac laughed out loud. "Now that's an awesome plot twist." He sat back in the driver's seat and laughed again.

"I thought I was the only one going crazy," I muttered.

"But this is perfect," he said, still chuckling. "We've got a possible case of babies switched at birth. If I were writing this book, they would have been twins, but I'll take what I can get."

"Oh, come on. Twins? That's nutty." I held up my hand like a stop sign. "No, it's worse than nutty. Twins separated at birth is a total cliché."

"Yeah, I know." He grinned. "But I still love it. And besides, sometimes a cliché is a cliché because it's happened a lot."

"That's true—although in this case, hmm." I smiled, but it quickly faded. "Look, I don't know if I'm opening a can of worms or not with this theory, but it's worth investigating. Don't you think?"

"Definitely. I think." His gaze zeroed in on me again. "Let me just say this out loud so I can be sure I'm following along. You actually think that Matthew and Petsy Jorgensen are raising Loretta's child as their own."

I gave him a nervous look. Hearing him put my thoughts into words made me feel even crazier. "Do I? I guess so. It's a little disturbing to hear you say it aloud. Because if it's true, it means that one or both of those mothers gave up their own daughter. I mean, there are dozens of reasons why a mother would need to give up their child, and most of them are heartbreaking. But this case is different. This is a situation where the babies might've been switched, either without the mothers' knowledge—or with their full agreement. And that's weird, don't you think?"

"From what you tell me about Petsy, the phrase *strong maternal instinct* is not one I would use in connection with her."

"True. Feral cats are warmer." I buried my face in my hands. "I don't know what to think anymore."

"As long as you're freaking out anyway, there's something else for you to worry about."

I snapped him a wary look. "What?"

His eyebrows lifted as he shot me a quick glance. "Amanda."

"Oh God." I closed my eyes. "Amanda. What are we going to tell her?"

"We don't have to tell her anything." Mac checked the rearview mirror and pulled back out into traffic. "Not yet, anyway."

"But who are her parents? Is she Matthew's daughter? Is Petsy her mother? Loretta?"

He nodded. "Too many possibilities and not enough answers. Wish it didn't take so long to get DNA results. I would assume her parents are the Jorgensens though, if we're going with the dark-haired-parents-giving-birth-to-a-dark-haired-daughter theory. But . . ." He frowned. "You're right. This is quickly moving beyond weird."

"I know. It doesn't make sense." I was completely baffled. Sure, I liked a mystery as well as the next person. But this was a mystery wrapped in a mystery wrapped in a— You get the idea. "But if it's true, did they switch babies deliberately? Or did Loretta pull a fast one on the Jorgensens?"

He came to a stop at a red light and gave a long, thoughtful whistle. "You mean, did she steal their kid and leave hers?"

I shook my head. "Who would do that?"

He frowned and his lips twisted in thought. "You know, all joking aside, we're grasping at straws here. Nothing is certain. And until we know more, we should probably just deal with the facts."

I touched his arm. "But blind speculation is so much more fun."

"I'm glad you think so," he said, grinning as he leaned over to kiss me. "I'm having a blast."

We showed the pictures of the suspects to four members of Jane's staff, but that didn't get us very far. They didn't recognize anyone and they had no clues or information to share with us. Jane explained that one of her desk clerks and two of her housekeepers had the day off, so we were welcome to come back tomorrow and show them the photos. Mac promised we would. I wanted to believe this would all be solved by then and a return trip wouldn't be necessary.

As we drove away from Jane's inn, I took a look at my wristwatch and realized it was midafternoon. I decided it would be a good idea to check in with my people at the Jorgensen house.

"To tell the truth, I'm a little concerned about leaving Amanda all by herself for this long," I explained.

"The Jorgensens aren't home?" Mac said.

"Oh, I'm sure they're home. I meant that I don't want her to be alone with them."

"Good thinking," he said. "If they had any clue that she could be their long-lost daughter, given up for adoption, who knows what they might do?" His frown deepened. "Would they be pleased? Furious? Yeah, too much we don't know."

"It worries me," I said, feeling once again like that mother hen. "If Amanda is Matthew's child and Petsy made him get rid of her all those years ago, what happens now? If Petsy finds out who Amanda really is, she might lash out at her."

"Or worse," Mac said.

I looked at him. "You think she might hurt her?"

"I've never met the woman, but from everything you've told me about her, it sounds entirely possible."

I'd been thinking the same thing and had sort of hoped that Mac would make me believe I was worried about nothing. I rubbed my stomach as it churned with anxiety. I told myself that everything would be fine once I got to the Jorgensens. I would check in with Amanda and make sure all was well. I also wanted to see the progress the guys had made on the orangery.

I turned to Mac. "If things are going okay with the Jorgensen job, I might stop by the Derry house and check on my guys."

He flashed a sardonic smile. "What you're really saying is, you're going to check on possible murder suspects Joan and Stan."

I smiled back. "You got it."

His smile faded and his eyes warmed. "Be careful, please?"

"Of course. Nobody's going to hurt me. I've got my crew guys all over the place."

"Your guys are great," he said lightly as he squeezed my hand. "And yet I'm not exactly comforted by that."

"But—"

"Hold on. Let me explain." He lifted my hand and planted a kiss there. "See, there's this vicious killer out there somewhere? And if you go looking for him—or her—you might find him. Or her. No big deal. Just thought I'd mention it."

I smiled. "Thank you for looking out for me. But not only do I have a crew full of big, protective guys; I also have a big pipe wrench and I used to bat cleanup in high school."

He grinned.

"I promise I'll be careful."

"Good." He pulled the car to a stop by the side of his house and we got out. "I'm going to swing by the county recorder's office and check on some birth records."

"Oh, that's brilliant." I thunked the heel of my hand

against my forehead. "I should've thought of that. I'm glad you did."

"That's why we make a good team. Besides"—he shrugged—"makes sense to check things out. And you can thank me by taking care of yourself."

"I will," I said, as we walked over to my truck. "And I'll call you when I get home this afternoon so you know I'm okay."

With a grin, he said, "If I don't get a phone call I'll come looking for you."

That was almost enough motivation *not to* call him.

When I walked into the Jorgensen house, it was quiet. But as I approached the dining room, I could hear what sounded like a muffled conversation. Was Lindsey home? Was she talking to Amanda?

I peeked around the archway and almost fell over. It was Petsy. She was sitting at the dining room table, chatting with Amanda. She looked almost . . . friendly. Was it possible? Was she on new medication? Had there been an apocalypse I hadn't noticed?

"Oh, hi, Shannon," Amanda said when she noticed me standing there. "We were just talking about the amazing history of this house." She turned back to Petsy. "I really hope you win the contest."

"That's why I hired all of you," she said cheerily, and flashed me a warm smile.

Okay, that was just wrong. Petsy was never cheery, never warm, and when she smiled she usually looked like a pit bull baring its teeth.

"As I told Shannon, I did my research," she was say-ing. "Shannon's company has worked on eight winning houses out of the last twelve years. I know you all will bring the magic this time."

I was completely blown away. I gripped the back of the nearest chair just to make sure I didn't fall over. I honestly couldn't remember Petsy saying any of that, but then that first day when Wade and I met her, she'd said a lot of things, most of which were rude and condescending. Maybe her "research" had crept into her conversation somewhere, but I doubted it.

I might've said something to counter her words, but then I glanced at Amanda and saw her beaming, so I composed myself enough to squeak out a happy response. "I don't see why we can't win. Your house is stunning. And I do like to win."

"I like to win, too," Amanda chimed in.

"That's a very good attitude," Petsy said, smiling brightly. "I think it's my year to take the grand prize and I'm happy to know I've got the best people working with me."

"You made a great choice," Amanda gushed. "Shannon is the absolute best."

I turned and shot her a quick smile.

Petsy stood and pushed her chair in. "Well, I'll let you girls get on with your work. The panels are looking wonderful, by the way. You're doing a very nice job."

"Thank you, Petsy," I murmured, and stared at her back as she left the room. As soon as she was gone, I whipped around to Amanda and whispered, "What have you done to Petsy?"

She held up both hands and shook her head. "Didn't do a thing, I swear. It's a miracle. She's being so nice.

I'm completely amazed. I actually enjoyed our conversation."

In my head I was questioning her version of reality, but I tried to smile anyway. "That's nice. Twisted, but nice."

"I'm not sure why she was so crabby up until now," Amanda said. "Maybe she was just nervous about having people in her house. But you can see she's really changed."

"I'll hold off singing hallelujah for a while," I said, trying to keep my voice down. Who knew if someone was listening in on our conversation? "I'm sorry, but after everything that's happened, I just don't trust her. Not yet."

Amanda stared down at a wood panel for a moment, then looked back at me. "I understand your feelings. But I really want to believe that she's a nice person. Especially if, you know . . ."

I touched her shoulder. "I know what you're saying, and I admire you for taking the high road. Pay no attention to me."

"Thanks, Shannon."

"But don't mind me if I stick to the low road until I get a little more proof that"—I dropped my voice to a whisper—"the witch is dead."

She laughed. "I think that's as good a compromise as we can make."

"So, what were you two talking about?"

"She started out asking me where I learned woodworking. I told her about my dad. And then she asked about my mom and where I was brought up and how I decided to move to Lighthouse Cove. You know, just small talk, really. But she seemed genuinely interested."

"I think that's great." I glanced around the room. The light coming in through the beveled bay window cast a rosy glow on everything, including Amanda. She looked so happy and I didn't want to destroy that. So instead, I did the best thing I could do in that moment and got to work.

Amanda joined me and picked up one of the panels. I took another one and set it on the end of the plywood table, where I began filing down the edges of the splintered vine pattern. As we worked, Amanda hummed softly and I knew she was thinking about the wonderful possibility that the people living in this house might be her family.

All the while, I couldn't help but think that Amanda was being played by Petsy. I wasn't normally a cynical person, but I had a feeling that it was just a matter of time before everything fell apart. And I didn't know what I could do to protect my friend from the fallout.

The next day, I spent some time helping Wade and Sean with the orangery. I had to admit it felt good to be working outside with my guys again. Our brick wall base was completely finished and the interior concrete floor surface was ready for a layer of subflooring. After that, we would lay down a dark wood laminate to match the rest of the house.

The steel framing was done and today we were going to start fitting the solar-controlled tempered-glass windows into the frames. We hoped to finish the pitched roof by the end of the day and I was eager to see the completed structure with all of its charming flourishes, such as the sunburst detail on the gable end facing the garden and the fleur-de-lis cresting along the top of the roof. This embellishment would not only give the orangery a true Victorian look but would also keep birds from perching on the roof.

That afternoon, Amanda and I planned to work on the faded stairway panel that Matthew wanted stained. I had purchased three different shades of wood stain and we would be testing them today.

Before we left for lunch, Sean set up the multiposition ladder on the stairway. It was the perfect ladder for this job, because we could shorten one side to stand on the higher stair and lengthen the other side to stand on the landing. Sean tested it until it was immobile, or wobble-free, as I liked to say.

Once we got back from lunch, Amanda and I laid down a small drop cloth on one of the steps and placed the stains and brushes on the cloth.

"If you need to help the guys, I can do this by myself," Amanda said as she climbed the ladder.

"Who's going to hand you the stains?" I asked.

"Oh, yeah." She grinned. "That would be you."

"Besides, I don't trust these carpeted steps," I muttered, clamping one hand onto the front side rail of the shorter side. "The ladder could slip. I'll hold it while you climb."

"Okay, thanks." She ascended quickly until she was facing the offending panel.

"You should probably go up one more step."

She did what I suggested. "I'm ready for the first stain."

"Here you go."

She leaned down and I passed her one can and a brush. I had already pried the cans open so she would be able to get the lids off easily.

She brushed the panel several times with the stain. "This might be too light. Let me try a darker shade."

She handed down the can and I passed the next one up to her with a new brush. We repeated that one more time.

"We'll need to let them dry," she said, "but I think the last one is the best match."

"Good."

"Oh, wait. It's dripping a little. Hold on."

She twisted around to pull a small cloth from her back pocket just, as Matthew started to walk up the stairs. "Hello, ladies."

Startled, Amanda began to teeter on the step. I grabbed both rails to try to stabilize the ladder.

A scream rang out from the top of the stairs. I whipped around to see Petsy rushing toward the ladder. Was she going to push it over?

"Don't!" I cried, tightening my grip on the ladder while I tensed up for the inevitable blow.

"Be careful," Matthew shouted.

He grabbed the lower ladder just as Petsy reached out to help me hold it steady. The three of us held on while Amanda descended. When she was off the ladder completely and standing safely on the stairs, Matthew clutched her shoulders. "Are you all right?"

"Of course," she said, laughing. "No worries."

"You were about to fall off," Petsy said, her voice tremulous. "You must be more careful."

"Took ten years off my life, seeing you up there," Matthew muttered, and gave her an avuncular hug.

"Sorry I scared you," she murmured.

"Good heavens." Petsy blew out a breath and straightened her shoulders. "Well, now that you're safe, please get back to work."

After watching Petsy freak out over Amanda's near fall, I was actually relieved to see she was back to her old self.

"Yes," I said, still feeling shaky, "let's finish this and get back to it."

Matthew patted Amanda's shoulder, then skirted the ladder and continued up the stairs. Turning once, he gave us a stern shake of his finger. "You girls be careful."

"Yes, Father," I said, joking. Honestly, I hadn't planned it or really given it a second thought. But now the words were out there.

It was as if time stopped moving. I heard Amanda's intake of air at the same time Petsy gasped. Matthew seemed to be the only one unaffected. He just chuckled and kept moving.

"Let's get this ladder out of the way," I said loudly, prodding Amanda back to the present.

"Right."

We folded the ladder and the two of us carried it down to the foyer. Since we would have to check the wood stain later, we left the ladder leaning against the back wall, out of everybody's way. I retrieved the cans of stain we'd left on the stairs along with the brushes and the small drop cloth. I set everything down on the dining room table and turned to Amanda. "Let's take a quick break. We can walk outside and check on the guys' progress."

"Good idea." She still sounded a little winded.

Once we were out on the veranda, I stopped and turned to her. "You should sit down."

"I'm fine."

"No, you're not," I said, and she seemed to agree, because she walked over to the first bentwood rocker, collapsed into the chair, and laid her head back.

I sat in the matching rocker. "Well, that got weird."

She smiled, then started to laugh. She bent over and buried her face in her folded arms. "Oh God. When will this be over?"

"We could force the issue," I said quietly.

"What do you mean?"

"I mean, we could simply ask them if they happened to give a baby up for adoption some thirty-odd years ago."

"I'm thirty-three," Amanda murmured.

"Okay, thirty-three years ago." I wasn't about to go into the babies-separated-at-birth possibility. Amanda was fragile enough as it was.

"I'm not sure I'm ready to bring up the topic yet."

"I understand." And I did, but it had gotten to the point where, like it or not, something was going to happen. "But it's getting close to the time when you've got to fish or cut bait."

"Is it?"

"We've got about a week left on this job, and after that, you won't be able to hang around here anymore. I mean, unless you want to hide in the bushes and be arrested for stalking."

She managed to chuckle. "I guess I'd better grow a backbone quickly."

"You have a perfectly strong backbone, Amanda," I said firmly. "You're just in an awkward, vulnerable position right now. It'll pass and you'll be back in fighting form any day now."

She opened her eyes and gazed at me. "I don't think I've ever met anyone as kind and loyal as you are."

Embarrassed, I straightened. "I'm not—"

"You are. I'm so lucky that you're on my team."

"Now, that's true. I'm Team Amanda all the way."

We both grinned and kept rocking.

"Hi, you two."

We glanced up and saw Lindsey standing on the steps leading up to the porch.

"Hi, Lindsey. We were just taking a short break."

"I'd love to join you if you don't mind company."

I smiled. "Please do."

"We would love it," Amanda assured her.

Lindsey sat on the railing facing us and sighed. "I just took the nicest walk through the town square, then over to the boardwalk and along the water. Sometimes I forget how beautiful this town is."

"It really is," I said softly.

"Do you have to go back to San Francisco?" Amanda asked.

Lindsey frowned. "I do. It's my home now. And besides, it's better if I'm there than, well, here."

"Don't you miss your father?" I asked.

"Yes, very much." Her features brightened. "But we talk on the phone all the time and he comes into the city every month or so to bring me his paintings. So it's like I have pieces of him with me when I'm there."

"That's really sweet," Amanda whispered.

Lindsey leaned against the rounded front porch column and her hair fluttered in the breeze.

"Lindsey, you have wavy hair." I stopped rocking. "I've never noticed."

"It's true," she said, with a rueful smile. "I usually try to dry it straight because Mother hates my unruly curls."

"I think they're beautiful," Amanda said.

"Thank you." She touched her hair self-consciously. "This morning I left for my walk and my hair was still a bit damp, so of course it curled. I'll have to use the flat iron to tame it back into shape."

I couldn't say a word. Yes, that her hair was wavy was just a little fun fact, but it was also one more piece of the puzzle that was Loretta Samson. Was Lindsey Loretta Samson's daughter? I still had no real idea, and clearly neither did Lindsey or Amanda. All I knew was that both of their lives would be shattered if we found out she was.

I just prayed I wouldn't have to be the one who told them.

That night, Mac called. "I tracked down the information I told you I was looking for."

"That was fast." I crossed my fingers that whatever he'd found would be good news. "What did you find?"

"Two baby girls, Lindsey and Amanda, were born a week apart. Both of their birth certificates listed the same address on Cranberry Circle."

"A week apart," I whispered. "And both babies were living in the Jorgensen house?"

"Yes."

I considered the significance of that. "I know I keep saying this, but that's just weird."

Mac sighed. "I couldn't agree more."

The next morning my crew arrived early to put a few finishing touches on the orangery. The landscapers were arriving sometime after lunch to start planting flowers and bushes around the structure so that the side yard would look like a spring garden in full bloom. It was going to be spectacular.

Amanda and I spent a few minutes admiring the orangery, then went around to the front door and rang the doorbell.

"I think the last wood stain I used on the panel was the best," Amanda said while we waited at the door.

I nodded. "I agree. Let's set you up to finish that job. Then I can help you with the dining room wainscoting for the rest of the afternoon."

"Good morning," Lindsey said as she opened the door. Her hair had been flat-ironed, and she was smiling and dressed casually in black slacks and a cream-colored blouse. "Come on in. My mother and father are both out, but I'll be here all day if you need anything."

"Thanks, Lindsey," I said, ignoring the obvious fact that this family seemed to leave their house as often as possible.

We put our stuff down in the dining room and went to get the ladder. The process would require some prep work: first removing some of the old stain with a fine-grit sandpaper, then using a tack cloth to wipe away any bits of dust and sand. Once the wood was smooth and clean, Amanda would apply the first coat of stain.

During breaks from the wainscoting work, she would add two more coats later in the day. I planned to be her assistant, staying close by the whole time to make sure the ladder was stable and that Amanda had everything she needed.

By midmorning we had finished the stairway panel and were working quietly in the dining room, when there was a knock at the door.

Petsy was home by then, and she answered the door. While I couldn't hear her exact words, I could tell she was agitated. Finally she said, "Oh, fine. Come in. But we're very busy here."

I watched and waited to see who would enter the house, and seconds later, the police chief walked into the room.

"Eric," I said, surprised. "What's going on?"

He looked uncomfortable and threw a glance over his shoulder at the hovering Petsy. "I'd like to ask Ms. Walsh a few questions."

"Me?" Amanda gave me a quick, puzzled look and then said, "What can I help you with?"

"I'd like to know if you own a set of chisels. The kind you might use to do your woodwork."

Petsy was right behind Eric and managed to maneuver her way into the dining room until she was standing in front of him, almost blocking him from moving into the room. I had the oddest feeling that she was trying to protect us. Or, more precisely, Amanda.

"Don't be silly, Chief Jensen," Petsy said. "Amanda

has every tool known to man, including whatever it is you're looking for. What's your point?"

His eyes focused on Petsy. "Someone killed Joe Scully with a chisel."

"Good heavens, that's grim." She laughed harshly. "Don't tell me you're accusing Amanda of killing Mr. Scully. I wonder just how many chisels there are in the state of California."

He smiled tolerantly. "I just want to see her set of chisels, ma'am."

"Amanda just moved to town recently," Petsy said. "She didn't even know Joe Scully."

I bit my tongue. Amanda *did* know Joe Scully. Back when she was following me around, she had approached Scully to ask questions about me.

"I'm speaking to Ms. Walsh," Eric said softly. "I don't want to ask you to leave the room, but I will if I have to."

I wanted to warn Petsy. That quiet tone of his was more frightening than if he were yelling.

"Do you work with chisels, Ms. Walsh?" he asked, staring past Petsy.

"Of course," Amanda said. "I use them for sculpting wood. I'm using one now."

"May I see it?"

She held out the tool and Eric walked over to look at it. "Is this part of a set?"

"Yes. The others are here in my toolbox."

She knelt down to get them, but Eric stopped her. "That's okay. I'll take a look."

She stood and waited. Petsy folded her arms across her chest indignantly and tapped the toe of her elegant pink pump against the wood floor so quickly, it sounded as if an agitated woodpecker was loose in the house. "This is ridiculous, Chief Jensen. Not only is it a waste of your time, but you're wasting my time by interrupting their work."

He gazed at her with the patience of a man who had dealt with far worse characters than Petsy. "A human being is dead, Mrs. Jorgensen. We want to find his killer before that person strikes again. Don't you want to help us rid the town of a vicious killer?"

She rolled her eyes. "Of course. But you're not going to find a killer in this house."

He grinned. "I'm here to make sure you're right about that."

Petsy seemed to realize her complaints were useless, so she turned on her heel and stomped out of the room.

Eric stood up, holding a sturdy plastic case that held five chisels of increasing size and weight. He took the one Amanda was using and slipped it into its spot in the case. "Looks like they're all accounted for."

He handed her chisels back. "Thank you for your cooperation."

"You're welcome." Amanda looked relieved and I couldn't blame her. Even when you knew you were innocent, it was scary to have the police question you.

He nodded a goodbye at me and began to leave.

"I'll walk out with you, Chief," I said, and followed him out of the house, down the steps, and along the walkway.

Finally he turned. "What's up, Shannon?"

"I just wanted to make sure you already checked Johnny's and Colin's tool chests over at the Derry house."

"I did, and they checked out." He winked. "So don't worry."

"Oh good." I let out a breath of true relief. Not that I'd really been worried about my guys, but it was a good thing to have them cleared. "Thanks." I continued walking with him.

"Did you have something else to say?" he said, biting back a smile.

"It's just nice to hang out with you for these few short moments." I winced. Okay, even I wouldn't believe that.

"Yeah, right." He laughed. "Now spill. What is it?"

"Okay, fine." I glanced around to make sure we were alone. "I hate to be a snitch, but there's someone else who uses chisels in the Jorgensen house."

"Who's that?"

"Matthew Jorgensen is a painter and a sculptor. He has dozens of tools in his art studio on the third floor."

"Really?" Interest gleamed in his eyes as he shifted to look at the house we'd just left.

"Yes. Unfortunately they're not in a tidy little case like Amanda's. They're mixed and matched and scattered everywhere around the room, so I'm not sure you could ever really know for certain if the murder weapon came from his studio."

Eric stared long and hard at the house, then gave me a brief smile. "Good to know. Thanks."

I saluted. "Your friendly neighborhood snitch, always at your service."

He chuckled as he climbed into his SUV and drove away.

Chapter Twelve

By two thirty, the orangery was completely finished and it was beautiful. The landscapers had already arrived and I could see from their placement of plants and flowers that the yard was going to be truly stunning.

My guys had worked straight through lunch, so I told them to take a long meal break before moving on to the other jobs we had to complete in time for the Home and Garden Tour in two weeks.

Amanda and I had six more panels to finish. It was slow going because of the intricate work, so we had been averaging one panel a day, which meant that we would be here another week. That still left Petsy with plenty of time to get her house ready for the tour. I wasn't sure who would be happier when we finally packed up and left, me or Petsy. But personally I couldn't wait for this whole experience to be over.

The following morning I rang the Jorgensens' doorbell and waited, hoping that Lindsey or Matthew would answer. I was bummed out when Petsy opened the door. She glanced around, then frowned. It seemed we were both doomed to disappointment this morning.

"Amanda will be a little late today," I explained, after forcing myself to smile at her.

She looked stricken. "Is she sick?"

"No, she's fine," I said, wondering at her reaction. "She just had to take care of some personal business this morning. She'll be here later. But I'll get to work right now."

"Very well." She swung the door wide open and I walked into the house. I mentioned our tentative schedule for finishing the job and she basically grunted, letting me know she'd heard what I said. Then she walked away.

"Feeling the love," I muttered, and strolled into the dining room to prep the next panel.

An hour later, Amanda arrived. I went out to open the door but Petsy beat me to it. Lindsey had come halfway down the stairs to get the door and we both watched as Petsy grabbed Amanda's arm and pulled her into the house. "I was so worried when you didn't show up earlier. Is everything all right?"

"Yes, I just had some personal things to take care of," Amanda said, looking a little flustered by Petsy's attention. That made two of us. Petsy was really being weird. Even for her.

The older woman weaved her arm through Amanda's as they crossed the foyer. "I've never offered you girls any coffee or tea, but if you'd like something, I'll be happy to bring it to you."

Lindsey looked as shocked as I felt. "Mother, what are you doing? Let the girls get to work."

Petsy scowled. "Go to your room, Lindsey, if you can't be pleasant."

Lindsey saw me watching and rolled her eyes. She turned and walked back upstairs.

"I'm fine, Petsy," Amanda said. "Please don't go to any trouble."

"It's no trouble. I'm home all day if you need anything."

"Thanks." Amanda rewarded her with a big smile, then walked into the dining room. Once Petsy had moved on into the kitchen, the two of us exchanged a quick look.

"Everything turn out okay?" I asked when she got settled.

"Oh, yeah. Sorry I had to take time off. I'm looking for a new apartment, so I had to meet a landlord and check one out."

I was relieved to hear the news. "Is it nice? Where is it?"

"It's beautiful, over by the marina."

"I love that area," I said, then added, "My father has a boat in the marina." I grinned, realizing that was the first time I'd said that. I wondered if Dad was on the boat right now and made a mental note to give him a call later.

"So," Amanda whispered, "did you get the whole welcome-wagon treatment from Petsy, too?"

I shot a look over my shoulder to where the woman had disappeared, then looked back at Amanda. "Hardly. She saved it just for you."

She frowned a little, and I couldn't help but join her. What was going on with Petsy? Lately she seemed to go totally manic around Amanda. It might have made sense if she believed Amanda was her daughter, but I couldn't be sure of that yet.

We settled into work, and while I appreciated the silence, I loved being surrounded by construction noise.

When Amanda pulled out her power drill and attached the latest panel to the wall, it made me happy. The sounds of industry, as Matthew had put it. I liked that.

Once she was finished attaching the panel, it was silent again for a while.

Suddenly there were hurried footsteps on the staircase and Lindsey shouted, "Mother, please just stop!"

"Oh, Lindsey." Petsy's displeasure was obvious. "What am I going to do with you?"

"Nothing, Mother. Absolutely nothing. For God's sake, just leave me alone."

I looked up and met Amanda's gaze. I imagined I looked as stunned as she did. We'd both heard the two Jorgensen women bickering before, but this sounded more serious. And uglier.

"All I said was that you could stand to lose a few pounds. I'm just trying to help."

"That's not being helpful," Lindsey snapped. "That's nagging. That's belittling. As always. Besides, you're wrong. I'm at the perfect weight for my height. For some reason, you can't see that, but ask any doctor."

"I'm sure you can find any number of doctors in San Francisco who will tell you what you want to hear."

"I could lose a hundred pounds and you'd still give me grief, so just stop talking."

I tiptoed closer to the door but Amanda held back. I

couldn't blame her. This was getting nastier by the second and I imagined it might get worse. I hoped they wouldn't catch me watching but I felt I had to see and hear what was going on. It seemed like they were finally showing us the real dynamic of their relationship and I hoped that would give me a clue as to what else had happened here in the past. Peering around the edge of the doorframe, I saw the two women still on the staircase. They were too involved in their argument to notice me.

Lindsey's mother looked her up and down. "Well, if it's not your weight, then maybe it's your choice of clothing. It doesn't flatter your shape. You always look a little . . . dowdy."

Lindsey sniffed at the insult. "At least I have curves. I'm not a stick figure like you are."

My eyes widened at the verbal slap. Not that I could blame her any.

"How dare you!" Petsy's eyes flashed and her shocked tone changed to pure sarcasm an instant later. "Haven't you heard? You can't be too thin or too rich. Sadly you're neither."

I saw Lindsey's face turning red. Her eyes looked both hurt and furious.

"What did you ever do to deserve being rich?" Lindsey wondered bitterly. "Besides marry my father, I mean. Was his money the only reason you married him? It couldn't have been for love."

"Shut up!" Petsy shouted, and in her fury, she looked more dangerous than ever. "Your father—"

"Don't you say a word about my father," Lindsey said through clenched teeth.

Petsy slapped Lindsey hard enough to make *my*

cheek hurt. I glanced at Amanda and saw her wince in sympathy.

Lindsey screamed, "I hate you!"

"Well," Petsy said imperiously. She was flexing her fingers behind her back after slapping her daughter so hard. "That's convenient, because I hate you, too. When are you going back to San Francisco?"

"Not soon enough."

"At last we agree on something," Petsy sneered.

Amanda let out a little gasp of despair. I knew it was for Lindsey. She had been holding out hope that the woman would stay in town, but Lindsey obviously had a very good reason to leave.

Both women turned at the sound of Amanda's gasp.

The jig was up, so with all innocence, I stepped out into the archway. "Is everything okay out here?"

Lindsey's shoulders sagged slightly, but Petsy immediately stood straighter. She walked the rest of the way down the stairs, stepped onto the polished marble floor of the foyer, and set her purse on the credenza. "Why am I not surprised it's you sticking your nose in our business? I'm so sick of you skulking around here, interfering in our lives."

I blinked. "You hired me to work here. I didn't realize I was skulking. As for interfering, we were simply doing our job before you ladies came downstairs."

"Then get to work and mind your own business," Petsy shot back. "I've never seen so much lollygagging."

"If you're not happy, I'll be glad to take my crew and leave. You can find someone else to finish the job."

"Fine. You can go. I'm hiring Amanda," Petsy said haughtily. "And you can drop dead."

I glared at her. "Amanda works for me."

Lindsey smiled as if she was really enjoying seeing her mother on the defensive.

"Oh, really? With one word I could hire her away from you like that." Petsy snapped her fingers.

"I'd like to see you try," I said, feeling like a ten-year-old on the playground, fighting over a dodgeball game. But what else could I do?

"Amanda, dear." Petsy's voice was gentle and calm now. "Come here."

"I think I'll stay right here," she said, but she did inch closer to the archway.

"I have something important to tell you," Petsy said, flashing a truly nasty grin my way.

My spine was tingling with nervous anticipation. Was she really going to say what I thought she might say?

"It might come as a shock," Petsy continued, "but I'm sure my news will make you very happy. I'm your—"

"No!" Amanda cried, backing away as if she couldn't bear to hear whatever it was Petsy was about to reveal. "Don't say it."

Lindsey glanced from her mother to Amanda and back. Walking the rest of the way down the stairs, she approached Petsy and said quietly, "Mother, leave Amanda alone. Let the girls go back to work."

"Stay out of this." Petsy physically pushed Lindsey away. "And I want you to stop calling me that."

Lindsey took a step back. "Stop calling you what?"

"Stop calling me Mother!" Petsy shouted, furious again.

Lindsey looked both puzzled and fed up. "If only I could," she muttered.

I almost grinned. Lindsey was getting in some good punches, whether she knew it or not. And she needed to know now.

"Why don't you just tell everyone the truth, Petsy?" I said. I didn't want to hurt Amanda, but things were about to come out now anyway and my friend couldn't hide forever. Better if I was with her when Petsy dropped her bomb. As for Lindsey, I had a feeling she was strong enough to take whatever Petsy handed out.

Petsy whirled around, checking each of our expressions. Did she realize she was trapped? Surrounded by at least two women—possibly three, if Amanda was finally coming to her senses—who neither liked her nor trusted her?

Petsy's gaze narrowed in on me. "What are you talking about?"

Enough games, I told myself. I was tired of tiptoeing around this woman. Heck, I was just plain tired of this woman. "I know what you were about to tell Amanda, and I know you're living a lie. You've been deceiving Lindsey her entire life." I took a step closer. "I know who you are."

Petsy stared at me, taking deep breaths in and out. I stared back, and as I watched, something seemed to click within her and her eyes grew even colder. She tossed her hair back and walked over to the purse she'd left on the sideboard. She opened it, pulled out a gun, and turned to point it at me.

"I thought I could avoid violence, but you've driven me to it." She sounded unusually calm and a bit weary, as though the burden of being rational had been a heavy one. "Honestly, you are terribly annoying. Has anyone besides me ever told you that?"

"No," I muttered, staring at the gun, sincerely rethinking my whole *get everything into the open* strategy.

"Mother," Lindsey said with a hiss, her face contorted in fear, "put that away."

"I told you to stay out of it, Lindsey. Now it's too late." Petsy pushed her hair back, then primly smoothed the front of her blouse as though she were about to pose for a photograph.

We were witnessing a woman diving off the deep end—and there was no water in that crazy pool.

I took a tiny step backward and gauged my chances. If Lindsey distracted her long enough, would I be able to dash to the front door before she got a shot off?

Clearly I wouldn't make it. My only option was to try to talk her down. But she had evidently reached her boiling point. Would she listen to reason?

"I hadn't planned on having to deal with all three of you," Petsy said, then added in a blasé tone, "But, you know, desperate times . . ."

Call for desperate measures, I thought, finishing the line. Did that mean she planned to kill all three of us? Would she spare Amanda, whom she actually seemed to like? Or had that been a lie, too? Perhaps she would simply use us as a shield to get to the nearest airport— or wherever psychotic killers went when they'd reached their limit.

"Mother, please," Lindsey said, trying to speak calmly although her faltering words betrayed her. "Whatever you're thinking, don't. Let's talk about this. I'm sorry I upset you."

But Petsy didn't seem to be listening. Instead, she appeared to be calculating her next move.

I was almost afraid to say anything, because I clearly annoyed her, but since the feeling was mutual I felt I had nothing to lose by trying. "You really don't want to do this, Petsy. Think of the Home and Garden Tour. I know your house is going to win this year, but if you hurt us, it'll ruin your chances."

She smiled, apparently amused by my ploy. "I can still win."

"Oh yeah? Good luck with that."

"Stop arguing with me!" Petsy grabbed from the credenza an expensive vase filled with beautiful spring flowers and smashed it on the marble floor.

Lindsey screamed. "What are you doing? What's wrong with you?"

"It was so sad," Petsy said, her tone vague as she glanced around. "I came home only to find that burglars had broken in. It was a home invasion in progress. My lovely daughter and two others lying dead on the floor." She moved over to the wall, never turning her back to us. Reaching up, she maneuvered an original seascape off the wall and tossed it onto the floor, breaking the glass.

"Don't do that, Mother." Lindsey sounded a little panicked. I couldn't blame her. "You're scaring me."

Petsy sighed dramatically. "Lindsey, stop being such a baby."

"I'm sorry, Mother, but—"

"And I've told you not to call me that," she said through clenched teeth.

"All right. Um, Petsy." Lindsey tried again to keep her voice cool and composed. "You need to put the gun away."

Petsy ignored Lindsey, instead turning to look at me. "I think I'll shoot you first." Switching back to Lindsey, she added, "And you'll be next."

I glanced at Amanda, who looked absolutely petrified, but I knew she was stronger than that. Meeting my gaze, Amanda gulped. When I nodded slowly, she returned a slight nod, and I knew she would be ready to fight this woman when the time came.

"So you're going to kill all three of us," I said. "You're going to leave our dead bodies in the foyer. And then what?"

Petsy blinked. Her nostrils flared as she breathed in and out rapidly. It was clear she had no idea what to do next.

"We're going upstairs," Petsy said all of a sudden.

"Why?" Lindsey said.

"You really need to stop questioning me." She jerked her gun toward the stairway. "Now move it."

"What happened to you?" Lindsey asked as she led the way up the stairs. "You were always harsh and unreasonable, but I never thought you were insane."

Petsy shook her head in frustration, her gun hand falling to her side. "And you used to be more compliant. Your moving away was wonderful for me, but it's ruined you. With all your opinions and ideas that no one asks you for. You need to be more like Amanda and keep your sarcastic mouth shut."

Lindsey glanced over her shoulder at Petsy. "How do you suggest I be more like Amanda? We barely even know Amanda."

"Of course we know her, you dolt," she said. "She's my daughter."

Lindsey stopped abruptly. "What did you say?"

Petsy jerked the gun back up. "Keep moving. In case you couldn't tell, I'm in no mood to be defied."

Amanda looked completely dumbfounded, so I grabbed her arm, and the three of us jogged up the steps ahead of Petsy. We stopped when we reached the second floor.

"Keep going," Petsy said. "Third floor."

She wanted us to go to Matthew's studio? I almost smiled. In that room, there were a million items that I could snatch and use as a weapon. If only I could get the chance before she shot us all.

"Amanda, do you work out?" Petsy asked.

"Yes."

"You see, Lindsey? That's how you get a perfect figure. Amanda is in great shape and she's smart and beautiful, and she's very artistic, too. Unlike you, who couldn't paint your way out of a paper bag."

"Lindsey is beautiful and talented, too," Amanda insisted.

Lindsey smiled at Amanda and scowled at Petsy. "Thank you, Amanda, but my mother—I mean, Petsy— thinks I'm insipid and frumpy."

"You're not," Amanda murmured.

I felt like I was in a three-sided Ping-Pong game and the referee held a gun.

"Petsy," Lindsey said, apparently no longer fearful of facing her mother's wrath, "do you know why Amanda is all those things you admire? Because she wasn't raised by you. If she'd been living in this house, you would've picked her apart, just like you've done to me my entire life."

"Shut up, Lindsey," Petsy muttered, and added under her breath, "Sharper than a serpent's tooth . . ."

Apparently the Jorgensen house was the place where irony had gone to die. But at least Petsy knew her Shakespeare.

We reached Matthew's studio and stopped. Petsy lifted her gun to point at us again. "Keep moving."

"Where?" I said, although I had a suspicion.

She pointed the gun toward the tower room. "Out there."

So, she wanted to end this out on the widow's walk. I thought of Ernie, Loretta's poor husband. Had Petsy forced him to walk out onto the roof? More irony? I wondered.

As I made my way through the studio, I bumped against one of the tables hard enough to cause a few of the jars and cans to topple.

"Be careful, you oaf," Petsy snapped. "I don't need Matthew whining about his precious paintbrushes on the floor."

It was enough of a distraction that I was able to sneak a razor-sharp, curved gouge off the table. The tool was about eight inches long and I figured Matthew used it to cut through clay. It would draw blood if I had the chance to get close enough to Petsy. I slipped it up inside the cuff of my shirt and kept walking.

I just hoped I would get the opportunity to use it.

"Amanda, dear," Petsy said, "open the French doors, would you? We're going out on the roof."

Reluctantly she did as instructed and walked out first. I followed her and whispered, "Once she steps out here, I'm going to try and grab her."

"I'll be ready," she murmured.

"This is hardly going to look like a home invasion," I said out loud.

"True." Petsy shrugged. "That would've been nice, but this shows more dramatic flair."

"I see," I said. "Since they're going to arrest you for murder anyway, you might as well make a show of it?"

Her smile was smug. "That's right."

"That's sick," Lindsey said.

"Shut up and get out there," Petsy ordered.

We walked outside and waited for Petsy's next move. I suddenly remembered Matthew's words the other day when he tried to explain Petsy's sour attitude. Appearances were everything, he'd said.

I took a deep breath and said, "This is going to look really bad to the people on the tour. Nobody's going to vote for this house."

"On the contrary," Petsy snarled, "everyone loves a sensational murder story. We're sure to win."

"No, the police will close off the house while they do their investigation," I insisted. "It'll be disqualified."

"You're wrong," she shouted. "I'm going to win."

She was so close to pulling that trigger. I had to disengage or I would be shot. I forced myself to look around. The air was cooler than usual up here, but the sky was clear and blue. I could smell the briny ocean and taste a hint of salt in the crisp breeze coming off the water. It was a perfect April morning on the Northern California coast. An ideal day for dealing with a murderous psychopath, I supposed.

Petsy pointed the gun at me and then jerked it to the right. "Get over there."

I had been standing as close to the door as I could get, hoping for a chance to use the gouge I had hidden in my sleeve. Cursing inwardly, I moved to the opposite side of the widow's walk.

Before she could say anything more, I demanded, "Why did you kill Loretta?"

"Don't be silly. She committed suicide."

"Naked? In a bathtub? With the cord of a hair dryer wrapped around her neck?"

Petsy smiled.

"No," I retorted. "You killed her. You tossed a television set and a hair dryer into her bathtub and nothing happened, so you strangled her. I know it was you. You're trying to get rid of all the loose ends."

"It was her own fault," Petsy insisted with disgust. "She pushed me to it. She's been showing up here every year, demanding more and more money. She's the problem, not me."

"Why did she demand money?" Amanda asked. "What did you do?"

"She sold you," I said matter-of-factly. That was a guess, but it was a good one, given Petsy's reaction.

Petsy's face was red with fury. "You don't know what it was like."

"Then please tell us, *Mother*." Amanda said the word derisively, and I couldn't have been prouder to see her strike back. "What was it like to sell your own daughter?"

"You don't understand! I wanted a baby more than anything. Loretta didn't. She was horrified when she found out she was pregnant."

Lindsey looked completely mystified. "What does that have to do with anything?"

"It wasn't fair! Loretta ended up with a perfect angel, and I ended up with . . ."

"Me," Amanda said flatly. "You ended up with me."

"You were a horrible baby," Petsy shouted. "You wouldn't stop crying. You were colicky and noisy, and your skin was washed-out."

"That sounds perfectly normal," Amanda said.

Petsy took a deep breath and composed herself. "My mother wouldn't come to the house. She insisted that you were defective."

"Defective?" Clearly shocked, Amanda yelled the word. "What a horrible thing to say."

"You can express your outrage all you want, but it's water under the bridge now. I'm very proud of the woman you've become. I really should've kept you, I suppose. But the colic. Oh dear God, I couldn't take it. And my mother was adamant that . . . Well, it was important that she accept my child, and there was no way it was going to happen with the constant whining and crying. And your skin was so awful. You were practically yellow!"

Lindsey sputtered in outrage. "Jaundice is very common in newborns. Everybody knows that."

"We aren't *everybody*," Petsy said, her arrogance returning with a vengeance. "My mother had very high standards, and I couldn't blame her. It was an unpleasant situation."

"Unpleasant?" Lindsey said. "She sounds ghoulish."

"*Ghoulish* is too nice a word," I said. "Your mother sounds as awful as you, Petsy."

She ignored me and reached her hand out to Amanda, who flicked it away and stepped back a foot.

Petsy tried to regain her composure, such as it was.

"I'm pleased to see that you overcame your early short-comings. It shows you have a strong genetic makeup. I can take some pride in that."

"Shortcomings?" Amanda cried. "I had colic. Plenty of babies have colic. It lasts a few months, and then it's over."

"As I said, it was all very unpleasant," Petsy said, sniffing defensively.

"And that's why you *sold* me?" She shook her head, still in disbelief. "So, you couldn't take it. You're a wimp. There's no way I inherited any strong genetic makeup from you, because you don't have any. You're sick. I wasn't the *defective* one. You were."

"You're learning," Lindsey said. "Your *mother* is a selfish pig."

Petsy continued as if she hadn't heard a word either of them said. "The sad part is that Lindsey was simply the most beautiful child." Her lips curved up as she reminisced. "She was blond and blue-eyed, and she smiled all the time. She had rosy cheeks and was so well-behaved and cheerful. Everyone loved her. I wanted her."

"So you made a deal with Loretta," I said.

"She would do anything for money," Petsy grumbled. "And she didn't want you anyway."

"You paid her a lot of money," I said, "to take your colicky baby somewhere far away and give her up for adoption."

"And you kept Lindsey," Amanda said in amazement, shaking her head.

"I'm curious," Lindsey said. "How much was it worth to you?"

"Drop it, Lindsey," Petsy said, her teeth clenched tightly.

"I want to know, too," Amanda said. "What was the going rate for baby swapping back in the day?"

Petsy sniffed. "Fine. I gave her a hundred thousand dollars to make you disappear forever."

"But she didn't disappear," I said. "And neither did Loretta. She kept coming back, asking for more money." And that was what those dollar signs indicated in her appointment book, I thought. Loretta was in Lighthouse Cove to collect her yearly blackmail money. Had she deserved to die for that? I was no longer able to judge. And speaking of dying . . .

"Why did you kill Scully?" I asked.

"Oh, that horrible man. He was angry when I made him leave, so he followed me to Loretta's hotel the next morning. When he saw her, he just about flipped. But then he saw me and knew I wouldn't play nice like Loretta always did, so he ran off. I thought he would stay away, but then he showed up again and wanted to talk. He remembered Loretta from years ago, and somehow he knew all about the babies. He was always sniffing around, meddling in everyone else's affairs. Do you know he actually tried to blackmail me? Idiot. I had to kill him." She pointed an accusing finger at me. "And don't you pretend you weren't happy to see him go."

"So you lured him to the Derrys' house," I said, ignoring her claim. "Why go over there?"

"Because everyone on the street heard Stan Derry yelling at Scully that day. I figured it would be easy enough to pin the murder on him."

"Yeah, that's what I thought. How did you get into the orangery?"

"Joan hides a key under a fake rock by the sprinklers." She rolled her eyes at that obvious stupidity.

"Where did you get the chisel?"

She snorted. "In case you didn't notice, Matthew has a thousand of them scattered in that pigsty of a room he calls his studio."

"He makes a pretty nice living in that pigsty," Lindsey said in her father's defense. "Enough to keep you in designer knit suits, anyway. You shouldn't be criticizing him."

"Besides, it's not a pigsty at all," Amanda said loyally.

Petsy's chuckle was dry and raspy. "Go ahead and take his side, both of you. He didn't put up much of a fight when Loretta left with you."

Amanda frowned. "Did he even know what you did?"

She seemed to consider the question, then shrugged. "Not really. I suppose he could tell the difference between the two babies, but I explained to him that the baby was simply growing out of her ugly infant stage." She gave a grunt of disgust. "What did he know? He was working long hours at the bank, so he was rarely home." She sighed. "I wish he still had that job. At least he wore a suit and worked in a place that carried some prestige with it. Now he's a stupid painter, working out of his home. Always wearing those dirty jeans and shredded denim shirts." She shivered delicately. "And why does he have to smell like turpentine?"

"Amanda," Lindsey said, turning her way, "how does it feel to be the daughter of a psychopath?"

Petsy gasped. "Lindsey, shut up. Don't taunt Amanda."

"Why should I do anything you say?" Lindsey asked. "Apparently you're not my mother. But you are definitely psycho."

Petsy gave her a look of pure hate, but said nothing.

"Who is Lindsey's father?" I asked. "Is it Matthew?"

Her nose wrinkled in disgust. "I thought it was. He pretended to be so devoted to me, but I saw him looking at Loretta when he didn't know I was watching."

"So is he my father?" Lindsey asked, her voice tremulous.

"No," Petsy grumbled. "Your father died soon after you were born."

I glanced around the widow's walk. "Is this where you pushed Ernie off the roof?"

Her eyes grew wide. "Ernie? How do you know about Ernie?"

I hadn't known she was responsible for Ernie's death until I saw her face at that moment.

"I know everything," I said. "And so do the police. Trust me, you'll be in jail by this afternoon."

"You're bluffing."

I smiled. "Try me."

Her eyes widened in fear. "Ernie confronted me. He wanted to take Lindsey away from me."

"Because he was her father," I said.

"What did that matter?" she said, stomping her foot. "I paid for her fair and square."

"Oh my God," Lindsey muttered. "This is a horror show."

"Ernie was a fool," Petsy insisted. "Loretta only

married him because he got her pregnant. She didn't love him. He was a chauffeur, for heaven's sake. She wanted more. The money I gave her was like manna from heaven. She couldn't wait to get out of town. But Ernie was going to expose the whole thing."

"So you had to kill him."

"Whatever. Enough of this." Petsy raised her gun with two hands and pointed it directly at me. I ducked, and without warning, Amanda made a dive right at her. The bullet missed its target—me—and hit the far side of the roof. Amanda knocked the gun out of her hand and fell down on top of her. Petsy struggled to push Amanda off, but Amanda held on to the woman as they rolled across the surface. When they hit the fragile railing, I heard the wood crack.

"No!" someone shouted from inside the house. Suddenly Matthew came rushing through the doorway. He grabbed hold of Amanda's shirt and yanked her away from Petsy. After helping Amanda to her feet, he whirled around and stared wide-eyed at Lindsey. "Are you all right, honey?"

"I'm fine, Dad." He grabbed her in a fierce hug and she held on for dear life. Over her shoulder he stared at me. "What in the world is going on?"

"She tried to kill us," Lindsey said, pointing at Petsy.

That was when I realized that Petsy was clinging to the broken rail and was starting to slip. I moved as fast as I could and grabbed her foot, yanking her back to safety.

I wasn't sure why I'd saved her, but there had already been enough death. And I wanted to make sure she spent some quality time in jail.

As far as I knew, the gun had flown off the roof somewhere, so I felt sure we were relatively safe from stray bullets.

Turning to Matthew, I said, "Your wife planned to kill all three of us."

He shook his head slowly. "That can't be true."

"It's true, Dad," Lindsey said, still clutching Matthew's arm. "She told us that she's really Amanda's mother and not mine."

"Lindsey's real mother is Loretta Samson," I said. "Petsy killed her and Joe Scully, too. I guess we became loose ends and she decided we had to die, too. She said she was going to make it look like a home invasion where the three of us were murdered by burglars." I glared at Petsy. "Do I have the story straight?"

She ignored me and stared off at the horizon. I had no idea what was going through her mind, and in that moment, I really didn't care.

"I'm sorry," Matthew said. "I'm having a hard time following this. Petsy said she's Amanda's mother?"

"Yes," Lindsey said. "And . . . and this woman Loretta is my mother."

She let go of Matthew's arm and took a step back. She tried to smile but the tears were starting to fall. "So I guess you're not my father after all."

"Don't you ever say that again," Matthew said gently, pulling her back and giving her a hug. "I will always be your father."

"But . . ." Lindsey wiped the tears off her cheeks. "I think you're actually Amanda's father."

"What?" He gazed from Lindsey to Amanda and back again. He looked down at Petsy, frowning. "Petsy, is this true?"

She didn't speak right away, so I jumped in. "I think that's a yes."

He stared at Amanda for a brief moment, and then he held out his arm for her to come closer.

Amanda was suddenly shy, and her steps were tentative. Matthew grinned and wrapped his arm around her shoulders. "Two daughters. I guess that makes me the luckiest man in the world."

We were all sniffling back tears until I finally managed to speak. "I think I'd better go call the police."

"Too late," Amanda said, looking delighted as she pointed toward the ground below.

I turned and almost cheered when I saw Mac and Tommy standing on the side of the yard near the orangery, staring up at the action on the roof. I waved at them to let them know we were okay. I had a feeling Eric was nearby, too, and wondered if he was on his way up to the widow's walk.

I took a quick look at Petsy, who hadn't moved from the spot where I'd pulled her away from the edge. I still didn't trust her, and I hoped that Eric would get up here soon.

I grabbed Amanda and hugged her. "Thank you for saving our lives."

"Yes," Lindsey said, "thank you. You're okay, despite your horrible mother."

Amanda looked completely wiped out as she turned to Lindsey. "I'm so sorry for everything you've been through."

Lindsey's eyes suddenly widened. "What am I saying? It sounds like my *real* mother was just as evil as this one."

I grimaced. "I thought she was nice when I met her, but considering what you've both been through, I'm afraid you're probably right."

Lindsey glared down at Petsy for a moment, then said, "No, Loretta was even worse. At least Amanda was raised by nice people, but I ended up with Petsy. And that's Loretta's fault." Her eyes began to tear up. "I didn't even know the woman, and it's probably wrong of me, but I'm not sorry she's dead."

Amanda weaved her arm through Lindsey's. "Looks like we've got more in common than I thought."

"You're right." Lindsey smiled sadly. "Neither of us hit the *mother* jackpot, but I sort of feel like I've gained a sister."

Amanda sniffed back tears. "I couldn't be happier about that."

I had to admit I was sniffling again, too.

"We should go downstairs," Matthew said, then turned and looked at his wife, who hadn't tried to move from the dangerous edge of the widow's walk. "Petsy, can I help you up?"

"Stay away from me."

"We can work this out, dear. I'll call my lawyer."

"Um, Dad? I mean, Matthew?" Lindsey gulped. "Apparently she killed my father, too. Someone named Ernie."

He blinked. "What? No. Ernie fell off the roof. It was an accident."

"I'm sorry, Matthew," I said. "Petsy already confessed to pushing him off the roof."

Breathing slowly, he gazed at his wife as though he'd never seen her before. He looked back at me and his eyes grew sharper. He seemed to be waking up. He turned to Lindsey. "Ernie—your birth father—was thrilled when he found out he and Loretta were going to have a baby."

"At least someone was happy," she muttered.

"He was a good man, Lindsey. He worked for us for many years and died tragically. I'm sorry."

He grabbed his daughter in another hug. Amanda was sniffling and I felt tears springing to my eyes.

"Shannon," Mac shouted from the backyard three stories below us, interrupting the moment, thank goodness. "Everything okay?"

I gazed down at him, gave him a thumbs-up, and shouted back, "We might need some help up here."

"Eric's on his way up."

I gave him another thumbs-up and turned to Matthew, Lindsey, and Amanda.

"If you all want to go downstairs, I'll wait here for Eric to come up and get Petsy."

I turned and watched the woman trying to stand up.

"Better watch her," Lindsey warned.

Amanda nodded briskly. "We'll stay with you."

Petsy was still clinging to the cracked wood railing.

"You need to get away from the edge," I said, and moved to help her.

"Stay back," Petsy said, and stared directly at me, giving me the strangest look. "Finish my house. I want to win."

"Honestly, Mother," Lindsey said, then waved the word away. "I mean, whoever you are. Forget about the contest. You're going to jail."

But Petsy kept gazing at me. "I mean it. I want to win."

"All right." I nodded slowly, trying to placate her. "I'll do what I can for the house."

"Good. I deserve to win."

"Oh," I assured her solemnly, "you deserve a lot more than that." She had definitely gone off the deep end, but I supposed that was what happened when you had carried around a dark, evil secret for most of your life.

Lindsey and Amanda stared at each other and shook their heads, mystified by Petsy's request. I gave them a puzzled look, then glanced back in time to catch an unholy gleam appear in Petsy's eyes.

"Watch out!" I shouted. "Grab her!"

But it was too late. Petsy let go of the broken railing and threw herself over the edge, falling to the ground below.

"Petsy!" Matthew shouted.

"Mother!" Lindsey screamed, forgetting that Petsy had never been her mother.

Amanda screamed, "No!"

Down on the ground, the police and Mac were shouting as well, as they scrambled to get equipment and men to help.

We all exchanged looks of dread. I gritted my teeth and leaned over the railing to see where she had fallen. It was only three stories, I thought. She could survive it.

Lindsey gasped for air. Matthew grabbed both girls and held them tightly. He didn't look down.

"Oh my God," I whispered as I stared at the sight. I couldn't stand it, and I had to turn away, too.

Amanda began to sob.

"I'm so sorry," Lindsey whispered, as though we might've blamed her for the woman's ugly, twisted behavior. Amanda grabbed hold of Lindsey's arm and held her close.

I sighed and stared out at the sweeping coast. The lighthouse stood sentinel in the distance. The choppy ocean waves caught the sun and sparkled like jewels.

After a few steadying breaths, I glanced down again. She hadn't made it to the ground. The beautiful new orangery had broken Petsy's fall. Her body was splayed on top of the glass roof, where the row of fleur-de-lis embellishments jutted up like spears along the main frame. The sturdy steel flourishes acted as spikes, piercing her body along her spine. Petsy Jorgensen was dead.

Chapter Thirteen

Mac and I hung on to each other as we sat on the tailgate of my truck, watching the police and EMTs do their jobs. Neighbors gathered in clusters on one another's lawns, whispering among themselves and barely concealing their lurid excitement that something newsworthy had occurred on their quiet little cul-de-sac. To be fair to them, Petsy hadn't exactly made a lot of friends among them. She'd managed to offend just about everyone in town at one point or another, so the neighbors weren't really heartbroken by her death.

I had spent a few minutes commiserating with Joan and Stan Derry, who were observing the activities from the relative safety of their lovely front porch. They gave me a dozen quick examples of Petsy's hostile behavior over the years, and I shared with them exactly what had happened up on the roof. I figured I owed them a little prurient insider information after continuously suspecting them of murder for the last few days. I didn't mention that part out loud, though.

Mac hadn't let go of me from the moment I ran through Matthew's studio and straight into his arms.

"How did you know to come here?" I asked him, when I could finally think again.

"I was over at Jane's," he explained, "showing photos of the suspects to her other two staff members. It turns out that the part-time desk clerk recognized Petsy. It was the night Loretta died. He had just delivered flowers to another room and he happened to see her strolling down the hallway toward Loretta's room. And he also remembered seeing Petsy with Loretta the same day Scully was there."

"That's amazing." I realized in that moment that Petsy might have known all along that Amanda was her daughter. From the first day Amanda showed up to work with me, Petsy had stared at her with so much scrutiny, it made me wonder. And then the Regency painting in the hallway was a clear giveaway. It was shortly after Matthew showed us the painting that Petsy began to treat Amanda with a lot more respect than before. Perhaps around that same time, Loretta had verified that Petsy's daughter was indeed back in town. Had Petsy's mind begun to unravel at that point? Had she decided right then and there to kill Loretta? She had already killed Scully, so what was one more dead body in the scheme of things? My own mind was starting to spin with all the possibilities, so I shut off the speculations and gazed up at Mac. "I'm so glad you remembered to go back to the inn. I hope Jane gives that desk clerk a raise."

"Yeah, me, too." He grinned. "So, needless to say, I called Eric immediately and we all came over here. His plan was to take Petsy in for questioning and I came along to make sure you were all right."

"Thank goodness you did."

"I don't know," he said, studying my face. "It looked like you were handling things pretty well on your own."

"I guess I was for a while, but then it got ugly." I shivered and shook away the image of Petsy aiming her gun at me. "Amanda really saved the day."

"What did she do?"

I inhaled deeply and exhaled. "Just as Petsy was about to take a shot at me, Amanda jumped on her and helped deflect the bullet. She could've been badly hurt. And I could've been killed. I really owe her."

Mac stood in front of me and leaned in close, pressing his forehead against mine. "I do, too. I'll owe her for the rest of my life."

My heart fluttered wildly for a second or two, then settled into a steady beat. That was what Mac did for me. Kept me steady. Kept me grounded. Then he wrapped his arms around me and we stayed like that for a long time. Finally he stepped back and touched my cheek. "I wish I'd been there."

"Me, too." It was true. I really did. Still, he was here now, and that was a gift. "But I survived. I'm okay. And Amanda and Lindsey are, too. I think they'll both be fine." Hedging my bet, I added, "Maybe after a little therapy."

"So, I guess this blows my theory that the most obvious suspect is always innocent."

"Completely." I laughed, then shook my head. "I'm just glad it wasn't Matthew or Lindsey."

"Or Amanda," he added.

"That would've been awful."

"From now on, I think you should trust your instincts on these things," Mac said. He tipped my chin up so our eyes met. "You liked Amanda from the start and trusted her, too."

"And," I reminded him, "I couldn't stand Petsy."

"For good reason, as it turns out."

I sighed. "Still, I've met some pretty bad people who came across as perfectly nice at first."

He nodded. "Yeah. Me, too. So we'll just have to be more careful from now on."

"Right. Although I doubt we'll have to confront another cold-blooded killer anytime in the near future." As soon as I said the words, I wanted to bite my tongue. I scrambled across the truck bed and grabbed a two-by-four. "Knock on wood."

Mac was laughing at me, but I noticed that he reached for the piece of wood and rapped his own knuckles against the surface, too. You just couldn't be too careful around Lighthouse Cove these days.

After the police conducted a preliminary investigation and spoke briefly with everyone involved, the fire department was able to remove Petsy's body from the roof of the orangery. I strongly suggested to Matthew that he contact a hazardous-waste company to come out and clean and sanitize the entire structure.

Matthew was moving like a man in a dream. He looked confused, worried, but he, too, would survive, I knew.

Once the structure was cleaned, my guys would be

able to replace the two pieces of glass that had been cracked by the force of Petsy's falling body.

It was almost unbelievable, but the fleur-de-lis embellishments had not been damaged by Petsy's fall. They looked as straight and strong and good as new. I suppose that would've made Petsy happy—as if anything in life had ever made her happy.

Two weeks later, the day of the Home and Garden Tour arrived. The town square was festooned with bunting and streamers and flags. A few dozen booths were set up across the wide expanse, promoting everything from beer and soda, to chocolate fudge and hot dogs, to flowers and pottery and puppies. Especially puppies. The animal adoption booth was always a huge success.

The fourteen homes that had been selected for this year's tour had been polished to a fine sheen and their gardens were bursting with blooms and lush greenery. Banners announcing the big day were hung on storefronts and picket fences and porches all over town. There were pots of flowers hanging on every light post. On the side streets around the town square, trolley cars and trams were lined up, ready to drive the tour-goers to each of the houses on display.

After days of worrying and debating, Lindsey and Matthew Jorgensen had decided to keep their house on the tour. Their reasoning was that they wanted to recognize all the hard work Amanda and my crew had done to make it look so beautiful.

Lindsey had decided to sell the gallery in San Francisco and had begun the slow process of moving back to Lighthouse Cove. She and Matthew had invited Amanda to live in their house and she had accepted joyfully. With three stories, eight bedrooms, and nine bathrooms, each of them could have their own wing and all the privacy they wanted. But it seemed that all they really wanted was to get to know one another better.

Happily, in the span of two weeks, the three had grown as close as any family could be. Amanda was already calling Lindsey her sister and she admitted that she hadn't been this happy in years. Matthew insisted on painting her portrait and he promised to hang it in the hall next to his Regency ancestor's painting.

And it was all thanks, in a strange and disturbing way, to Petsy.

The tour hadn't yet started when I spotted Jane checking on the line of trolleys and I called to her. "Anything I can do to help?"

"Oh, Shannon." She grabbed me in a hug. "I so wish you were working with me on this event."

"Me, too. But I've kind of had my hands full."

"We've got to get together with the girls and talk about everything." She stared at me, scanning my face for cracks, maybe? "You look great, but you could be faking it. Are you all right?"

I laughed. "I'm not faking it. You might've heard I had a close call last week, but everything's fine now."

"I'm glad. But I really want to sit down and hear everything that happened."

"You already know that your desk clerk saved the day, right?"

"Yes. Mac stopped by to let me know that Ricardo was very helpful. So that was exciting."

"I'm extremely grateful for Ricardo's sharp eyes."

She smiled as she gazed around, taking in the festival scene. Suddenly she did a double take. "Oh my. Is that Marigold's new friend?"

I turned and saw Raphael holding Marigold's hand up to his lips and kissing it, right in the middle of the sidewalk.

"It sure is. That's Raphael Nash."

"Wow. He's just as gorgeous as you said he was." She smiled softly. "She looks so happy."

"Doesn't she?" In fact, Marigold looked radiant. I had a sneaky feeling Raphael must have assured her that she would never have to milk another cow for as long as they both lived.

The tour was a huge success, as I had known it would be. Everyone who viewed the houses gushed over all of the glorious Victorians. People chatted about the fun of walking through these marvelously overwrought homes built so many years ago, when decorative excess was king.

The more intellectual types could be overheard comparing the High Victorian style to the Early Gothic, while the kids enjoyed exploring the wraparound verandas and climbing the stairs to the bell towers.

Each person on the tour filled out a ballot with the names of their top three favorites. These were handed over to the official festival booth in the town square. That afternoon, after the flamenco dancers and the spoon ladies had performed and all the puppies and kittens had been adopted, the mayor walked onto the stage. He welcomed the crowd and thanked everyone for coming.

Then he said, "Ladies and gentlemen, I want to offer our thanks to our official celebrity judge, MacKintyre Sullivan, who helped us tabulate the ballots."

Mac had joined me in the crowd and he waved to everyone as they applauded.

"And now," the mayor continued, "I am pleased to announce the winner of this year's Lighthouse Cove Victorian Home and Garden Tour. The most beautiful home and garden in Lighthouse Cove is . . . Drumroll, please!"

The band complied, and the mayor grinned. "The winner is . . . the Jorgensen house!"

"What?" I was frankly astounded. I stared at Mac, and he laughed out loud. Grabbing me in his arms, he swung me around until I was dizzy and laughing with him.

"You won!" he shouted, hugging me again. "Well, the Jorgensens won, but only because of your work. Congratulations! I'm so proud of you."

"You knew!"

"Of course I knew," he said. "I'm the official celebrity judge. I know everything."

My eyes narrowed. "You didn't rig it, did you?"

He laughed again. "No. All I did was count the ballots. The Jorgensen house won fair and square."

"Wow. That is fantastic." I grinned at him. "I honestly don't think the win had much to do with me, but I'll take it."

I had to wonder what the crowd had been thinking. Had they been influenced by the adrenaline-charged thrill of exploring a house where a vicious killer had once lived? Or had they simply been drawn to the beauty of the house itself? I hoped it was the latter, but whatever their motivation, the people of Lighthouse Cove had chosen the Jorgensen house as this year's winner. Either way, I was stunned. And a part of me was sure that Petsy knew and was right now lording it over everyone around her—wherever she was. After all, just because you were dead didn't mean you suddenly got nice.

After a few more minutes of celebrating, the crowd began to disperse. I would try to find Jane and my other friends later, but for now, I was happy to be with Mac.

He frowned introspectively. "So, why didn't you enter your house on the tour? It's got to be one of the prettiest ones in town."

"Thank you," I said. "Or are you just sucking up?"

He raised an eyebrow. "Is it working?"

"I believe it is." I leaned over and kissed him. "The truth is, my house won the tour a few years back, so I retired from the competition."

"Hmm." He scratched his ear, thinking. "Maybe I'll enter the lighthouse mansion next year."

"Oh, you should," I said, excited at the prospect. "Really. I'll do whatever it takes to get you that first-place ribbon."

He thought for a moment, considering the idea. "That's nice of you. And actually I have been thinking about landscaping the yard and adding on a room one of these days. Maybe off the kitchen, where you put in those beautiful French doors."

My eyebrows lifted and I smiled. "Wonderful. A sitting room? Or another bedroom?"

"No," he said, his eyes twinkling with mischief. "I was thinking it would be nice to have an orangery."

Read on for an excerpt
from Kate Carlisle's new Bibliophile mystery,

BURIED IN BOOKS

Coming from Prime Crime in June 2018.

"The name is Wainwright," I said to the conference volunteer seated at the registration table before me. "Brooklyn Wainwright."

The young woman gave an absent nod and began to skim the thick row of envelopes standing upright in the box in front of her. Not exactly friendly, but the crowd was huge and the woman was probably feeling overwhelmed. Halfway through the row, she stopped suddenly and stared up at me. "Wait. You're Brooklyn Wainwright? I signed up for your workshop."

"Oh." I smiled. "I hope you'll enjoy it."

"I know it'll be fantastic," she said brightly. "I'm like your biggest fan."

"That's so nice. Thanks."

For the fifth year in a row, I had been asked to present the bookbinding workshop for the annual National Librarians Association conference. I was thrilled that the conference was being held in San Francisco this year so I wouldn't have to lug all of my supplies and equipment halfway across the country.

Sighing inwardly, I admitted that I would've been looking forward to the workshop a lot more if I hadn't botched up my schedule so badly. But nobody here needed to know that.

The volunteer flipped her pink-streaked hair away from her face and continued to stare at me as though I were a rock star. Her former bored interest had turned into wide-eyed excitement. It was fun, but also a little intimidating. She knew me and my work. What if she hated the workshop?

"I saw your pop-up display at the Covington Library," she said. "It was amazing."

"Thank you." I sensed the people in line behind me getting antsy to move things along. I turned and flashed an apologetic smile.

But my new biggest fan didn't seem to notice the impatient crowd. Instead, she leaned forward and whispered loudly, "Everyone says you're going to dish about the murders during the workshop. I'm so psyched!"

"Uh . . . what?"

She nodded eagerly. "Is it true you found a body inside the Covington? What a rush!"

"Umm, no, I . . ." I had no words. The fact was, I *had* found a body inside the Covington. More than once, to be honest. But I wasn't about to discuss the details with a stranger.

She frowned at me, clearly confused by my reticence. Then she began to nod slowly as if she and I were in on a secret together. "Ah, I get it. You're saving the gory details for the workshop. I understand. Don't worry. I can wait."

Snapping back into work mode, she pulled a manila envelope from the stack and handed it to me. "Here you go. This envelope contains your badge and your program book. It's got all the events listed as well as the speakers' bios. And there's a map inside the back cover. This place is huge, so we don't want anyone to get lost." She pointed toward the opposite side of the massive hall. "You can pick up a book bag at the south end of the auditorium."

I peered at her badge to catch her name. "Okay. Thanks, Lucy."

"Enjoy the conference, Brooklyn." She gave me a conspiratorial wink. "See you at the workshop."

"You bet." A little dazed and a touch breathless, I stepped away from the registration table, feeling like I'd just run a sprint.

An enormous woman in pink bumped into me and kept walking, obviously in a hurry to get her conference bag. I hardly noticed.

Was someone spreading the word that I would be talking about murder? Seriously? I didn't even like *thinking* about the bodies I'd stumbled across, let alone using them as filler in my workshop program. It wasn't going to happen. Which meant that no doubt there were going to be some disappointed people—like Lucy, for instance. I sighed and shook my head. The conference just got more complicated.

I'm a bookbinder specializing in rare-book restoration, which means I make my living refurbishing old books. I also enjoy creating handmade books when I'm feeling particularly artistic. Unfortunately, in connection with my work, I happened to have stumbled across more than a few dead bodies over the past two or three years. And yes, the victims were all connected to the various books I had been working on at the time.

But that didn't mean I knew anything about the subject of murder! And I absolutely refused to draw attention to myself because of my weird proclivity for finding dead people. So why would anyone think I would take time out of a bookbinding class to talk about murder?

When it came to any connection between rare books and murder, the only bit of information I was willing to offer was this: If you thought that books weren't worth killing for, you were dead wrong.

I scanned the enormous hall, noting that in the time it had taken me to register, hundreds more people had arrived for the conference. Dozens were waiting in line to register. Some peered around anxiously, trying to get their bearings. Others were gathered in small groups, chatting and laughing and, in the case of the cluster of five women closest to me, shrieking.

I did a quick mental calculation as I studied the diverse crowd. There had to be at least eight hundred people milling around this cavernous space. Probably closer to a thousand. No wonder the noise level was deafening.

The racket didn't bother me. These were my people. Librarians. Book nerds. "And apparently a few murder fans," I muttered to myself.

I headed toward the south end of the convention center, asking myself all the way: Did I really need a book bag?

More importantly, did I really need to be here at all?

It had been months since I'd first agreed to give the

bookbinding workshop. Then somewhere along the way they had also roped me into giving a speech on book conservation. And if that wasn't enough, I had also said yes when they asked if I'd like to donate a raffle prize. I was all for fund-raising for librarians, but I couldn't just give a basket of books or a gift card. No, I had offered to take twenty lucky librarians on a three-hour "Booklover's Tour" of San Francisco. We were renting a bus and everything. Good grief. What had I been thinking?

Of course, all those months ago, I had never dreamed that I would be getting married to Derek Stone this weekend.

My gaze softened and I sighed happily at the thought of marriage to Derek—and almost crashed into a gray-haired man minding his own business, reading the program booklet.

"Sorry," I muttered, and kept walking. It wasn't the first time I'd spaced out and almost injured someone lately. Whenever I thought of Derek and our imminent wedding, I sort of lost consciousness for a few seconds.

I had considered canceling my conference events this week, but after talking it over with Derek, we decided that it would be a good idea for me to keep to my original conference schedule. Because amazingly, every last detail of the wedding was taken care of. And Derek had pointed out that attending the conference would—hopefully—distract me from any prewedding jitters I might have been susceptible to. He had a good argument there, seeing as how I was more than a little overwhelmed by the fact that his entire family—including his parents, four brothers and their spouses and children, and various aunts and uncles—would be arriving from England any minute now.

My entire family and my friends would be arriving as well, but I wasn't worried about them. We had all grown up in Sonoma and knew San Francisco intimately. And my parents and brothers and sisters had been more than willing to show Derek's family around town while I was busy at the conference. Derek insisted that his family would take my occasional absences in stride. They were all looking forward to exploring the best parts of San Francisco and the wine country. They didn't need me to play tour guide.

It had all sounded good in theory. But now that I was here, I began to wonder if there wasn't something I should've been doing to prepare for the wedding. I checked my watch. Would it be wrong to leave after I'd just arrived?

Not just wrong but stupid, I silently lectured myself as I made my way through the crowd toward the book bag counter. Attending this conference would be great for my business and my career, I reminded myself. I would make new contacts, possibly acquire some new clients, and reacquaint myself with old friends.

So I was here to stay. At least for a few hours. As I wound my way through the crowd, I grinned as I looked around and realized that despite my neurotic compulsion to check all of my wedding lists on an hourly basis, I was happy to be here. I always enjoyed this conference, and I was grateful to the organization for all the good things I'd received by being a part of it. Besides, being among all these librarians always made me feel nostalgic for my postgraduate years. Those were good times.

Even though I'd never planned to work as a librarian, I knew that starting out with a degree in Library Science was one of the best routes to a career as a bookbinder. Consequently, everyone I'd known in school had been working feverishly toward their Master of Library Science degrees back then. I had to admit it was daunting to be surrounded by all of those highly intelligent, compulsively organized, overwhelmingly detail-oriented people. I coped by wearing T-shirts that said things like: *Did you wash your hands today?* and *Do you spell anal retentive with a hyphen?*

Instead of the quick laugh I always expected when I showed up wearing one of my dumb T-shirts, my gifted friends would actually spend an hour or two discussing whatever statements I was displaying.

God, I missed them!

I finally snagged my book bag and was headed for the coffee kiosk when I heard someone call my name.

"Brooklyn?"

I whirled around and stared at the red-haired woman standing a few feet away. "Yes?"

She laughed and ruffled her short hair self-consciously. "I know it's been years and I've changed a few things, but I don't look that different, do I?"

I blinked. "Oh my God. Heather? Heather Babcock?"

"Yes!" She squealed and grabbed me in a crushing hug. "I was so afraid I wouldn't find you!"

"I was just thinking about you," I said. Absolute truth. She had been one of my favorite people back in the day. "I didn't realize you were coming. Why didn't you call me?"

"I didn't know I was coming until two days ago, and then it was like a whirlwind, trying to get ready for the trip."

"Wow. What a stunner. A good one," I added quickly, grinning to hide the fact that I was in complete shock. Heather had been one of my college roommates and a best pal from the good old days. She was always so beautiful, but today she looked . . . haggard. "Gosh, it's been . . . how many years?"

"Ten, maybe? You look fantastic."

"So do you."

"Yeah, right." She chuckled ruefully. "I do own mirrors. Let's not get carried away."

"Don't be silly. You're beautiful," I insisted but quickly changed the subject. "Do you have time for a cup of coffee?"

"Of course."

I bought two caffe lattes and two biscotti, and we found a small table in the far corner. Within seconds we were talking and laughing like the old friends we were, as if ten long years hadn't passed since we'd last seen each other.

Heather and I, along with our best friend, Sara Martin, had been roommates back in Library School. We had clicked from the get-go and become so inseparable that our classmates took to calling us the Three Musketeers. Sadly, though, one week before graduation, Sara and Heather had a major falling-out when Heather found out that her boyfriend, Roderick, had been cheating on her—with *Sara*.

Heather was inconsolable, especially when Sara and Rod ran off and got married. About a year later, I heard through the grapevine that Sara had caught Rod cheating on her. This was not a big surprise to anyone since Rod was adorable, but very shallow and prone to believing his own hyped-up PR. But in the end, Sara forgave him, and they were still together, as far as I knew.

Heather and I avoided the dreaded subject of Sara and Roderick. Instead, Heather talked about her fulfilling job at the local library in her small town, and I told her all about my adventures in bookbinding and my upcoming wedding to Derek. After thirty minutes of chatting and catching up, we both sat back and smiled.

"It's really good to see you," I said wistfully.

"You, too." Heather's smile turned enigmatic. "So, are we ever going to mention the big fat bitchy elephant in the room?"

I reached over and grabbed her hand. "I didn't want to ask."

She raised an eyebrow. "But you're dying to know."

"Sorry," I said, wincing. "But yeah, I would love to know if you've had any news or run-ins with . . ."

Heather inhaled quickly, as if she were about to take some horrible-tasting medicine. "No. I haven't seen Sara in ten years. But I have a friend who has a friend who knows her, so I hear things."

I frowned. "Do you think she'll be coming to the conference?"

"I sure hope not," Heather said. Her jaw tightened, and her eyes narrowed in unrepressed fury. "Because I swear, if I ever see Sara Martin again, I'll kill her."